✳

BLUE CHRISTMAS

EDITED BY
JOHN DUFRESNE

B&B
Press | A Project of Books & Books

Published by B & B Press | A Project of Books & Books
www.booksandbooks.com

A Motherland production in association with the Lavoie Agency, New York
adea@themotherland.net
www.lavoieagency.com

Designed by Cindy Seip
www.splashfoto.com

Library of Congress Cataloging-in-Publication Date

John Dufresne
Blue Christmas / Edited by John Dufresne

For information about special discounts for bulk purchases,
please contact www.booksandbooks.com

First Edition
1 2 3 4 5 6 7 8 9 10

ISBN: 978-0-9839378-1-4

BLUE CHRISTMAS

TABLE OF CONTENTS

INTRODUCTION

As a child I harbored decidedly mixed feelings about Christmas, equal parts breathless anticipation and suffocating dread. School was closed, and that, of course, was liberating. But everything else was closed as well (Massachusetts/blue laws), and that disruption in the social routine I found distressing. What if I needed batteries for my new transistor radio? What if we ran out of milk? We went to Mass—as a family for once—and then piled into the Fairlane and drove through the slushy and abandoned streets to the grandparents' apartment to gather with the aunts and uncles and all those excitable and frightening cousins.

We kids got toys and games, and we all amused ourselves for hours playing with them until we grew bored or they broke or some tiny cousin swallowed the dice. We spoiled our dinner with ribbon candy that looked like spun glass, didn't so much taste as tickle, and stained our fingers red and green. And then the delicious meal itself with the turkey and the mashed potatoes and the cranberry sauce and the pies, the pies! But then as the dads fell asleep on couches and chairs, lit cigarettes burning in their fingers, and the weary moms, who had had it up to here, tried to mollify their whiney toddlers, and the fearsome cousins hunted through bedrooms to find their boots and scarves, I'd look outside and see that it was dark already, and I'd realize that this day of extravagant indulgence was ending and wouldn't return for another year, and when it did, it wouldn't produce quite the thrill it once had.

It's a tough job sustaining the pretense of holiday joy. And it's getting harder. What had been a day of celebration has become a season of furious consumption and profligate spending. (Or maybe it always was, but I was oblivious or stingy or both.) It's become our civic and patriotic duty to fuel the commercial Yuletide engine that drives our sputtering economy and to do so with a smile. We can buy happiness, we are assured. We can wrap it up and put it under the tree. All of our cultural holiday images and all those recycled stories on TV and in the movies insist on our seasonal happiness and on the miraculous and transformative power of the Lord's humble and unprepossessing birth. Don't be a Scrooge; don't spoil it for everyone else, and please don't call it *Xmas*.

Well, Christmas turns out to be the best of times and the worst of times, more or less equal parts mirth and heartache, cheer and gloom, a time when we embrace the love we have found and grieve for the love we have lost. And these stories about Christmas are simply trying to tell that truth. They won't deliver a message but a meaning. They may not make you feel good, but they will make you feel. Lord, save us from cynicism and deliver us from sentimentality! This is Christmas for the rest of us.

—John Dufresne

AMERICAN SWEATER
Diana Abu-Jaber

After Gram heard about the Arab men who got taken off the plane because the crew thought maybe they were what terrorists looked like, she sat down and knitted me and Hani American sweaters. She kept saying, "Look at your hair! With this hair of course they will think you're terrorists."

Hani's hair was always like that; he didn't do it on purpose.

His sweater had a blue square full of white stars over the shoulder, and then these white and red stripes that started on one arm, went across the chest, and ended up on the other arm. Gram tried to get the right number of stars and stripes, but she ran out of room. The best part was she knitted in red, white, and blue, "God" "Bless" "America!" across the back.

"Sweet," Hani said when he saw it.

My sweater had a jagged green Christmas tree that started on the back and stretched around one side to a point with a white star on the front, and underneath in red, "God Bless USA."

"What does a Christmas tree have to do with it?" I complained.

"Never mind, don't ask so many things. I been American five times as long as you." Gram slid her hands higher on the steering wheel.

Dad calls himself a "crusader Arab" because of his dark hair, skin, everything, and then these killer-blue eyes that drive women crazy, according to him, and are the true reason for his downfall, according to Gram. He used to live with us and Gram, but he had to move to Baltimore to make a mint, he said. He had this idea for a dotcom start-up called Tribalrootz.com where they figured out what tribe you originally come from. He and his friend Frankie Colicello, who lived in Baltimore, were going into business together.

"You be careful," Gram said. "Don't take these off, these sweaters."

"We won't," Hani droned.

At the turn-off to the airport road, she said, "There are good things about all religions, no matter what."

"The Christians get to have Santa Claus and Easter bunny," Hani said. "We don't get anything."

Gram's knuckles looked big on the steering wheel. Usually she only drove to Lane Bryant twice a year for a new dress. Otherwise, she walked. It was hard to drive in Syracuse. This year it had started snowing on Thanksgiving and now it was December 22, and the sky seemed like it hadn't taken a breath. The snow curled in slushy columns behind the wipers then suddenly spread a blurry fan across the windshield.

"Damn it, damn, damn." Gram hunched close to the steering wheel, her lips moving like she was telling it a secret.

I looked up; the white misting unfocused my eyes: it looked like the sky was dissolving. "Gram, does Dad really know we're coming?"

Her lips kept moving; her eyes were low and narrow over the steering wheel. I thought: if anyone in this car looks like a terrorist, it's her.

"What? Of course he does. Why do you think you're going? *Ya'Allah*, stop talking all the time."

We pulled in front of the building: there was a Santa Claus by Arrivals, smoking a cigarette. Gram scowled and crossed herself to keep away the Evil Eye. She wasn't going to park; if she had to drive, she wouldn't park because somehow that made it into two drives. Once she got home, she'd lock the car in the garage then go lay down for the rest of the day. Hani kissed her a million times and hung on her arms. I wanted to also, but I just said, "Bye, Gram."

She held my shoulders, her dark eyes wet. "Don't talk to anyone. Don't take off those sweaters. Listen to your father. Even when he talks crazy." I kissed her cheek which was like kissing a handful of Jean Naté talcum, and whispered, "I love you, Gram."

Gram whispered, "Don't forget the Christmas wish!"

We'd gone over it and over it, trying to explain there *is* no Christmas wish.

She didn't care; she wanted us to wish for Dad to come home.

Things were bad right after Mom left, but then they got better, and then things had been sort of fine for a long time. Dad and Gram got us to school and to bed, and Gram had her tea and backgammon gang, and Dad had a million girlfriends and phone calls to Mom where they still said I love you—I heard them say it lots of times. But then Dad decided to take his big idea to Baltimore where his friend Frankie said he knew a guy.

We waved to the back of Gram's Rambler, then went inside, dragging our suitcases behind us. I don't mind flying alone. Airports are like dream worlds. You walk inside of one, and it's like you've left town, but you haven't arrived anywhere yet either. You're just floating there, like somebody dreamed you up, and you don't quite exist yet. They were playing "Have Yourself a Merry Little Christmas," which is somehow like the saddest song in the world; everyone looked tense, shoulders up, eyes moving quickly. I knew what they were thinking—everyone was thinking it: is it going to happen again?

There was a big blinking tree, and for some reason, right away I wanted to take my sweater off. Ever since I'd turned twelve things were like that for me: things that I thought were super-cool one second suddenly looked completely geeked the next. Hani was adorable in his sweater, but he was eight. Everywhere it was flags and trees, trees and flags. I'm not saying this to seem unpatriotic or anything: I'm Greek-Jordanian-Irish-Welsh, born here, and just as proud-American as anyone. But after a while, the trees and flags just looked like colors to me, the same colors repeating everywhere, like a pattern I couldn't figure out, and I didn't know if it meant *you belong here* or *get the heck out.*

The ticket agent was wearing a Santa hat; he was pretty funny, moaning, "Until then our troubles will be miles away!" But when we got to the counter, he looked over our heads for a second. "Where're your parents?"

My face turned hot, and Hani slipped his hand into mine. We flew a lot: Mom had moved to Tempe about six years ago because she said she needed a break, so Dad shipped us to her once or twice a year—even though she spent most of our visits dragging us around shopping malls. But we hadn't flown since Dad moved in June, and then, of course, September happened. I got scared; I didn't know if they would let us on the plane without a grownup around. The guy's nametag said, "M. Rodriguez." He was one of what Dad called "the eight other brown-skinned people in town." (That wasn't true, there was a ton of brown people in Syracuse.) Anyway, I got a strong feeling, and I stood up straight. I was pretty tall for a twelve-year-old, and people thought I was older than I was. I looked into his coffee-colored eyes—the same color as mine and Hani's. "My mom's just in the bathroom. She's really scared of crowds, 'cause of—you know, everything in the news—and she's got these bad stomach problems. She told us to come over here and get our tickets before it's too late. Please, sir, we just want to see our grandma." It was such a huge, stupid lie, I couldn't believe it came out of me. Hani kept the death squeeze on my hand and nodded.

M. Rodriguez stared back at us a long, long second. His eyes caught for a moment on our sweaters. Then he nodded and muttered, "The damn terrorists." He started pushing buttons. When I saw those boarding passes printing, my knees sagged with relief.

He asked us a million more questions, if we were carrying anything flammable or liquid or had anyone given us any mysterious packages. But he did it in an official voice, like everything was settled. Then we went to security, which was crammed; guards were running wands over people's arms. They made us take off our sweaters, so we were shivering in our t-shirts. "Oh my gosh!" this one guard said. "Where did you get this?" She held out Hani's flag sweater. "This is *darling*."

Even though I didn't want to wear it, all at once it was like I had to get our sweaters back right away, and I stood there not moving while the guards read them and shook their heads and said they'd both order sweaters if Gram ever went into business.

We were at the gate about twenty hours early, of course. There were more guards and soldiers—two of them saluted at Hani—and all the people who finally got through security looking even more grim. I had my Christmas tree on, and Hani wore his flag, and people gave us little smiles and looks and one old man said, "God bless you, children."

"I'm gonna wear this every day from now on!" Hani proclaimed. When it was time to board, we didn't get randomly selected for extra questioning, even though they seemed to pull anyone darker-skinned out of the line. The gate lady just lifted her eyes at Hani and said, "Merry Christmas, cutie!"

The first flight was a little bumpy plane that blared the whole time like a lawn mower. At JFK we walked a million miles, and we asked people directions until a Delta lady took us to the gate. She gave us candy canes in plastic sleeves and said, "Those are the sweetest little sweaters."

I couldn't remember if people were always that nice to us at airports, but I didn't think so.

Every year growing up, I wanted a Christmas tree, but Dad always said that was just the Western colonizer taking over my imagination. "It's not bad enough that they steal our land and oil, they have to take over our culture too." But when we asked Dad about how the Muslims celebrated stuff, he wasn't sure because he was also half-Greek, born in America, and when you come right down to it, total American. Gram told me they celebrated Eid el Fitr, which was like the big feasting that came after all the fasting for Ramadan. She said they made dainty pancakes sprinkled with sugar and rolled up. And you'd get a new set of clothes, and people would go walking all over, visiting each other and bringing food. It sounded awesome, only we didn't do any of the Muslim things in this country: it was too much work. Stop everything and pray five times a day? Like that's going to happen. So, the way I saw it, why *not* have a tree?

The second plane was huge; it was going on to LA after Baltimore, and it was packed with guys in white suits and women carrying shopping bags filled with wrapped things, and at least two people wearing Santa hats. A flight attendant dressed up like an elf gave us coloring books and crayons, and even though I was twelve, I was kind of happy to get them. There had been all these rumors that another really bad thing would happen around the holidays; everyone looked stressed, their eyes skating everywhere, checking each other out, the darker-skinned guys had their heads tucked into their shoulders like they were trying to shrink. I looked at Hani's springy black hair and thought, please, please, please, don't get any older.

We were sitting in one of those center aisles, four across, Hani on the end, then me, then this lady, and some guy on the other end. The lady was wearing a cute pink suit with pearls and pink shoes. Her skin was this creamy cocoa color, and her hair was black and smooth as wax. She opened a tin and offered us cookies in the shapes of reindeer and angels. Hani tried to take like a thousand, but I was like, "Uh-uh. *One.*" She laughed and said "It's fine—take all you want." She admired the perfect little Gram stitches on my sweater, running the lower edge between her fingers. "My mother does work like this too."

When we started rolling down the runway, though, she stopped smiling, her eyes moving back and forth like everyone else's. "I never liked flying and—now especially . . ."

She wasn't the first grownup who'd said something like that to me. Hani and I had flown something like ten times since Mom moved away, so I patted her arm and said, "Don't worry—there's really nothing to be scared of." Hani leaned forward and said in his high voice. "Flying is the funnest. After you get back on the ground, then it's less fun." Then he was done and sat back.

Her lips parted again like she was surprised, her smile white as porcelain. "Are you going to spend Christmas with your granny?"

I nodded: it was easier to go with what people expected than to try to explain things. She could've been a sky marshal in disguise. Gram said they were on all the planes now—she might compare what we said to what we'd told the ticket agent.

Her name was Theresa, and she was going to Baltimore to get married. She twisted a diamond back and forth on her finger. They were getting married at a nice spot on the river front on Christmas Eve. "All my people are back in Maryland."

Hani, meanwhile, was in heaven. He'd discovered the seats had screens with stuff like Super Nintendo. He played with the video game, jumping around, holding the controls in both hands, making stupid little laser sounds.

"Pioo, pioo, pioo!" His head twisted sideways. "I made it to Level 3! Sami, did you hear me? I got to *Level 3.*"

For a while, we all sat back. Theresa was sewing a satiny thing that she said was her something-blue. I flipped through a magazine that someone had forgotten in the seat pocket—it was pages of Christmas stuff that you could make or buy: angel-shaped cards, rum-spiked eggnog, Santa stencils for your kids' walls. After a while, I noticed Theresa put down her sewing and start kind of looking over her other shoulder. I wasn't paying a lot of attention though because Hani had started giving me these long, watery, old man looks. He was like that more and more—one second he'd be eating Bearitos and watching SpongeBob, the next he'd be worried about Gram's cough, or what was he going to wear to school, or did anyone make our lunches. Now he said, "Why are we spending Christmas with Dad?"

"'Cause—I don't know—he's our dad and we don't really do Christmas, anyway."

"Why doesn't he come *back* for Christmas? Why do we have to go *there?*" His little voice got higher and louder. "What if they're going to make us *move* to Baltimore?"

"Don't be *mejnoon.*" I said a Gram word, which was usually pretty persuasive, but Hani still looked old and sad. And I felt this angriness start inside me, like a trembling, like I almost didn't want to see Dad at all, when I felt something clap down on my arm. I jumped. Theresa's face was close to mine; her eyes were full of tears. "I think the guy sitting next to me—I think we've got to call the flight attendant!"

"What do you mean? What's wrong with him?" I leaned over to look, but she grabbed me again. "He's holding—I think it's one of those holy books. And he keeps standing up and sitting down and staring out the window."

"Did you try talking to him?" I heard Gram's voice come out of me.

Theresa shook her head; her face looked tight, like it was wrapped on. "I tried—a couple times! He just ignores me. He's not normal. I don't think he speaks English. He just keeps looking in his holy book!"

I let my eyes skim over her shoulder. I saw the guy had wooly, knobby hair like Uncle Ziad's, his skin just a shade lighter than Theresa's, just a touch darker than mine and Hani's. He was bent forward so I could see the bow of his back, an old black book open in his hands: he looked like he was praying. Then he got out of his seat, crouched, and stared out the window, like at the wing of the airplane.

My throat felt cinched up like someone had pulled a drawstring, and my breath got smaller and smaller until it was just tiny puffs. Pictures started coming back to me from the news that day. Fire and smoke like black curtains.

We were supposed to have been at school that day, but Hani and I were both home with chicken pox. We were still in pajamas watching Gram's game shows when the news came on. Dad ran to call Mom, and Gram went out in the hallway, knocking on doors, checking on the neighbors, like she thought that curtain of dust was going to roll all the way up the state. Hani and I kept watching the TV. Hani kept asking, "Is this a movie or for real?" I couldn't get my voice to come out to answer him. Gram was crying, talking to Turkish Mrs. Krickorian next door, saying, "Please God, don't let it be the Arabs."

The green elf flight attendant jingled up the aisle. I saw Theresa's eyes follow her. Her eyes were lit up, her voice tight as a little metal coil. "We've got to go back. We have to turn the plane around."

"What's she saying?" Hani held my arm with both hands. He wanted me to tell him, and he didn't want to know. For weeks after we saw the pictures on the TV, I woke up in the night, coming out of sleep that felt sharp and twisted, like a corkscrew. If I heard Hani whimpering in his bed next door, I'd go climb in with him. Sometimes Gram would come and put the cool cloth on our heads like we were sick—it smelled like mint and cucumber. I usually slept a little better after that.

If I were a grown up, I might have tried to put a washcloth on Theresa's face, or rubbed her palms—another Gram thing—and told her to breathe, breathe, and said, remember, the world is basically good. Even when lots of bad happens, the world is okay. Which was something that I'd figured out to tell myself, and it helped even when the washcloth couldn't.

Instead, I whispered, "You think he's one of *those guys*?" We both looked again, and now the man was leaning into his book and his face looked like he was furious.

I'd heard it myself on the airport speaker system: "If you see or hear anything suspicious, speak up!"

Theresa stood and climbed past me and Hani, going fast up the aisle after the attendant. For a second there was this empty space she left behind, like a little whoosh of fear, and I was scared too because now there wasn't anything between me and the terrorist. I felt this slot open in me that was so cold all I could feel was how angry I was with my dumb dad always trying to hit it big and our dumb mom whose motto was: what's good for Mom is good for the kids.

Anyway, I saw Theresa snag the attendant-elf; they were whispering like mad; then other attendants seemed to be magnetized by their discussion and came over. All these people in the seats near ours started looking at us, and the guy and Theresa, their heads twisting and their faces hard as glass. One woman said in a wavy voice a few rows away, "What's going on?"

Then the guy at the end of our row looked over at me and my heart felt like it actually jumped out of place, like it could bang right out of my chest. I wrapped my arms around myself and felt the silky yarn under my hands. I thought: Gram made us the wrong kinds of sweaters.

Finally I glanced back, and that was when I realized that the guy was sort of a kid too. Slowly, my heart calmed down, and I told Hani to chill. Theresa's cookie tin was on the floor. I picked it up and pried off the lid. It was red with green holly leaves. Gram always said the most important thing is to *offer*. I leaned over Theresa's seat and said in my horrible, terrible Arabic, *"Bitheb bascote?"* It was like buying a chance at a raffle. Even if he actually spoke Arabic, I didn't think he'd understand me. The only words I knew were the little things I heard Gram saying on the phone or when she visited with Uncle Ziad or Aunt Leeli or Aunt Nuri, usually just crying about why did she ever move here, fifty-two years ago.

Anyway, the guy almost flinched like he thought I was going to hit him.

Hani was hanging on me going, "What are you *doing* Sami? Don't *do* that." But then the guy smiled and said something that I realized meant, "Hey, you speak Arabic? Where are you from?" Then he took one of the reindeer cookies and asked, "Is this a gazelle?"

We had a little conversation: it was little because I didn't know the language, though he kept saying I did—and the whole time, I could see Theresa and the elf and about five other flight attendants watching us eat cookies. He said his name was Fareed, but we could call him Fred, and he was a student in Morocco. He was studying mechanical engineering—the book he was studying was a textbook full of diagrams. He'd been watching the wings of the plane to see how the flaps operated. He was going to meet the rest of his class in Washington D.C. and tour the Smithsonian, and had I ever been to the Smithsonian? "Spirit of St. Louis!" he said in English.

He asked where we "started from," which I liked; it seemed like a better way of saying, I know you didn't learn that Arabic in Syracuse. He said Morocco was a long way from Jordan.

He shook hands with Hani, who showed him the game controls in the seat and then it was so much for Fred's textbook, and he started playing the same game. The elf flight attendant came back with Theresa, and they stood there half-way smiling. The elf leaned in and rested an elbow on the seat back in front of us. "So, how're we doing here?" Fred had to put down his controls and shake hands with everyone again. I introduced him to Theresa after she got back into her seat and he said in English, "These cookies? I get fat! Ho ho ho! Yes?"

She smiled, then turned, clutching the tin almost like she had a stomachache. "I'm so ashamed," she mumbled to me. "My people have been racially profiled for years, and I just turned right around and did the same damn thing."

I realized that everyone in our row was a slightly different shade of brown or tan. All of us eating reindeer cookies.

Dad was waiting for us, smiling so hard I almost didn't recognize him at first. "There they are," he said. "My good-luck charms!" He gave me a squeeze that pushed the air out of my lungs. "Thank God you made it! Was Grandma mad you came? I didn't think she'd let you come. Did they give you a hard time at security? Did you get *randomly selected*?" He made that gesture of curling his fingers in the air.

Hani tried to tell Dad about the people we met on the plane, but Dad was on the phone a lot. Being successful—he kept saying—was a lot busier than not being successful.

A week later, after we got back to Syracuse, we told Gram that the best part of the trip was back at Dad's condo. I smelled it when we walked in the door, but I didn't believe it until we got to the living room, and there it actually was: almost touching the ceiling, with bright flashes of blue-green, then dark, secretive boughs. There weren't many ornaments, but there was a white star on top, like the one on my sweater. "Oh yeah." Dad had rolled his eyes, but I could see him trying to hide his smile. "The girl friend 'doo joor' made me get that. I don't know. It's annoying, but it's just another pagan symbol, right?"

I tried to explain to Gram how seeing that tree made me feel like there was this wonderful stranger in the room with a secret to tell me.

"What was this secret?" Gram asked, not really listening, winding her yarn. We constantly had to wind her skeins into tidy balls.

"I don't know," I said. We'd forgotten our sweaters back at Dad's place and hadn't gotten around to telling her yet. "That's what made it good." I'd figured out at least that much: you couldn't actually know the secret. You had to just enjoy it. It looks like one thing or another but maybe it doesn't necessarily mean anything. And as soon as I saw the tree, I didn't feel so mad at our dad anymore.

"So you get your magical Santa wish," Gram said. "Congratulations." She made her snuffling sound which means, *well that's enough of that*. "And what about the boy on the aeroplane? What happened to the *meskeen*?" Poor thing.

We kept rolling yarn, thinking about the meskeen. Who knew what happened to that guy? I saw him getting a suitcase at baggage claim—he looked lost and a little scared in the whirl of holiday music and travelers, and then he was gone. Would he be okay? Would Theresa get married and be happy? Some things you know and some you never really figure out—those are the scary rules for being a grownup.

But I wasn't really ready for all that yet.

I stood near the window, winding, watching the evening come; outside, a Christmas tree lay toppled on the corner. Snow scattered over it in the blue evening. Even though people were done with it, the tree still looked beautiful to me. It was deep green against fading white, its branches soft and full of old light. It murmured to me as I stood in my window, like a promise or a secret, like something silky, unfamiliar, and new.

I AM DRAGON
Preston Allen

Once upon a time, there was a dragon who took the form of a man.

And the dragon who looked like a man lived with his wife and three children until they could not take it anymore and they left him.

His eyes were too big for his head. His hands, though they looked like hands, reminded them of hooked talons. And always, there was the smell of smoke about him. Smoke and blood. A smell like human flesh cooking. Their house, though it was a modern house with a TV, refrigerator, and store-bought furniture, was cold and empty like a cave. The ceiling was too high; animal noises came from the walls. Their house—it was a cave!

And so they left him, and he was alone, and not very old yet. In dragon years, he was only 473. A mere child. In human years, he was thirty-five.

And so he did what dragons do when they are lonely, or just alone; he went out and hunted for treasure, and when he found it, he hid it in the basement of his cave.

Her name was Mary.

Her name was Mary Elizabeth Gaskins, and she was six. But she was sickly and died after only two years in the basement.

He put her remains in a sack and put the sack in the trunk of his car and made the trip from Miami up to Alabama and partially buried the sack in a shallow hole he dug on the grounds of a memorial for Confederate Dead. There was no significance to his selection of this particular spot that they knew of, though after they discovered Mary's body, with her little feet sticking out of the half buried sack, the authorities up there spent many years chasing a murderous specter they dubbed "Bloody Rebel." The Alabama authorities were certain that Bloody Rebel would strike again, but he never did.

The dragon, however, did strike again, beginning his next hunt immediately after the death of Mary Elizabeth Gaskins, whom he had loved very much.

It was Christmas again, the season of tinsel and holly, and he found her at the mall in the company of her older siblings, but he quickly lured her away.

Her name was Alexandria Tamara Bonophileos, and she was six and he hid her in the basement of his cave where she remained for a decade.

A decade later, when the dragon reached the age of forty-seven in human years, his human form had become seriously ill and he sought the advice of a friend, who was a doctor at the hospital. The doctor informed him that the cancer had spread to the bones and had reached such a stage that really there was nothing that could be done at that point—now, if the dragon had sought treatment five or six years earlier, maybe something could have been done. Chemotherapy. Radiation. Something. So the dragon had about six weeks to live—and he must be hospitalized immediately.

"Immediately," the dragon roared. "No! I have to go home right now. There are things that I need to take care of. Let me go home, and I shall return. I have treasure in my basement that needs to be secured!"

He fought against them, but he was under the sedative influence of various medicines, and so his fighting amounted to little more than the feeble flailing of his limbs as they wheeled him down to radiation.

Now there was an orderly on duty who had heard the dragon say "treasure."

The orderly was young and of a character that was not entirely wholesome. The orderly flirted with the head nurse until she opened the dragon's file, whereupon he quickly memorized the address. Then the orderly and a friend staked out the house for thirteen hours until they were certain no one was inside and that no one would be coming home—they had concluded correctly that the dragon lived alone. Using the tools of burglary, the orderly and his friend entered the dragon's home through the back door.

There was not much to steal. An old black and white TV. An old stereo system. A few hundred dollars in a jar marked "groceries." But the treasure, the orderly knew, was in the basement.

Now where was the basement?

It took them more than two hours to find the door hidden behind the false fireplace, which the orderly's friend had pushed aside accidentally while taunting the orderly: "There ain't nothing here. That man was delirious, talkin' crazy. There ain't no basement in this house. There ain't no basement in none of the houses in this neighborhood."

But the friend, speaking thus, leaned against the fireplace and there was a slight movement. The orderly jumped with joy when he saw that.

They pushed the false fireplace away from the wall and discovered behind it a small door. It was made of reinforced steel with the hinges on the inside and no grooves, no cracks, nothing they could stick a sharp tool into for purchase. It had a coded spin dial on it. It was as impregnable as a safe.

"Now what we gonna do? We ain't got nothing to open this," the orderly's friend complained.

But the orderly said, "The wall itself! We can cut through the wall. Or we can break the damned thing down."

The friend guarded the wall while the orderly snuck out and using the money they had lifted from the jar marked "groceries," went to the hardware store. He came back with sledgehammers and a hacksaw. Twenty-five minutes later the hole in the wall was large enough to crawl through if they got down on their hands and knees, which they did.

They stuck their heads inside. There was a light on in there—and two big blue eyes blinking back at them.

They screamed like little girls and flung themselves backwards as a cheerful voice from the hole in the wall said, "Hi? Hello? Are you there?"

Outside there was the sound of sirens. One of the neighbors had called the police because of all of the banging with sledgehammers. Now the police were banging on the front door.

They heard the noise of other police officers coming in through the back door, shouting, "Get down on the ground! Show us your hands! Show us your hands now!"

They heard the voice from the hole in the wall say again, "Are you out there? Hello? Hello?"

The police officers were in the room with them now and they heard it too. Guns were drawn, but no one spoke as the blond-haired, blue-eyed Alexandria Tamara Bonophileos, brushing back the crumbling masonry, crawled out of the hole, stood up and waved at them with her fingers.

She looked wild with all of that long uncombed hair, though still beautiful. An innocent smile played across her lips. Of course, she was completely innocent after ten years in the dragon's basement. She had gone from six to sixteen. She was ghastly pale but beautiful.

She was completely naked.

At the prison wing of the hospital, the dying dragon explained to the police, a priest, his court-appointed legal counsel, and his ex-wife, "I was lonely. I tried not to hurt her too much."

"What are you talking about? How could you hurt her any more than you already have? You're a monster," his ex-wife sobbed.

"Was there anyone else?" asked the police captain.

The dragon said, "Yes," and proceeded to tell them about Mary Elizabeth Gaskins, who had been unearthed up in Alabama, and about another girl, a girl about the age of his eldest daughter, buried in his backyard, and another one from way back, a girl whom he had kept during his high school years, a girl who, he assumed, was still resting in a small pink box in his parents' attic in Coral Gables. Sarah Gayle Rosencrantz. Heard of her? And another girl, the first girl, who had been named Kaitlin Fitzgerald. Fitzsimmons? Something like that. Buried in an abandoned field near her elementary school.

He had not meant to strangle Kaitlin Fitzgerald. Fitzsimmons? Fitzpatrick? The strangling had been an accident due to his inexperience back then with gags. He had not meant to hurt any of them. These girls—they were treasure. They were to be guarded and treasured.

He asked the police representatives if they understood what he was trying to tell them. They said they did, but he knew that they were lying. It is not easy to lie successfully to a dragon. They were trying to close the book on as many cases as they could before he died, and the dragon was telling them all of this in exchange for a favor.

He wanted to see his treasure one last time.

Now in most cases, such a request would have been rejected, but Alexandria, back at home three weeks and having a real hard time getting to know a family that she had long ago forgotten even existed, wanted to see him too. The dragon was the only human she had known for ten years, the greater part of her life, since he had never let her up out of the vault except on the Fourth of July to see the fireworks and on Christmas to see the blinking lights.

He had imprisoned her in the vault, the small basement he had built beneath his false fireplace, and he had taken advantage of her sexually, but, in her words, she had grown to "love him."

She called him the nicest man in the whole wide world and the funniest too. She said that he came down and made her laugh every day. If his silly jokes didn't work, he would tickle her.

He had kept her well fed and read books to her at night before she went to bed. When she was good, he would bring down the TV and allow her to watch it for a while, but not too long. He warned her that TV was bad for her and too much of it would make her stupid.

In the basement, which he had furnished for her like a playhouse, he lavished her with gifts. Dolls and dollhouses and pets. In her whole life, she estimated, she had had at least a thousand goldfish, six parakeets, three bunny rabbits, and one dog, a black Labrador retriever whom the dragon got rid of when it attacked and ate one of her rabbits, which made her sad. He never liked to see her sad, and she made sure always to smile for him whenever he came down, even if she wasn't feeling too well that day.

She was innocent, illiterate, and completely in love with the dragon, whom she called "husband."

And she promised them that she would kill herself if she were not allowed to see him before he died.

It was an evil thing he had done to this girl. Evil.

So they brought her in to see him. He was very sick. She sat beside him and took his hand.

She said to him, "I thought I would never see you again, husband."

He said, "I thought I would never see you again, little one."

There they sat, exchanging private smiles.

And she came by again the next day and sat with him all day. They heard her singing to him. They heard him singing to her. They heard them singing together. Christmas carols. Indeed, it was Christmas again. The season of tinsel and holly. The season he hunted them. The season he took them. The season he had taken her.

That night, in the company of a trio of select print reporters and a dozen armed guards, they were allowed to go outside.

She sat in a chair beside the dragon's wheeled bed, holding his hand. Watching the blinking lights, neither of them spoke.

When she came in the day after that, they informed her that he had died in his sleep the previous night.

The girl, Alexandria Tamara Bonophileos, age sixteen with the mind of perhaps a nine-year old, was the only one who shed tears when the dragon died.

Then she went back to her strange new home and tried her best to learn to love her birth family again.

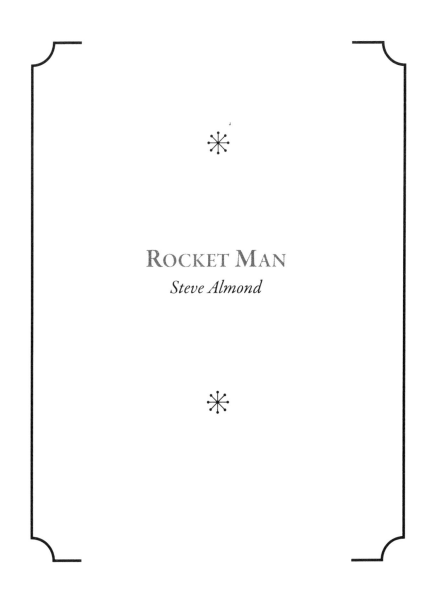

ROCKET MAN
Steve Almond

In 1974, my parents gave me a Gemini Titan Flying Model Rocket for Christmas. I had been talking of nothing else for months. The Gemini Titan wasn't as big as the Saturn, and it didn't have the excellent detailing of the Patriot or the Mercury Redstone, but it had become central to my existence. I was ten years old that winter. My brother Dan was thirteen.

We lived in the Central Valley of California, where it never snowed, where the fields outside of town threw up fumes of garlic. The holidays were always something of a stretch. We were Jews, technically, but we didn't celebrate anything. We had lost our loyalty to the ancient myths.

I asked my father once whether he believed in God. He closed his eyes, as if the question made him very tired. "I believe in problems," he said slowly. "And I believe in proofs." He was a theoretical mathematician, brilliant but, for the most part, unreachable.

We had come to California because his father had secured him a position at the local university. I didn't know this at the time. The move was explained to me mostly in terms of weather. Columbus was cold and dark. The sun never set in California. My mother took a position with the state. They both spent long hours at the office, my father compiling material for the manuscript he hoped would win him tenure, my mother providing counsel to the families of infants in jeopardy.

Dan and I did our homework. We had a few tentative friends. Mostly, we spent long sunny afternoons in front of the television. We hung blankets from the curtain rods to cut the window glare and set ourselves adrift in the bright colors and canned laughter, borrowed notions of coolness, desperate smiling commercials.

Christmas happened at the insistence of my grandmother, a German Jew who, for complicated but not unprecedented reasons, wanted nothing to do with the religion of her birth. It was a holiday in keeping with her notions of family, a ritual that celebrated innocence and hope, and involved a large, mid-day meal, to which she invited a variety of ecumenical strays. Her home was haunted by relics she had smuggled out before the Second World War, photos of her as a girl in Bavaria, wearing a white dirndl and staring sadly at the camera. My grandfather, a famous astrophysicist, paid little attention to her, and she responded by leaving food on their kitchen counter till it turned.

I can't remember what we ate that year, though I feel safe in reporting that it was under spiced and overcooked. My brother was already showing signs of his genius. He and my grandfather huddled at one end of the table, murmuring in their private language of exoplanets and dwarf stars. I was trapped between my grandmother and a homely graduate student from Sweden. My parents sat across from one another, eating in silence. Toward the end of the meal, my mother glanced at my father with a misery that startled me. She got up, rubbing her eyes, and went to the bathroom.

I assumed that she was merely bored and irritable, because the Christmas meal was understood, even then, as an obligation, a way of pretending that if you gathered around a table laden with food, on the prescribed day, that meant you were a family.

Among the photos taken that day is one of me, snapped at the precise moment I unwrapped the Gemini Titan. I had figured out I was getting the rocket. I knew the precise size of the box, and I also knew that my parents felt guilty for moving us to California, for leaving us mostly to our own devices. But I still had to act surprised. That was part of the deal.

You can't see the rocket in the picture, just that I'm cradling something in my arms. My eyes are bugged out and my mouth is stretched into a gaping zero. What I remember when I look at that photo today isn't how hard I was selling the moment, but the disorienting sensation I felt inside, of my yearning suddenly reduced to nothing. I look, in fact, horrified.

There's no sign of Dan in the picture. But he was there, just outside the frame. He waited for me to exhaust my gratitude, for the questions from parents and grandparents to be asked and answered. Then he leaned in and whispered to me, "It's a shit model, Eli. Shit shit shit."

Dan had always been tough on me. And now that he was in middle school, on the brink of puberty, his disdain had blossomed into something closer to cruelty. I could tell I was losing him—younger brothers always can—and this made me obsequious, which only deepened his disgust. He hated that he had to sit around each afternoon and watch television with me, because he was a lowly seventh grader, studying with, as he put it, "a bunch of retard Mexicans." So I suffered his insults and occasional beatings. I certainly wasn't going to tell on him.

The big question, as far as I was concerned, was whether my parents would allow me to launch the Gemini Titan that day. It was mid-afternoon, another three hours of light, and there was an open field behind my grandparents' house, where I'd launched two smaller rockets.

I looked at my mom, who looked at my dad. He was lost in thought, tumbling through one of his equations.

"Bernie," my mother said tiredly. "Earth to Bernie."

"Right here," my father said. "Yes. What?"

My grandmother began to fret that the rocket might hit a neighbor's home.

"It's a rocket," my grandfather said, "not a bomb."

Which seemed to settle the matter.

I took the kit to the garage. The Gemini Titan was my first "level four" rocket. I won't bore you with the technical details. It's enough to know that the instructions consisted of ten pages of small print. According to the specs, the Gemini would exert eight newtons of thrust at launch, with a maximum flight altitude of 250 yards. The parts themselves composed a kind of nerd poetry: *shock cord, nose cone, launch lug.*

I had gotten into rockets not because of any inherited aptitude for astrophysics, but because Dan had been into them a few years earlier, and had allowed me—on our mother's orders, no doubt—to accompany him on a few launches.

He'd since moved on to more adult pursuits: chess, electrical engineering, astronomy. Dan cycled through hobbies like this. He pursued them furiously, obsessively, mastered them, moved on. To me, the lonely kid brother, the kid who had to struggle at things, his abilities seemed limitless. It didn't take me long to recognize that the Gemini Titan was beyond my expertise. I sat, lost in a scattering of components.

Inside, the adults were drinking wine in the living room. A fire was going and my grandmother had hung a silk tapestry over the hearth, as she did each year, of the tiny baby Jesus in his mother's arms. This had been a gift from one of her strays, and it made us all feel uncomfortable, as Jews, as non-believers, which was, I think, its purpose.

I was looking for my dad, but he was out back, staring at the pool.

Dan was in the study with my grandfather, having already put together his gift, an electric Ferris wheel.

"What is it, honey?" my mom said.

"I just wanted a little advice from Dad."

"Please don't disturb your father right now."

"Why? What's wrong?"

"Nothing." She sipped her wine and smiled. "I'll tell him, okay?"

A silence descended on the room. My mom glanced at the tapestry of the mother and child, that milky vision of love that looms over Christmas. She seemed on the verge of weeping. I knew I'd walked in on something, but I couldn't tell what, so I went back to the garage.

A few minutes later, Dan appeared in the doorway.

He looked down at the half-assembled recovery unit in my hand, and sighed with a towering disappointment. "You're fucking that up," he said.

"Bullshit," I said.

"You got to pack the wadding tighter, or the engine's gonna melt the parachute."

"What happened to the Ferris wheel?" I said.

"Why the fuck would I want a Ferris wheel?"

"Maybe you could make it into something else. Like a roller coaster."

Dan looked at me and shook his head.

I had to accept this about Dan. He wasn't going to like me. He wasn't going to teach me. He was here because it was Christmas Day and he was trapped, and because my mom had ordered him to help me out. And still, for me, it was enough. Enough to be in his presence, to watch his restless hands at work, to smell the Mennen Speed Stick he'd begun wearing under his arms. It took him maybe five minutes to rig up the recovery unit. He didn't look once at the instructions. He built a launch pad using a sundial and wooden blocks. Then he began rooting around in the shelves above my grandfather's workbench.

"What are you looking for?" I said.

"Propellant," he said.

"What do you mean? It's done. Let's launch it."

Dan kept rooting around.

"Seriously. It's getting dark."

"You want this thing to get air or not?"

"Duh," I said.

"Then stop being a fembot and help me look."

"For what?"

"Fertilizer. Pressurized gas. Anything with nitrogen."

Dan came up with a concoction that was mostly fertilizer, along with a little gasoline and powdered sulfate. He packed it into four thick cardboard tubes, each the size of a roll of quarters. These he taped around the rim of the original engine pack. He held the rocket up for inspection. "Quad boosters," he said, looking at me and smiling. "This thing is going to outer space, bro."

I had a strong sense that our parents should be consulted. But I also knew we were doing something wrong, and we were doing it together, which is the dream of every younger brother—to be taken into confidence, to pass from a state of hindrance to collaboration.

We went back into the house. I figured my father, or grandfather, would see what Dan had done and put an end to it. But the only person we could find was our grandmother. She was in the kitchen watching her maid, Wilma, wash the dishes. The strays had found their way home. My parents were taking a walk. My grandfather was asleep at the desk in his study.

"What do you think, Grandma?" Dan said.

"It's quite big, isn't it? Look at this, Wilma. My grandsons just built a rocket."

"Real nice," Wilma said.

"We're going to launch it in the backyard," Dan said.

My grandmother got a pained look on her face. "Oh, Danny," she said, in her German accent. "I wish you wouldn't. It's nearly dark."

Dan smiled and set his hand on our grandmother's arm. It was a debonair gesture, as if he recognized, beneath all her social efforts, the essential loneliness that ruled her life. "Eli's been waiting for this for months," he said quietly. "Don't worry, Grandma. We'll be super careful. It goes straight up and comes straight down."

What was she going say? We were practically all she had in this world. The rest of her family was long gone.

"We'll be back in half an hour," Dan said. "Less." Then he opened the cabinet where she kept her cookie tins—he was tall enough now—and grabbed a half dozen frosted Lebkuchen.

Dusk was coming on and we hurried past the pool and into the dirt field. Dan was carrying the launch pad. I had the rocket. It was cool and windless. We could see the colored lights strung up from nearby houses. Dan picked up a rock and hurled it over a stand of trees, toward the big house on the other side. It landed with a thud. I wanted to say something, to caution Dan against bringing trouble down onto us. But I also knew that he was going to do what he was going to do; that his delinquency was, in this sense, another invitation to me, a chance to demonstrate I was worthy of his company.

He picked up another rock and hurled it and this one landed, much more loudly, with a hollow ringing.

"Shit," I said. "Dude."

"Fuck it," Dan said. "Rich fucking assholes."

We walked to the middle of the field and Dan stomped on the dirt, to create a solid foundation for the launch pad. "It's got to be perfectly level," he said. "If there's any deviation, even a degree or two, you're fucked." He set the launch pad down and motioned for me to lower the Gemini Titan into position. It was dark enough now that the silver and white decals shone against the sky.

The rocket launched via an electronic switch box. I worried that Dan was going to want to flick the switch. But he handed the box to me and said, "All right, bro. Let's see what this mother is made of."

As we stepped back from the launch pad, I couldn't help but to start imitating the broadcasts we'd watched, as much younger kids, of the moon launches. "Houston, do you read me? This is G-T One, counting down for launch."

"Roger that, G-T One," Dan said. "Flight path set. Extra boost capacity implemented. This is your moon shot, you little fembot. Quit holding your pud and count that shit down."

"No longer holding my pud, Houston. The pud situation has been remedied. But I'm pretty sure I just pooped my pants."

"Roger that, poopy pants. Shit sensors activated."

I started laughing, hysterically, and Dan farted, something he was able to do at will.

"You are one smelly little fembot, G-T One. Did you have beans for dinner? All right. Let's lock it down. No more poop talk. We've been working toward this launch for years."

Dan handed me a cookie, without looking at me, and I thought I might die of happiness, that he was next to me, acknowledging my feeble wishes, which seemed, most often, a faint echo of his own. I started the countdown. At four, a scream knifed in from behind us.

We wheeled around and there stood our parents, maybe fifty yards away, squared off near the diving board.

"I won't be accused like this," my father roared.

"This happened, Bernard," my mother roared back. "We're both responsible."

My father gazed out into the field. I thought for sure they were talking about us, that he would come marching out now to collar us. But neither of them moved. They stood in the undulating blue light of the pool, their bodies stiff with rage.

"What the fuck?" I said. "What's going on?"

"They're fighting, you queeb."

"Duh," I said. "About what?"

Dan was chewing on a cookie. He turned away from the pool and squinted at the houses across the field. "She had a fucking abortion," he said. "Don't you get it? Don't you get anything?"

"I *get* it," I said. "Duh. Abortion."

I had a vague sense of something medical, a condition perhaps. This was another one of those moments—they were happening more and more—when the gap between my age and Dan's felt vast and unbridgeable. It wasn't just that he knew things I didn't, but that he knew things about our parents. I was jealous of him, because he was closer to them, to their unhappiness. That's how young I was.

"Mom was going to have a baby," Dan said, "and now she's not."

"A baby?"

"A *wittle* bundle of joy," he muttered. "A Christ child."

I didn't get it. I was ten years old, after all, still murky on the entire question of how babies got made, let alone unmade. I understood what I could see: that my parents were in a fight, that the mysterious tensions of the past months had erupted, at last, into something visible. I watched them step toward one another and embrace, as if they'd fall apart forever if they released their grip.

"What should we do?" I said.

Dan turned away from my parents and spit on the ground. "We should launch your piece of shit rocket."

It was severe purple overhead now, and a first star appeared. In just a few minutes, it would be too dark to see anything. "Okay," I said. "Houston, I'm going to initiate the launch sequence."

"Just do it, queebo."

I flicked the switch. For a second, nothing happened. Then I heard the familiar sizzle of the propellant coming lit, and the orange contrails appeared. The Gemini employed an A-83 engine, those eight newtons of thrust, with another three for the second stage, when the recovery capsule released. But Dan had added his homemade boosters, and they detonated a hundred yards up, four monstrous yellow explosions, one after another, sending the rocket zooming toward space.

"Fucking A," I said. "Houston, are you seeing this shit?"

"Roger that," Dan said.

For a moment, it looked like the rocket was never going to stop at all, was going to achieve escape velocity, that holy threshold where earth's puny gravitational field gives way to the unseen mass of the universe and orbit becomes possible.

It occurred to me, as we watched the fuselage become a tiny white point above us, why I'd become so fixated on the Gemini Titan in the first place, which was because the Gemini rockets, the real ones built by NASA, were designed for two men. Our grandfather had explained this to us one afternoon, just after our arrival in California, a time of great hope. He showed us pictures of the cockpit, the twin seats abreast like thrones, and I imagined Dan and myself, strapped in together, steering our vessel toward an eternal serenity.

We heard a faint pop, which was the recovery unit detonating, then the thin hiss of debris falling from the sky. The fuselage whistled down and landed ten feet from the launch pad, mangled and smoking. The extra heat had melted the checkered parachute into a clump of plastic.

"Holy shit," I said.

"Fucking moon shot," Dan said.

"Should we look for the nose cap?" I said.

Dan laughed. "You crack me up, little man."

It was getting darker. I kept expecting someone to call us into the house. But no one did. We stood there watching the stars appear one by one, then all at once. Dan had been studying the charts, not just the constellations, but the nebulae and distant suns that reveal themselves, on clear winter nights, as a kind of enveloping celestial dust.

I looked down at the smoking husk and sang out, *Rocket man, burning out his fuse out here alone.* It was the wrong thing to do, of course, because it broke whatever spell we'd been under, and reminded Dan that I was young and sentimental, still eager for some childish version of love, which is to say, a faggot.

"Shut up, faggot," he said.

"What should we do with the rocket?" I said.

"Bury it."

I did so and we marched back toward the house, until we were close enough to see my grandparents through the back window. They weren't hugging exactly, but their bodies were pressed close and this was striking, because my grandmother shied from physical contact.

Maybe all Christmases are sad in retrospect, because we expect them to be so happy. Or maybe this is the theory of a depressed person. I hope not.

In any case, my hallowed innocence did not die that night. It's only my memory that sees it that way. This is what our memories do. They organize the emotional chaos of our lives into discrete stories. They are the unsung editors of consciousness, because they always know more than we did at the time.

It would turn out, we say. It would turn out that my mother and father separated six months after that Christmas, and divorced a year later. It would turn out my grandfather was, unbeknownst to all but his wife, losing his way, his famous brain eaten by disease. And it would turn out that Dan never treated me as kindly again, as I'm sure you've figured out by now. He was growing into himself, becoming someone sealed off from love.

Years later, having failed out of college, married too young, fathered a child, and driven his family from him, Dan called me. He was in Olympia,

Washington, for reasons he didn't feel like discussing, standing, it sounded like, in a sopping rain. He wanted me to invest in a project he was putting together, something involving fuel cells. The individual sentences he spoke made a terrible kind of sense. But none of them fit together. He used the mocking tone of our childhood. It was a way of reaching back, a panicked reflex.

I asked him if he remembered building the Gemini Titan with me, all those years ago, the booster cells he'd made from fertilizer.

"What are you talking about?" he said. "You're such a weird little dude, Eli."

A few weeks later, he would call again, this time from jail. It was late at night and I went out onto the porch and listened to him run frantic circles around the truth. The stars were out and I gazed at them and thought about my wife and baby, asleep inside.

They were my family now, and I wanted to pretend that Dan had nothing to do with them, or with me. But every person lives within his own small pleasures and larger sorrows, which are inflicted early on, which we are helpless to erase or undo. However fiercely we cling to one another, our hearts orbit alone.

Some people have a talent for forgetting. I am not one of them. No matter how old and wise I grow, the essential part of me is still ten years old, standing in that field next to my brother, watching him disappear.

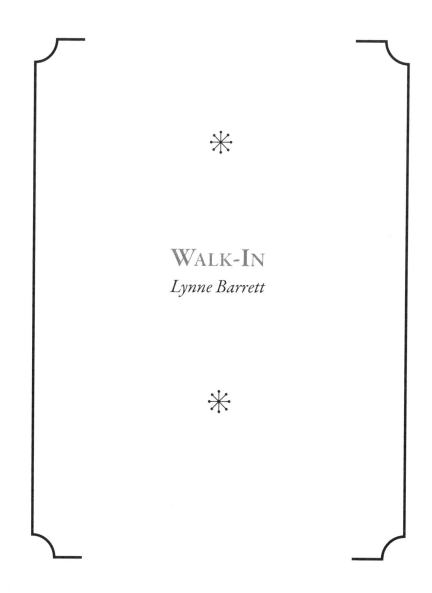

WALK-IN
Lynne Barrett

W hen Joelle sees him step into the Silver Scissors on the Saturday after Thanksgiving, he's just a tall silhouette in a quilted canvas jacket and a long-billed cap.

Joelle's stacking clean towels on the rack beside the sink, and her uncle Jerard is sitting cross-legged in the salon's window space, bedecking their three-foot tree. They have almost nothing booked this morning. Their regulars got spruced up before Thursday, and the college kids home on break, planning around their hangovers, scheduled afternoon appointments. Jerard is happy to use the time to get the salon shining. But she's still got debts, so when she came down from her place above the shop, before she got the coffee and music going and started a load of wash, she put out the sign that says: *Walk-In Appointments Available With Joelle.*

Which means he's hers.

She asks the stranger's name and what she can do for him, and he says, "Kyle Davies. Just a haircut," and takes off the cap. His dark hair is shaggy around his ears. "Could be now, or I can come back."

"Now's fine. Put your things there," she says, indicating the coat rack.

Behind him Jerard gives her the signal for "damage," a finger brushing his eyebrow. No matter how far she's traveled she'll always be his teenage apprentice from back when it was Jerard's Unisex. For years he worked alone, not trusting itinerants, but he welcomed her back when she needed a new start. She ushers Kyle Davies into her chair and lets it down a couple of inches. She sees his hair is colored a flat dark brown with one of those home products. It's coming in just a bit lighter at the roots. She says, cheerfully, "Now, how short do you want to go?" and puts her fingers through to feel: cottony. More than ordinary damage.

"Trim it close all over," he says. "It's been growing fast since I got here."

"That's the Eastern Shore. Comes from eating all that protein in our crab and oysters." She shakes out a blue nylon cape to wrap him in. When she leads him to sit with his head back over the sink, she sees his face, the long jaw and tight mouth, and places him. He's the man with the camo limo.

As she wets his hair, she notes that his roots are a warmer brown, with threads of gray by his high cheekbones. The damaged hair is truly fried. It's had nearly all the color lifted out—it must have been taken all the way down to pale yellow, she guesses—and then re-dyed. She wonders what the story is, but she takes her cue from the customer, and so far he's not a talker.

She uses the shampoo for color-treated hair, lifting his head up to lather underneath. When she washes someone's hair, she can't help but feel tender: the skull so vulnerable, the weight of the brain in its shell in her hands. Yes, she's a fool, forgetting all the bad things a brain can think up to do.

She digs her fingers in for the second lather, and he grunts a little and relaxes. Most people do, even the most dignified. It's a deep pleasure. She works a pearl of conditioner through, leaves it in, towels his hair and follows him to the chair.

She cuts it close, trying to get rid of all the bleached/dyed stuff and leave just the natural, which is healthy, thinning a bit at the temples. At a guess, he's past forty, older than her thirty-eight. The roots have grown in a good three-quarters of an inch, more in the back, which always grows faster. Could be nearly two months since the dye. It was mid-October when he arrived with the camouflage limo, parked it right in front of the Tarrant Creek Tavern with a big sign on the windshield saying "Limousine & Driver for Hire." It was an older Caddy, not a stretch limo but long enough to hold five in back with jump seats, and the local guides went right into competition over who'd have his services, though few doubted it would be Billy Peasy who'd win, since he had the slickest website, the most acres under hunting leases, and the deepest history with the rich hunters who come in on the weekends from D.C. and beyond. She's not really interested in hunting, but the men customers talk about it. Word is Billy Peasy's kept him busy doing airport runs and fetching parties to and from restaurant dinners so no one drives drunk. She realizes why he's off today. Yesterday was the last day to hunt waterfowl before the mid-season break—no more Canada migratory geese till December 15th, though in just a couple of days they'll resume taking light geese, which are overpopulated.

"So, Kyle," she asks, "are you here for a while?"

"Depends how long the work I'm doing lasts," he says. "Then I'll go back to Florida."

"I was working out west myself till last spring, but the economy got so bad, I decided to come home."

"Tough times," he says.

And that's it. Uncle Jerard has emerged from the window to get hair products which, tied with red ribbons, will sit under the tree as suggested stocking stuffers. Her uncle looks like other Innes businessmen, with a trimmed beard and a belly straining his plaid shirt. He's gay and no one cares, her mother has said, but then again he's always been discreet. And careful—who would have thought he'd be thriving and her tough father the brother who died.

She asks Kyle, "Clippers?" and he nods, so she buzzes his nape clean and shapes around the ears. After using the blow dryer, she rubs finishing paste into her palms and works his hair against the grain and then back. It looks good, cut according to the growth pattern. The whorl at the crown looks like a kind of fingerprint when the hair's this short. She shows him himself in the mirror and he nods. His face seems younger but harder. She wonders whether his jaw might have been broken, sometime—it's off symmetry on his left side. Still, he's a handsome man.

She unsnaps the cape, and Uncle Jerard takes him to the desk where he pays with cash. She looks away when he's tucking something for her into a tip envelope. She's sweeping up the shorn hair when she notices Kyle watching her while he snaps up his jacket. She dumps his hair—the bleached and darkened mystery of it—from the dustpan into the white plastic trash bin. "Hope you stop back," she says, and smiles, and he flashes her a glance so for the first time she thinks he's noticing her as a woman.

"Guess it depends," he says, "how much protein I eat."

He leaves. She leans into the window, pretending to check out Jerard's tree. Kyle's crossing the town green toward Tarrant Street on foot. She wonders where he's living. She'd probably know if she'd been going out at night, but she's been staying in, keeping out of trouble, trying to get over all her hankerings.

Sunday, just past noon, Kyle carries a sack of groceries into his furnished one-bedroom rental. The Sunrise Apartments, available by the month, are on the marshy side of town not far from the high school and Bell's Market. Buggy in summer, he bets. He did wash yesterday afternoon, in the Sunrise laundry room. The one dryer was broken, so he hung his clothes on hangers along the shower curtain rod, but nothing is all the way dry yet. Maybe it never will be. The weather's been dank and gray all week. He puts on water for coffee and unpacks ham, cheese, rye bread, half and half, Dutch pretzels, a six-pack of pale ale from a brewery in Philly, and the Easton *Star-Democrat*. He's left the limo, adorned with a banner advertising Billy Peasy's services, parked by arrangement near the gas station everybody passes as they take the turn across Tarrant Creek onto Innes Landing Road, the only way on and off of Innes Neck, if you don't count boat access. Billy's daughter and office manager Molly loaned him one of the company jeeps, but he hasn't taken it anywhere. He's sick of driving.

He spoons in coffee in from the bag of dark roast in the freezer into the filter of his travel mug and waits for the water to boil. He rubs his hand across his head, feeling the clean bristle, and thinks that the woman who cut it yesterday surely noticed it had been colored. But she didn't say a word. He liked that, as he liked her blue eyes, russet hair, and curves.

He assumes the men around haven't thought anything but that maybe he uses Grecian Formula. Men aren't observant in that way—they notice the limo, mainly, wanting to know details of the paint job and what it cost, which he lies about. He used to do a lot of crazy stuff to his hair, starting when he got into rock and roll in high school in Erie. The best band he had was called Kyryl Dragovich, his great-grandfather's original name. While his pal John Tucci, the one with the talent, shredded on lead guitar, Kyle got to prance and strut and intone seductive phrases. He'd enjoyed theater in college, but went for a communications major so he could get a TV internship, where he learned the value of being smooth. In the nineties he was on many a Good News team from Harrisburg to Savannah. In those days he spent a lot on haircuts and his teeth and clothes. He wasn't really excited enough by local disasters to get ahead as a reporter, but, when a contract wasn't renewed, he'd do a good interview and land something else. He was willing to try anything. He'd been a weatherman, done voice work for radio ads, acted in dinner theater, reviewed dinner theater, been a phantom gourmet. When all else dried up, he did his livery paperwork and, with his still-good appearance, found work driving limos in the Palm Beaches. It was just another kind of acting: Enter the chauffeur.

He takes his sandwich and coffee to the recliner he's moved over by the window, picks up his cell, and leaves a message, just, "Tooch. Call me." He'd told Tucci he'd be off this weekend and to call anytime, but Tucci has this whole rigmarole now: Kyle has to leave a message, then he calls Kyle back within an hour. Tucci is back up in Erie, working on a book, which is going to be an e-book, showcased in a blog, and then become a bestseller, or that's Tucci's plan. All about Phillip Vanneman and Vanneman Media, Vanneman's empire, which Tucci insists has ruined his life and Kyle's as well.

Kyle's career path and Tucci's crisscrossed here and there, but the one time they worked together was in Orlando, five years ago, at a free tabloid thick with real estate ads. Tucci, who'd taken a buy-out from the *Miami Herald* but just couldn't give up writing, was covering politics, and Kyle did movies, celebrity news, and wrote the astrology column under a woman's name. Then Vanneman Media bought their rag and converted its format to make it a small weekly full of filler, part of a chain they owned between Tampa and

Daytona Beach. They kept the ad team and laid off everybody else. Kyle couldn't complain; they got decent severance, better than you'd get now. But when Tucci called him this past August, he insisted the deal had been about Tucci's reporting. Did Kyle remember that series he was doing on voting and demographics in the I-4 corridor? Tucci'd been tracking all the small elections to school boards, zoning boards, town councils, and county commissions, probing why, despite the fact that these areas should be getting bluer, with younger people moving in and taking service jobs, the votes cast kept shifting right. Voting machine records were dubious if they existed at all. Well, what was the I-4 corridor but the belt across the state that Vanneman's weeklies covered, or failed to cover? And Vanneman Media, which owned display advertising, radio stations, and small papers all over the Southeast, was in good with the right wing. In other words, in response to his political pals, Vanneman bought them to shut Tucci down. He felt bad that Kyle had suffered for it.

Kyle said those were the breaks, but Tucci insisted on reminding Kyle how much he'd lost, which Kyle usually preferred to forget. In Orlando he'd been living with Bonnie, a business reporter on local news, but all he could find next was an early morning show in Melbourne, and Bonnie didn't want to live there, so they split, and she soon moved to Atlanta en route to her gig on cable now. And the next year, when he was on his way to work, pre-dawn, a couple of lowlifes carjacked him at a red light two blocks from the station. Though he hopped out and handed over the keys, the one with the pistol gave him a quick tap across the chin that cracked bone. The surgeon put in a titanium plate and screws, working from inside his mouth, and wired his jaws shut for three weeks. No scars showed, but he didn't look quite the same on camera, and even after a stint of therapy his jaw sometimes wanted to lock up. Not long after that—after the phantom gourmet job—he began driving for hire.

Which wasn't so bad, Kyle tried to tell Tucci, but Tucci was obsessed. Tucci'd had a couple of short-lived newspaper gigs, but the print world was shriveling even before the economy tanked, and he'd missed his chance to make a name with his exposé. He went back home, started a blog people sometimes donated to on PayPal, and was living cheap while writing his book. He claimed to have figured out that, big as the country was, everything depended on what he'd identified as "the small pivot points of power," a phrase he repeated with great intensity on each "p." And one of the invisible ones controlling these pivot points—in Florida, the Carolinas, Virginia, Maryland, Delaware—was Phillip Vanneman. Tucci insisted it would be a whale of a book, but he needed more on the personal angle. So he asked Kyle to do him a favor and go check out Daniel Vanneman, son by Philip's first wife, a guy in his early thirties who was currently living in Key Largo, as Tucci's learned from Daniel's mention on some culture and society blog. Tucci had the idea he was a well-off wastrel. He'd lived in Italy, Miami, and New York. No way could Tucci get close to him, but Kyle could, couldn't he? Kyle could easily look like the kind of person Vanneman's son would know. Tucci could pay some expenses, say for a week down there, if he'd go undercover and find out any details about his old man's habits, his vices, his opinions, family anecdotes. Anything at all would help to fill out the book.

Late summer is the season of not much work for hired drivers in the Palm Beaches, and September, with its peak chance of hurricanes, is the absolute doldrums. And to "go undercover"—that appealed to Kyle. In Largo there were people with boats and lots of others who worked on them. Kyle decided to be a boat bum, bought a couple of linen shirts at late-summer-in-Palm-Beach sales, got a spray tan, bleached his hair, and started on the path that led him here.

When Tucci calls, Kyle can hear music in the background—Santa asking Rudolph to guide his sleigh—and he asks where Tucci is, thinking maybe a mall, but Tucci says he's home.

"Hey, that town has webcams," Tucci says. "Did you know that? It's on their website: Innes Harbor Cam, Old Town Green Cam. They take a new picture every ten minutes. You can go back and watch things change on their slideshows, past hour, past day."

"What're they for?" Kyle asks. Tucci is on the Internet all the time, but Kyle avoids it.

"It's a way to show off how pretty the place is. To draw visitors. And maybe the people who vacation there like to check on it from afar, keep them connected. The one on the green shows a big Christmas tree. If you stand by it, you'll be in the picture. Has to be on the tens, though, 3:10, 3:20. That'd be cool. I can see part of one street to the left—some cutesy shops there. Looks like a safe little place."

"The town is," Kyle says. "Everybody's shooting guns off all day out in the fields and woods and ponds from here to Delaware."

Tucci says, "Right, right. Getting their rocks off. So, what I want to know is, are you sure, absolutely sure, Vanneman is coming?"

"I asked the boss's daughter, who handles all the bookings, what work I can expect coming up after this week, which looks a little slow, and she was happy to fill me in on who'll be here. Vanneman's arriving with some business friends a week from Friday, after Canada goose season resumes, hunting Saturday and Sunday, leaving Sunday afternoon. They've taken the top package. Wherever they want to go, I'll be on call."

"Will they take one of those photos they have on the website, the proud goose-slayers with their dead birds?"

"They all do. They make their daily bag and then line up for group pictures with their kill. After that Billy has the birds cleaned and they can take the game home with them or have it shipped, frozen."

"I've looked at all the pictures from past years," says Tucci, "but Vanneman's not there."

"Those are just samples—people happy to have their photos up. Why? Is Vanneman camera-shy?"

"In the past decade," Tucci says, "there are very few pictures. Mainly you see the one where he has a cigar in the middle of his face, like he's sticking out his dick at you."

Not for the first time, Kyle thinks Tucci has seriously gone around the bend. But he's been sending Kyle fifty bucks a week on PayPal for "expenses," while Billy Peasy is paying him a good rate and covering the gas, and he's been getting nice tips from guys who love riding in the limo. They line up to take pictures with it, too. Peasy has hinted he'd be interested in buying the limo, if Kyle doesn't want to take it back with him. He has nothing to lose by staying for now, though work will pick up in Florida after Christmas.

"Saturday of the weekend he's coming they have their holiday lights festival here," Kyle says. "I saw posters for it in town yesterday. A lot of candles in glass jars, what do they call them, luminaries? Rides in horse-drawn carriages. One last chance to pull in visitors before Christmas."

Tucci says. "So how about in the town? Do people know him? He's been coming for a long while, the son said, right?"

"I haven't had much time to spend in town till this weekend, no chance to develop any sources. But what does it matter? I'll be driving Vanneman and his friends, hear what they say."

"You could try, couldn't you? Why don't you go now?"

"Tooch, is this just so you can see me on the town green?"

"No, no, I was just thinking that you could get friendly, hang out, buy somebody a drink. But take a look at the town tree, why not? You'd have to do it before the sun goes down. It says on the site they just use the last daytime picture during the night. From the angle, I think the webcam must be in that building at the end of the green. It's got a hexagonal tower with some kind of cupola on top."

"How do you know that?"

"Oh, I saw the town layout on Google Earth."

Kyle is silent, looking out at the soft dun colors of the marsh.

"Look, Kyle, I'm not going to sit glued to the computer or anything. I've got other stuff to do here, research. But if you go I can scroll back through the slideshow to find you. That'd be kind of fun. My end of this is boring."

"Okay," Kyle says. "I can use a walk." When he gets off the phone, he switches to a clean pair of khakis, still damp. If he's staying well into December, it's sure to get colder. He could use some heavier clothes, a couple of flannel shirts, maybe get a parka. He'll make a list on his walk back into Old

Town center. He can use Tucci's money.

Sunday afternoon, Joelle goes with her uncle to visit the graves of her grandparents and dad at Star of the Sea cemetery in Chawton, a few miles inland. Jerard has ordered winter grave covers, evergreen blankets adorned with red bows and pinecones, which they pick up at the stand outside the gates. She lays the double-sized one over her grandparents, and Jerard tacks it down with metal skewers so it won't blow away. Other Bowen graves here, some looked after by distant cousins, date back to the 1800s. Jerard maintains that an early Bowen came over with the Catholics who founded Maryland. While Joelle has long since lapsed, her uncle is a Catholic who deeply criticizes the church but goes to Mass. He loves the past, antiques, the whole history of the Chesapeake. He's not a Conservative, he says, but a Traditionalist, which is a matter of memory and ritual, not politics.

They move to her father's grave. Chiseled dates show the span of his forty-seven years. There's space on the headstone for her mother, but, widowed, she followed well-paying nursing work to South Carolina and remarried there. She's never coming back.

Joelle knows her uncle wants her to understand this will be her duty someday. As things stand she'll be the last of their line. When she was sixteen she had a pregnancy scare. Her father would have wanted to hold a gun on the boy till they married, and her mother was too intimidated to be trusted. Her uncle was the only one she could tell. Jerard offered money, secrecy, and his help in finding a safe place to go if she needed an abortion. But she went to an Ocean City fun park, tried all the rides, paid to bounce for forty minutes on a trampoline, and the next day she got her period. She's never been sure she actually was pregnant, but since then she's always been on guard, one way or another, against her fertility. There was a time, a few years ago, when she and her then husband talked about maybe getting started trying, but when work disappeared, so did he. She still feels young, but something's ebbing.

When she stands the wind buffets her. Canada geese fly across the silvery sky, honking like a bunch of crazy clowns. She wills them to get on through here and south before the hunting resumes. All around are corn and wheat fields where Billy Peasy has his blinds.

On their way back out, Jerard buys a holly swag. Forty minutes later, Joelle is outside the salon, handing her uncle pieces of florist's wire, while he stands on their antique bench and reaches above his head trying to fasten the prickly greenery around the decorative bracket from which the Silver Scissors sign hangs. Her uncle is not much taller than she is. She's about to suggest she bring her kitchen stepstool from upstairs when the man who owns the camo limo crosses Bivalve Lane from the green and stops.

"Hello, Mr. Kyle Davies," says her uncle, who never forgets a client's name. Kyle says, "Need help?"

Now, a week later, stretching in the warm bed Kyle has just left, Joelle grins, remembering. When she was younger, she felt like a slut if she acted on her desires. Not that that prevented her, but now she's in a different place. Nobody should expect her to be virtuous, a woman pushing forty with a not-too-bad body who's earning her own living. A man passing through, why not? And that he has some mystery about him just means he isn't going to be the same old thing.

So she was pleased when Kyle Davies invited them, that Sunday, to join him at the wine bar down the street. Jerard carried the conversation early, describing how dilapidated Innes was as recently as the late eighties. "Back then, you could buy an Old Town Victorian cottage for a song, as I did, and others, too, who saw the potential." Joelle has an idea Jerard might have found some of the buyers, that he had a secret life in the cities, with Philadelphia, Baltimore, and D.C. just a couple of hours away, not counting bridge backups. These new town fathers opened the first bed and breakfasts, a bakery, and an antique mall. As tourism flickered to life, the town acquired and removed the empty cannery and collapsing docks. For the first time, her uncle said, he heard the term "bay-scaping."

Joelle was worried he'd go on at length, but after the first glass of wine, he adroitly claimed he saw some friends and excused himself. After the second, when they came out to a dusk streaked with pink, she and Kyle walked down by the harbor front, where boats clanked at the floating docks. She described how tumbledown old fisherman's shacks on Innes Point used to look, before developers made that end of town a fantasy village of dark shingle and peaked gray roofs, with balconies facing the water and cute chimneys. He said he was familiar with the process; there were whole new towns like that in Florida. "In California, too," she said. "It's just odd to have it happen in the grungy place you fled at eighteen."

When he asked if she'd like to have dinner, perhaps at that seafood place on the water, she said, "Well, I have the makings of a damn good crab chowder at my place."

He paused, said, "I should be clear. I'm not going to be sticking around," and she answered that that was fine.

He looked startled, the first evening, when he saw the dozens of old carved and painted decoys, everything from paired eider ducks to geese with bullet marks to an oversize Victorian swan, ranged on shelves built into the eaves down one side of her main room. She explained that her uncle collected them when he lived up here, back when they were being sold off cheap by hunters turning to mass-produced plastic. With room for just a few gems in his cottage, he kept the rest here, hoping to donate them to an Atlantic Flyway museum he and his friends want to establish in the old custom house building on the green. "He cleared away a lot of things when I came home, but asked me to keep these," she said. Kyle chopped celery and onions for the soup, and after supper he washed the dishes and settled in to prove he had the experience of a good-looking man many before her had desired.

And now he's been with her four evenings out of eight, all through the night on the two when he didn't have to drive early the next morning. This afternoon he even brought his laundry over. He said he remembered when he first saw her, she was holding a bunch of fresh blue towels. Which is as close to a romantic thing as he's uttered, but it doesn't matter. She feels grand. An hour ago, when he stirred, and she knew he was getting ready to leave, she wrapped her legs around him, and they were enmeshed before he could think about a condom. After a few minutes he said, "Is this all right?" and she said, "No worries, I got it covered." Which was not true, she'd gone off the pill and relied on condoms the past few years, but at that moment she didn't care, she wanted naked risk.

Leaving Joelle's, carrying his laundry in a grocery bag, Kyle crunches the frosted grass under his boots, but he's not cold. When he'd mentioned that as a Florida guy he needed winter clothes, Joelle said it was ridiculous to pay full price, which he'd have to in season, before Christmas. She recommended a re-sale place in Easton, where he was amused by the multitude of camo patterns depicting grass, trees, field, and swamp, even fleece outer layers showing black bare branches against snow's blue-white, for winter hunting. His new parka is plain khaki green, perhaps the reason it had gone unbought. He paid full price for good lined leather gloves.

As he crosses the green, the lights on the big tree turn dark. Must be on a timer. It's midnight. Old Town Innes is lit by reproduction gaslights and a moon just past full. Tooch was gleeful when he saw Kyle last Sunday, standing in front of the tree, but since then, all week, Kyle's avoided that spot and the angle of the Harbor Cam. He doesn't like the idea of Tooch seeing him with Joelle, even though he could just say he was talking up a local.

He also avoided phoning, with nothing to report anyway. Then today, after he took a couple of departing hunters to catch their flight, he called, ready to leave his message, but a woman picked up and said, "Who the hell is this?"

"I'm sorry. I was trying to reach John Tucci."

"And who are you?"

"An old friend." Was this Tucci's mother? She sounded old and crazy. And he wasn't sure if Tucci would want him to give his name. "Is he there?"

"Are you a drug-dealer?"

"No, of course not," he said. "To whom am I speaking?"

"None of your damn." Her voice was gone. She must have hit something by mistake.

He remembered Mrs. Tucci as a nice mom, proud of her son, especially when he got a scholarship to Penn State. She let them practice in the basement. Used to feed them big plates of eggplant parm.

Within half an hour, Tucci called, saying he was sorry. He'd left his phone in his other book bag. Just found Kyle listed as a recent call.

"Who was that I spoke to?" Kyle asked, thinking, book bag? Other book bag?

"Must have been my grandmother. She's gaga. She's ninety."

Kyle had no recollection of a grandmother. "How's the book coming along?" he said.

"Well, it takes a long time, reading records of incorporation and so on. It's dry, the business side. You know I'm counting on you for something that adds juice."

After that, Kyle thought for a while and then called his parents' house. It was Sunday afternoon and his sister's whole family was there, so he had to say hi to his nephews and his four-year-old niece, and let his sister blast him for being so long out of touch. He exchanged a few words with his father, who was watching football, but eventually he had his mother and, after promising he was feeling fine, said, "Listen, Mom, you remember my old friend John Tucci?" Of course she did, the journalist. He said, "I hear he's back home, and I wondered if you knew anything about how he's doing."

"These days lots of people who were too good for Erie are back, looking for a free place to live. You thinking about it?"

"No, Mom. I was just wondering if he was okay."

She said, "You know you can visit. Come home for Christmas."

"I don't think so, Mom," he said. "I have work. But I'll call then. I promise. Meanwhile, if you hear anything about Tucci, call me." And he gave her his number.

Then he called Joelle. He wanted to be around her chatter, the hum of doing things. He took her out and drank more than he intended. He worries that he's seeing her too much, and worries more that they just had sex without protection. It was unwise. He's sure she's healthy, and he is, but he doesn't want to get stuck with child support payments. He likes to travel light.

He glances at the moon, barely lopsided, before he goes into the apartments. The forced heat in his place gives off a metallic burning smell. He feels the first throb of a headache. He's dehydrated, he thinks, and guzzles water before he gets into bed. He tells himself he should stay away from Joelle this week, but he probably won't.

On Friday, Kyle drives to the Salisbury-Ocean City-Wicomico Airport to pick up Mr. Phillip Vanneman, Mr. Edwin Bartell, and Mr. Dean McEachern, who are coming in on a commuter flight from Charlotte. He waits inside holding up Billy Peasy's sign. They shake hands all around: Phil, Ed, Dean, Kyle. He escorts them to where they pick up their checked baggage and loads it all, including the carefully packed weapons in their hard-sided cases, onto a cart. Ed and Dean laugh when they see the camo limo and slap Vanneman on the back.

In the car, he explains that the sliding window track is a little dinged up, so if they don't mind, he's leaving it open, and Vanneman says fine, a camo limo shouldn't be too formal anyway. There's a lot of talk—as there always seems to be—about the devices of hunting, the birdcalls, the decoys, the blinds. He's picked up enough to answer questions and deploy some facts Billy likes them to appreciate, for instance the thousands of dollars in taxidermy decoys and plastic ones that Billy's guide will lay out in huge stagings to lure in the geese. "He has an expert goose caller," Vanneman contributes.

The only personal remark is when Ed Bartell says to Vanneman, "Didn't I hear you got your start around here at one time?"

"When I was a kid I sold billboard advertising along Route 13, not long after they put the Bay Bridge Tunnel in," Vanneman says. "I was able to place a lot at the south end for attractions in Virginia Beach."

He's currently sixty-six years old, according to Tucci. He's over medium height, with a solid frame, hair still more pepper than salt. Kyle can't see much resemblance to his son Daniel, except that Daniel's hair is black.

Kyle turns in at the entrance to the Innes Lodge, which is on Innes Neck about three miles from the town proper. The drive is marked with brick pillars, and the brick facade of the lodge is impressive, with its four chimneys and modern addition at one side. He lifts their bags from the trunk onto the doorman's cart, while the men grab their guns. He follows them through the lobby, where a real, aromatic fire crackles, and turns them over to the desk. One other member of their party is coming, driving in on his own, due soon. They know that Billy will be there at four, meeting everyone in the taproom, to go over the arrangements for tomorrow. The Innes Lodge is dark-beamed, solid-looking, though Joelle has told him it stood empty for many years before it was completely redone and made deluxe.

A high boxwood hedge hides the parking lot. He pulls in there. He's arranged to wait here to be ready if Billy wants him to take the group anyplace. He spends a lot of time in the car this way, has his iPod, a set of puzzle books, and some nonfiction. He likes to read about adventures, past and present. He has a book he found at Joelle's about the 19th century Chesapeake Oyster Wars, where Marylanders snuck over to Virginia waters to dredge illegally. It could have been written in a more exciting way, he thinks, leafing through to look at the maps.

Now he's seen Phillip Vanneman, who's not what he imagined from meeting Daniel. But then meeting Daniel hadn't been what he imagined. Unlike the guy drinking his life away Tucci had led him to expect, Daniel wasn't so easy to get close to. He was staying in a private home on the bay side of the key and spent a lot of the day there. Still, there was only one main road in or out. Kyle hung around, followed his car and identified his patterns, which included listening to music at the old, funky Caribbean Club, with its statue of Bogey in his white dinner jacket. Daniel met up there with a casual crowd of floating regulars. The place was fun, and Kyle was just a blond aging goof-off on a permanent vacation. By being unpushy but smiling, Kyle had some of the women smiling back.

Then on Sunday, open mike night, Kyle did a number, "Look What the Cat Dragged In" (Mechanicsburg boys, Poison), and though he was terribly rusty and it was just acoustic on a borrowed guitar, he got applause and encouragement to do another, so he summoned up "Fallen Angel," and then he was one of the crowd. Two days later he reached the point of sitting at one of the picnic tables out behind the club with Daniel and an attractive girl who seemed interested in Daniel, eating pizza the crowd had chipped in for. Daniel was educated, his way of speaking elegant and lightly bitter. He was a painter. Kyle knew absolutely nothing about painting, nothing about the artists Daniel mentioned as reference points. He was painting skyscapes, he said, the past several days trying to catch the spectacular colors bounced onto the clouds from a fire burning across the water in the southern glades.

To steer away from painting, Kyle said he'd given some thought to writing a novel. It would be about growing up in Erie, about having a Croatian-American dad and an Irish-American mother, hard-working people but they warred over every tiny thing the kid might do until the boy felt smothered.

"Something like early D.H. Lawrence," Daniel said.

Kyle had heard of D.H. Lawrence. "Of course, with a lot of sex. But more about how the kid wants to be something else, somewhere else. Families are strange, you know what I mean?"

Daniel said, "My parents divorced when I was young, but it was civilized. I lived with my mother, and my father got me for visits. They'd be highly planned with lots of activities."

"Like what?"

"Oh, sports lessons, batting practice, golf. He took me bowling—he won bowling trophies when he was a kid. Golf—I liked that better. One year, when I turned twelve, he got me a junior waterfowl hunting license as a birthday present. That was prelude to a special trip to go shooting birds in Maryland." Daniel swigged his beer. "You see that white ibis there at the water's edge, just minding its own business? Why would you want to empty him of life?"

Kyle, whose father had never hunted, agreed. The girl said, "So was it brutal?"

"He told me he'd never forgive me if I cried in front of his guide—Big

Billy P—a horrible fat guy. I didn't cry, but I made sure I didn't kill anything. I think they gave me credit for what somebody else shot. After that Dad just got us tickets to baseball and football games. Eventually we sat in skyboxes. My father became quite successful."

"What does he do?" the girl asked.

"Well, you could say he redistributes trash." Daniel laughed, and Kyle tried to look like he didn't understand. "He has two other children by his second wife, daughters, in college now. I don't think any of us really fit his expectations. He does things with his business friends. He takes them goose hunting every year in that same place, in Maryland. I think he really likes to kill something before he has to see us all at Christmas."

Before Kyle could think of anything more to ask, Daniel said, "See, across the water, those anvil clouds? Ultramarine and umber." And the girl wanted to know all about how he would paint them.

While he left out details about Daniel he felt would easily track back to him if they were in the book, Kyle reported to Tucci: son estranged, father likes sports and hunting, had bowling trophies. No particularly interesting dirt. He was elated he'd managed to pull off his masquerade, but Kyle had no notion of going further. He dyed his hair back to brown and was getting some work for hotels. Maybe he felt a little flat, wanting more excitement, but it was just happenstance that a fellow driver invited him to an auction of used limousines and there was the 1986 Cadillac Fleetwood limo, its boxy shape somehow comical in camo. It had a blue interior, with a great inlaid wood dash. Plush back seat and fold up jump seats. Rear climate and radio controls. The exterior, originally white, had been customized fairly recently. The camouflage design was tan, gray, sage, tall grass suggested by paint scribbles—almost like some kind of abstract painting. It had a Mississippi registration—the auctioneer speculated it had been used to drive gamblers, but maybe hunters. Undercarriage, not bad. New tires. It was cool. And priced to go. He got it for just under $4,000. Of course, there was registration and insurance, and its 8 cylinder, 4.1liter engine drank gasoline. He could flip it for more on eBay, but he wanted to take it on a road trip first. And so he dredged from memory the guide Daniel mentioned, searched the web for him, and then asked Tucci if he should get himself established there ahead of Vanneman's annual trip.

Billy Peasy is a not so much big as broad, wide of cheek and neck and chest and gut, with sturdy legs. He's asked Kyle to join him in the lodge's dark-paneled bar. Kyle orders coffee, Billy a draft. Vanneman, Ed, and Dean show up with the fourth in the group, Frank Waterford, who drove down from New Jersey. While they have a beer, Billy runs through the agenda for tomorrow: Kyle will pick them up an hour before sunrise and drive them out to Billy's place where they will have a careful safety run-through, and then they'll go to the first location Billy has chosen, based on his scouting of the geese's patterns over the past weeks, the season, and all year. And all his life, he implies. "He can read a goose's mind," Vanneman said earlier in the limo. While they have reservations for dinner later, here at the diamond-rated restaurant at the lodge, Billy wonders if they'd like to ride through town first.

Philip Vanneman says, yes, he wants to show everybody Innes and leads them to the limo. Billy sits up front, beside Kyle. He takes up a good portion of the bench seat.

Vanneman has them stop first at the Tarrant Creek Tavern, on the way into town on Innes Landing Road. Joelle has told Kyle that when her father took her there, when she was a kid, it was a dark, smoky roadhouse. In the parking lot men traded in retriever puppies, hooch, guns, fresh-killed game and fresh-caught fish. Her father and his friends drank there daily until their bodies started to fall apart: livers, or, in her dad's case, lungs, one suicide, several buddies turning to AA. According to Joelle, the tavern went through a fern bar stage, and then, when Innes got redeveloped, emerged as a sports bar with decent food. It's got the legacy liquor license; it's where the adults go to drink. Joelle doesn't hang out there, but old friends of hers do. He wonders if Vanneman used to rub elbows here with Joelle's father, whether he saw the old untamed Tarrant Creek Tavern in this one where flat screen TVs blast sports highlights and Christmas commercials. There are vintage neon beer signs and what Billy says is some top-notch professional taxidermy—deer, a bobcat, and Kyle thinks he spots a falcon up in the rafters. They sit at the bar, and Billy introduces them to some locals.

While the others have a round, Kyle drinks club soda. He never drinks when he is driving.

Back in the limo, they head for Old Town to see the boats and water. Dean mentions that somebody in the tavern said the government was soon going to make everybody turn in all the currency for new money that will have micro-threads in it, so all transactions can be traced, the end of untaxed income. Recent bill redesigns are to set this up.

Billy chortles and Vanneman says, "They've been passing versions of that tale around here for more than twenty years. Keeping track of it all would cost more than it's worth."

Billy says a lot of the new people out on Innes Point are retirees from the military, mostly Navy. They like the water view. Some have telescopes on their balconies, as if they're keeping lookout for some invasion.

"Hard to imagine we'd ever have a naval war again," says Ed.

"It's all going to be about information," Vanneman comments, "not territory."

"Cyber wars?" Frank Waterford asks.

"I wouldn't be surprised if we see wars between corporations and governments, at some point," says Vanneman. "There are already terrorists attacking research."

Though they've said they were just going to take a spin through town, Vanneman has him park. Kyle finds a spot along the High Street edge of the town green behind the old customhouse. It's after five. The tall tree is shimmering, the sun completely down, but still throwing some glow up onto shreds of cloud. The others walk out on the green. Vanneman, standing very still, just looks out beyond it towards the water. Kyle realizes Christmas music is coming from the cupola of the customhouse, instrumental, an old traditional tune, "Greensleeves." Tasteful. He thinks Vanneman has paused to take it in. He wants to tell him he's driven in the Palm Beaches, that he knows his stuff, but instead he mentions that he's seeing a woman who works at the hair salon, just over there on Bivalve—for some reason he guesses Vanneman will like that he dates a local—and Vanneman suggests that he has time to run in and say hi.

Joelle is cutting the hair of Sharon Robertson, a fourth-grade teacher, taking her time, even though it's her last appointment. She takes pride in cutting for the weight and flow of the hair and the client's features, as she did when she was getting $115 for a cut in that place on Cahuenga Boulevard. Here, she's drawing new customers—a librarian sees a teacher with a flattering style, a woman returning books sees the librarian with subtle color. She leans in to sculpt Sharon's bangs in a way that will make people notice Sharon's eyes, and then her world lurches for no reason. Huh, dizzy, she thinks, and blinks a minute. She says, "Do you want some water," and without waiting gets cupfuls for Sharon and herself. And sips. She's fine. She looks up and there's Kyle, to say he's driving clients around, but hopes to see her tomorrow evening— take in the lights festival, eat a bite, if he can get free? He'll call. Yes, of course, she says, and goes back to Sharon's hair. She feels fine now, definitely.

When Kyle comes out of the Silver Scissors, Vanneman is talking to the others, in the middle of the green. It's too late, too dark, for the webcam, Kyle thinks. On the ride back, they are quiet as Billy tells stories, long histories of enticement and entrapment.

As soon as he gets home, Kyle leaves his message for Tucci, and, when Tucci calls, says, "You know, I don't want to promise I'm going to get anything solid."

"What do you mean? Are you backing out?"

"I'm just trying to be fair. They're not going to be with me that much, and there are four of them. What am I going to find out?"

"Noooo," Tucci whines. "Listen, what happened? Did he recognize you? I know you never met, but he could have seen you sometime on TV, right? Your face might ring a bell?"

"No, Tooch, nothing like that. I don't want to promise you that I'm going to get something you can use, that's all."

"Hey, always a gamble. I know. Just do your best. You've barely started."

Tucci tells him to get some sleep, but he sits up, looking out the window. Kyle only wishes Vanneman *had* recognized him, had said, "Hey, didn't you used do local news in Savannah?" He can't really explain it, but he likes the guy. No, like is the wrong word, and admire isn't right, either. Simply, Kyle wants his approval. It's not solely a matter of his success. Kyle has driven a lot of successful, rich people. Vanneman conveys a sense of concentration, almost as if he's hearing something you don't.

Impossible to explain why this makes him want to please Vanneman, to impress him. But he does. It just grew upon him today, his desire for Vanneman to see his worth. He wants Vanneman to say, at some point, "Son, there's a place in my organization for a man like you." He wonders if it comes, in some way, from his envy of Daniel. He'd be happy to be Vanneman's son. It's ridiculous. He might as well say he'd be happy to be his dog.

But one thing he knows: Tucci is a fool to think he can harm Phillip Vanneman. Vanneman can swat him like a fly. And Kyle isn't eager to be swatted.

There are still stars overhead when he drives to the lodge Saturday morning. The hotel has prepared hot coffee and sweet rolls for the men to have in the back of the limo during the twenty minute drive inland to Billy's HQ, an old white farmhouse with a string of outbuildings. He helps them carry their gear, then hangs around, watching the careful checking-over Billy's people put them through, looking at all their paperwork, briefing them on gun safety, describing where they're going, hunting conditions, weather conditions. The Vanneman group and another, three men and two teenage boys who are obviously all related, will soon head off with their guide and his helpers, men and dogs, driving towards the closest parking to the chosen field, where a trailer loaded with decoys went earlier. There they'll put on their camouflage and boots and walk out through frosted stubble to the pit blind. He's heard about all this, just never done it. Shooting can begin at sunrise.

He goes back home and has breakfast. It's barely eight so he tries to sleep for a while, keeping his cell off. Around eleven he calls in to see how the hunt is going. Molly Peasy reports they had some early luck, but then they had to move to a fresh location. While the team is setting up the decoy layout, they're eating lunch. By this point in the season those geese are wary, says Molly.

He notices he has a message on his phone. It's from his mother.

"Hi, Kyle," she says, "I spoke to Becky Lewis, who is a neighbor of the Tuccis, and she says, yes, John has been home for some time. His mother says he is freelancing. He has high blood pressure and some other health issues. Mrs. Tucci has her mother to deal with, too. Okay, love you. Remember, you're calling us on Christmas morning."

At two in the afternoon, there's a sharp wind, and Kyle's nose is running. Vanneman's three pals kneel, beaming. In front of them loll eight big dead geese. Vanneman's taking the picture. Propped by their feet, a sign says this is bag limit from a four-man party. Billy has these pre-printed to be filled out and included, to make sure no photo anywhere will make it look like anyone has exceeded regulations on a hunt of his. Vanneman hands the camera to Dean and takes his place. After a day outside the men look like big, ruddy boys. Kyle uses his phone to snap a surreptitious shot. But then it seems obvious where it was taken from, and he deletes it.

While he drives, they reminisce about the hunt. At one point, their guide, Decker, put out a couple of crow decoys as part of the array, because the geese trust the crows more than their own, Decker told them.

"Geese must know they aren't as wise as crows, which is itself a kind of wisdom," says Vanneman.

"So a hunt like this isn't a chase," says Kyle. "Would you say it's more of a close study of how to fool the geese?"

Vanneman says, "That's what hunting is, knowing your opponent. And your opponent knows you, too, as a predator, so you have to be careful not to give yourself away. But it's also about self-control, planning, waiting. You get in the pit, crouch in the dark, and then there's light when the cover is drawn back, or in some blinds you are popping up from under a thatch. You must aim fast, you shoot, and then you duck back into the dark. It takes steady nerves."

"I see," Kyle says.

"So you haven't hunted waterfowl?"

"I don't have the permits," Kyle says, "and I've never used a gun."

Vanneman says, "Tell Billy you're interested. He might gain a convert."

"I've always been more of a city boy," Kyle says. "Before this I was driving in Palm Beach." He's pleased to work that in.

But he's thinking. It's not about the birds, as Daniel thought. It's about the self. The sturdy sense of self you need to keep trying. Popping from darkness into the light and acting. It's like theater.

Since the men got up early, they want dinner soon. They're going to eat at the restaurant on the water. When Kyle gets them to the lodge, he calls Joelle to see if she can be free soon, then waits in the limo till they come out, cleaned up, in nice sweaters, cords, and coats. He drops them off by the restaurant, finds parking on Market, and walks two blocks to the Silver Scissors. Joelle is blow-drying a woman's hair. She's got a good thing here with her uncle, he thinks.

He sits on the padded seat that's placed along the wall near the window, for customers. Joelle says she'll be ready shortly. Where does he want to go?

"I thought we could go to the tavern and get something warm to eat. I'll be on call to take them back when they need me, but it won't be for a while. They want to walk around after dinner, see the lights."

She pauses, thinking about the tavern, he's sure, but then she nods. She's got some old Christmas pop on, "Boogie Woogie Santa Claus," must be early fifties. He flips through a magazine full of ideas for Christmas food and decorating. He's struck by how phony it all looks, the extra-shiny food and rich colors. He thinks it's about glamorizing winter, hiding from the terror of cold and darkness. Vanneman, he thinks, sees through that. He simply goes about his business.

Then Joelle's ready, winding a red scarf around the collar of her black wool coat, humming along to the music, now "Baby It's Cold Outside."

"Drive," he says, "or walk?"

Joelle chooses to walk. She locks up but leaves the lights on. Her uncle will be here and everywhere this evening. He's on the festival committee. At the tavern, not much is as she remembers except the structure itself. They get a booth and order the special, bison chili topped with jack cheese. He gets club soda, and she says, "Can't let you undrink alone," and gets it too. She has her little thought, about what that lurching moment was, but it's far too soon to say. And she knows Kyle isn't planning to stick around. She thinks how little he's told her. When she asked, in bed, why his hair had been bleached and dyed, he said he was in a play, and when she touched his chin and asked about that, he said he was in a fight.

He says, "Remind me to return that book I borrowed, about the Oyster Wars."

"Did you finish it?"

"More or less. They just went on over and stole Virginia's oysters because they'd run out of their own, right?"

"My illustrious ancestors, yes. When you think about it, at the start the Chesapeake was simply loaded with bounty. All people had to do to eat was learn some skills. But they were greedy. Now parts of the bay are dead. It's different with the birds, now. Everybody seems to go along with the idea of what has to be harvested and what conserved. No one wants to throw a natural advantage away again." She laughs. "I guess you could say there's a new crop, the people who've moved here. We've started to live off them, too. We may not be able to make it anywhere else, but we can, here."

"For now," he says. In the flickering of the TV lights, he looks serious.

"Right," she says, "for now." And Joelle clinks her glass against his.

On their walk back to Old Town Green, Kyle lets her lead him through the residential streets, the area of old restored houses and B&Bs, where there is everything from a single pillar candle in a chimney of glass to hundreds of small ones lining front walks and steps. When they come out on Water Street, Kyle can see that the Old Town shops are lit up. The wine bar is selling some kind of hot toddy outside, ladled from what looks like a cauldron. Joelle says she needs to light the candles her uncle set up for the shop—he doesn't want them burning without someone to tend them. They kiss goodnight and Kyle says he'll walk on down by the water.

A horse-drawn carriage passes him, and another draws up on Water Street between the Christmas tree and the harbor. The driver, in a high Dickensian collar, lets off his passengers. Kyle sees Phillip Vanneman and friends, bunched together waiting, are next, ready to step up and get aboard.

Carolers are moving down the Green. Strong clear voices shine in a roundelay:

> *Christmas is coming*
> *and the geese are getting fat.*
> *Please to put a penny*
> *in the old man's hat.*

> *Christmas is coming*
> *and the geese are getting fat.*
> *Please to put a penny*
> *in the old man's hat.*

Kyle notices behind them a strange figure, waving, a man in a Santa hat and a puffy red coat, jeans and black galoshes. He has tinsel around his neck, twisted around the strap of a camera, and he's lifting his camera because he's John Tucci, a pale and distorted John Tucci, taking pictures of Philip Vanneman and his friends in the horse-drawn carriage.

Kyle heads towards him, and, standing beside him casually, says, "Don't blow my cover."

"Don't blow mine," says Tucci. "I'm Santa Claus."

"What have you been drinking?" Kyle asks.

"Some hot spiced wine. Vile stuff, but it's cold out here."

The singers are marching across the green now, towards the Village at Innes Point.

> *. . . ...then God bless you! If you haven't got a ha'penny*
> *then God bless you!*

Kyle's phone rings. Dean says they're in the carriage, and he should bring the limo around to the harborside to pick them up in a few minutes. Kyle says, "Done," and clicks off.

"How did you get here?" he asks Tucci.

"Drove, how else? I'd been thinking about it, but last night when you sounded like you needed help, I thought I'd just get an early start and do it. Took me nine hours. I hit some traffic trying to come over the bridge after Annapolis. I parked at your building and walked over here. It really is a pretty little town."

Kyle says. "I have to go get the limo to take them to the hotel. Then I'll come back and find you. Don't get in trouble."

Tucci assures Kyle all he wants is photos. The Santa hat droops ludicrously across his face. Kyle sprints back to the car and pulls onto Water Street only a few yards behind the carriage stand, not legal parking, but no one minds a camo limo. Indeed, people applaud it and a woman asks him if it's available for rides.

He gets out and watches as the carriage with the Vanneman party pulls up. He sees they are smoking cigars. He's aware, but they seem not to be, with flickering flames in the darkness and the many other people taking pictures, that Tucci is capturing them in the carriage, stepping out, strolling, puffing, getting into the limo.

Kyle closes them in and drives. They continue to smoke, which normally he'd object to, but they seem absorbed in it and fortunately oblivious to other things. He has some Febreze in the trunk and he'll spray the upholstery down later.

After he delivers them to the lodge, he beats it back to town and circumnavigates the green until he finds Tucci is amusing himself by trying to get a shot back at the Old Town Green webcam.

"Tooch," he calls, "get in. You can ride in the limo."

Tucci comes over and gets in the back, and Kyle starts them moving.

"Hey, let me fasten my seat belt," says Tucci. Then, "Jesus, it stinks in here."

Kyle hits the buttons to open the windows in back. He can hear Tucci taking deep breaths. "Are you all right, Tooch? I heard you had some health problems."

"Who doesn't? Little hypertension, little anxiety. Hey, who's the chick you were with? I saw you tromping along together."

"Local businesswoman. Her father may have known Vanneman, a long time ago. I was planning to learn what I could. Really, Tooch, I haven't been shirking."

"You don't have a camera," says Tucci.

"No, I have a phone that contains a camera. It's far more discreet."

"Stand back," says Tucci, and he leans forward pukes into the jump seat. He keeps at it till he's just making empty gagging sounds and spitting. The smell makes Kyle's stomach turn—the chili sitting uneasily—but he opens his window and drives. He spots Tooch's car in the Sunset parking lot—a time-worn Honda with Pennsylvania plates.

He stays up late, cleaning up the limo. Some of the vomit has frozen, so he can just pick it out and toss it, but then he has to run the heat while he's washing the jump seat upholstery with dish detergent. Eventually he gives up and goes inside, hoping it will dry. He sleeps in his recliner while Tucci snores in the bed, and gets up two hours later, sprays the plush with Febreze, and keeps the windows wide open until he swings into the drive of the lodge at 6:10. There's a lingering smell of perfume and illness. He wishes he had a cigar to light to cover it up. But the men look a little the worse for wear themselves. Frank Waterford mentions they'd had some of the punch, which he said was called Negus: port, claret, burgundy, brandy, and spices.

Once he has delivered them at Billy's, Kyle drives on toward Salisbury till he hits a service station with a car wash and uses the vacuum to reclean the upholstery. He buys another can of Febreze. Then he drives back to the farmhouse and finds Molly Peasy, a hearty young woman who favors grape-colored camo, not good for hiding anywhere he can think of. He has a favor to ask. He has to be gone for a few days, to help a sick friend. He's sorry; he knows there are bookings. Billy can have the use of the limo and decide who will drive. He'll be back as soon as possible. Molly says she'll be glad to drive. She absolutely loves the limo. She promises they'll shelter it in the barn if it should snow while he's gone. After he drops Vanneman's party at the airport—he can stick around long enough to do that, can't he?—he can come back here, and she'll run him back home.

Kyle uses Phillip Vanneman's hundred-dollar tip (the others gave him twenties) for gas on the long drive to Erie in the Honda. Tucci has insisted that it was all just a bad reaction between the alcohol and his anxiety drug, but Kyle doesn't want him behind the wheel, even though he feels rocky himself. Pennsylvania's gray leafless trees on gray hillsides depress him. He misses the limo—it adds something to the world.

At two a.m. in Erie, he finds Tucci's been living in the family basement where they used to practice. Even now, amid Tucci's many stacked boxes of files, there are still some scraps of their band: tapes and posters and poseur photos with long hair. In one he's wearing a black shirt with ridiculous sleeves, thinking he's Hamlet. Tucci is eager to download the Vanneman photos onto his computer even though it's the middle of the night. Kyle flops onto the daybed. He remembers the rhythm of the furnace kicking on and off, and sleeps.

Tucci wakes him early, with coffee and news. He says that Frank Waterford checks out to be the owner of some papers in South Jersey, so probably Vanneman's looking to acquire them. Kyle thinks, looking at the photos of them in the carriage, that they must have sealed the deal. He's just glad that, since he's in some, it's clear he didn't take the pictures. For Tucci's sake, he hopes Tucci's blog is too obscure to bother Vanneman. Tucci has conceded on the drive that there isn't enough on Vanneman for a whole book. He'll expand it to be about all the small media outlets and their importance as the pivot points of power.

At home, Kyle is greeted as if he has pulled off a surprise holiday return of the sort they feature in commercials. Within a day he is full of the old feeling, that he doesn't belong to these people who are so overjoyed, demanding he stay through Christmas or why not New Year's. His mother has him assembling his niece's gift, a bright plastic pretend kitchen. It's impossible to get plane tickets to Philly, though there would be seats on the even-smaller plane that goes from there to Salisbury. Yes, it would be easier to get to Florida. But Kyle really wants the limo. The best chance to fly standby anywhere, the girl adds, will be Christmas day itself.

On Monday, the day after Christmas, Jerard and Joelle are opening up the salon, facing a booked-solid week. Her uncle is ripping foils in half in preparation for Mrs. Wells' appointment and arguing that Joelle need not tell Kyle Davies what she told him last Friday, after she asked him to take on her color appointments because she didn't want to breathe ammonia, that she has reason to think—

"To hope," says Joelle. She's making coffee, half decaf.

"To think about hoping you may have a baby. You can be perfectly fine here raising a child on your own, with work, a place to live, an accepting community—"

"You and all your friends."

"Your friends, too. It's a Christmas story. What is Christmas if not the holiday of uncertain paternity?"

Joelle says, "I don't know if I'll tell him. I may never have to. He may never show up here again."

"Exactly. He's here and then he dashes off—"

"He had a friend in trouble, that's what Molly Peasy said he told her, when she came in for her cut."

"He didn't tell you."

"No," she says, "you're right." She sniffs the coffee and doesn't want it. She's quite sure. It's fifteen days today, and she can take a home test soon. "And as I said, he may not come back."

"Oh, he will," says Jerard. "He has to get that limousine and whatever Billy owes him."

"If he turns up," says Joelle, "it's likely he'll leave after New Year's when things slow down. I could enjoy a little time with him, and he'd go on down to Florida and never know." In her heart, though, she can't see how she'll resist telling him, some moment when they're warm in bed. She'll assure Kyle he has no obligation, and he'll say, no, he's proud and happy. She's a fool, she tells herself, but she can't help but imagine.

"I know his type," Jerard says. "He's an itinerant. Which is to say, an unreliable opportunist. If you tell him, he'll be all ready to settle in, live off the fat of the land for as long as he likes, beget a couple more kids, and then, no doubt, he'll leave you."

She nods. It could be like that.

Jerard says, "I hope you're listening."

"I'll do as I please," says Joelle.

Which is when Kyle walks in.

CRUZ'S NEW PLACE
Tricia Bauer

On the way out the door I turn to Gramma's whisper telling me to take a good look around when we get there. I wink back at her like we do, and then I'm gone. My dad is driving us back to Cruz's new apartment because my cousin forgot to bring his Christmas gift for Gramma. If my mom knew where we were going, she probably wouldn't have let me leave, but she's busy in Gramma's kitchen. She doesn't like me near Aunt Terry's unless absolutely necessary. But this seems absolutely necessary. For Gramma.

"So how long have you all lived at the new place?" Dad is asking Cruz. "You like it?" My cousins—Cruz and his twin sisters—seem to move every six months. My mom has plenty to say about it, unlike Cruz, who doesn't say a thing, but just keeps looking back at Gramma's house like he's never going to see it again. Cruz doesn't talk all that much normally. He's twelve, two years older than me and twice my size, but everybody says he seems way younger.

I turn around, too, and watch Gramma's white house disappearing into the snowy sky. She has a lit candle—the kind you plug in, not like the old-fashioned ones from stories she's read me—in every window of her house. I count ten just on the front of the house. The long driveway is whitening with snow as we drive away. I keep looking until I can't see the little gold lights any more.

Gramma's house was cozy. I helped her make a fire in her fireplace. Cruz picked out the Yule log, but I wish it had been me, though Gramma reminded us that I did the picking last year. My dad's car still hasn't warmed up enough to send heat to the backseat.

"OK, show's over. Turn around, Daniel," my dad says. I think he wishes he was back watching the football with Uncle Chris. It's hard to believe that my mom and Cruz's dad are Gramma's babies. But that's what she says. I wish I was back with my presents, not the PJs so much, but the Xbox game Gramma gave me—Viva Piñata. She wouldn't get me Gears of War, and neither would my dad. I think Cruz got a game, too. Maybe it was something to do with Scooby Doo, which he loves so much I've never been able to stump him on a single Scooby detail. And I've tried.

The road is hilly with lots of curves, so my dad is on the brake more than normal. Cruz and I can see Christmas trees in the windows of some of the houses that are close to the road. "Wow," Cruz says at one house with three enormous evergreens on the front lawn—one lit totally with blue lights, one with red, and a small one with all white.

"They do it up big here," Dad says and checks me in the rearview mirror.

Cruz just keeps staring out his window. "Cruz" isn't his actual name. His name is Christopher like his dad. "Cruz" is what he started calling himself when he was a baby, and nobody stopped him. His dad tried saying "Topher" for a while, but even Gramma didn't like that.

Nobody can seem to figure out why they move so much. Cruz's dad has a good job as a corrections officer in Beacon. He was already drinking too much beer today, which is why Gramma wouldn't let *him* drive. Cruz said his dad is the first one to see the men when they arrive at the prison.

Maybe Cruz's new place will be really great. Gramma's told me not to hold my breath.

I know when we are getting close to Beacon because there are two huge smokestacks. Dad says it's only steam that pours out into the sky and makes one huge weirdly shaped cloud, but Mom doesn't buy it. When we get closer we can see MERRY CHRISTMAS, half of the greeting hung on each of the stacks.

There's a strange smell in the air, not like the fireplaces in Gramma's neighborhood. And somehow, the leftover snow looks grayer here. My dad says that's crazy.

When we first got to Gramma's, Cruz told me in private that his dad gave him a scratch-off that won twenty dollars on the spot. When Cruz promised his dad he would use the winnings for Christmas gifts, his dad took the card back and handed him a twenty. Cruz lowered his voice even more to reveal that he used almost all of the money on his present for Gramma.

Cruz has never mentioned that he gets an allowance like I do. My parents run the Subway close to our house. One or both of them is always there taking orders, making sure everything runs smoothly.

On Main Street there's a BAIL BOND/CHECKS CASHED. My mom has explained the entire process to me a couple of times, but I still don't exactly understand, so I've stopped asking. The candy store has gone out of business and is up for rent. There's a drugstore and a grocery with Spanish words on the front door, but neither is open right now. When my dad and I are alone in the car, he usually says the Spanish words and tells me what they mean, but today he doesn't bother.

"What is it?" I want to know. "What did you get Gramma?" But Cruz is silent.

An old man in a bright red coat is walking his boxer along the sidewalk. The boxer is wearing a red sweater. The dog keeps stopping and looking behind, and the man stops with him, doesn't pull the dog forward. Maybe because it's Christmas.

We make a right turn at a big stone church, then a left at the bakery that has a crack wiggling at an angle from top to bottom of the storefront window.

"This is it," Cruz says, and my dad stops the car.

"This is a liquor store," my dad says.

"Upstairs," Cruz says simply and opens the car door. I follow him.

"OK, boys. Hurry it up," Dad calls as he lowers the front passenger window.

Just to the right of the liquor store, Cruz goes to a door that I didn't even see at first, and there's only a big staircase, green hallway, broken tiles on the steps, a bunch of mailboxes like in the post office on the wall. One of them is open but there's nothing inside.

The air feels greasy. I can't be sure if the voices coming from behind some of the doors are angry or they are excited over their Christmas gifts because Cruz isn't "dawdling," which is one of our Gramma's words.

At the top of the third flight of stairs, Cruz is practically panting. He takes keys out of his pocket and unlocks the door in three places.

"You must have a good view from here," I say to be nice.

Cruz says, "Of what?"

So then I'm quiet as we step into the dark apartment that's not as cold as outside, but pretty close.

Cruz flips on the overhead light. The only thing in this main room, which looks to be the living room, is a big flat-screen TV and, in the corner, two blankets. The tile on the floor seems meant to look like yellow bricks.

C-R-E-E-P-Y.

A wooden table sits in the center of the kitchen, but there are only four chairs. Cruz's family has five, so I ask him which one of them gets left out, and as I'm talking I'm hoping it's not him. Cruz says it's not a problem because the only time they all eat together is at Gramma's.

Gramma's long table with the red tablecloth and the gold cloth napkins was already set for twelve when we left her house. There's nine of us, and then she invited three friends to come, too. One is a lady who now, like Gramma, is a widow. Gramma says "lost" her husband, but she means he died. I've never met her, though Gramma says I have when I was little. The other two used to take trips with Gramma and Grandpa when he was still alive. They went to places like Argentina and Kenya and the Galapagos Islands, places my mom got the map out for. Places my mom now says should have made Gramma more magnanimous. Magnanimous is my mom's word for "kind" when she talks about Gramma. Gramma says her brother, who last year married a young woman from Asia, might stop by to say hi. Gramma's eyes went up when she said "Asia," but I don't think she meant anything bad by it.

Cruz looks for his gift for Gramma as I glance around the mostly empty apartment for any evidence that somebody really lives here.

There are two bedrooms. He shares one of them with his teen-aged sisters. Cruz points to a single mattress on the floor, a set-up of WWE wrestling figures positioned near his pillow.

"Where's all your stuff?" I ask.

"My mom's brother couldn't get it up the stairs, so my mom told him to keep it." Seems like every time they move, they end up with less. My mom says most people move because they need *more* room.

"Shit," Cruz says. I have never heard my cousin use this word. "She got into it," he says with disgust. He's holding a bag of Godiva peppermint white chocolates and it's not wrapped. Or it's unwrapped. At first I try to figure how Gramma got her gift already, but then I understand that he's referring to his mother. For a minute I think Cruz is going to cry.

"It's the good candy," Cruz says softly. So I help him find a piece of wrapping paper in a Kohl's box near his sisters' bed. Girls always have wrapping paper, I tell him. First we cut the Godiva bag down just above the letters, then tie it with a red ribbon so it doesn't look like someone has already eaten half the present.

"How do you know your sisters didn't eat it?" I want to know.

"They would have finished it," he says.

As soon as we get back to Gramma's, my mom asks my dad what it was like at the new apartment. He tells her he doesn't know, that he waited outside.

"What?" she asks. "Wait," she says, moving closer to him.

"Waited," he says. "What?" he says. "I idled right outside of the front door."

"What were you thinking?" she says in her angry voice.

Then they go into the next room and even though they close the door, I smell smoke.

They have all talked about Aunt Terry before. How she's always buying something, spending, spending, spending, never keeping a job, how she used to be a fabulous cook, but now often dishes out Lucky Charms for dinner.

And how Uncle Chris just keeps drinking and working overtime at the prison.

Aunt Terry can't hear my parents because she's lying down with her eyes closed in a room off the kitchen in her fur vest, soft like some endangered hibernating animal. Her nails are painted bright red and decorated with Christmas trees. Cruz says her toes are, too. Cruz's sisters are texting each other from different rooms upstairs.

I'm telling Gramma about Cruz's new place because she's begging. "They won't let me inside," she says, then stops and looks at me. "Gloria has a Droid but no couch in the living room?"

Cruz comes in and hands Gramma her present to get her to stop talking about the Droid. She hugs him, and opens her arms for me. "And, Daniel, I love my perfume." My Gramma is warm and soft, and smells like soap and stuff cooking in the kitchen. And she has a tight grip on me for a minute.

"OK, boys, let me finish my stuffing and get the turkey into the oven."

My Gramma has the most beautiful Christmas tree. It's real, for one thing. And it's decorated in red and gold ornaments and then little gold and red bows, too. Every light is white. There are so many opened gifts beneath it. My dad is starting to pick up the wrapping paper and stuff it into a black plastic bag. After two scoops, he takes a break and sits down. My mother has already told me that Aunt Terry is going to return everything and get the cash. I hope not the wrestling ring we got for Cruz's WWE characters. "Why would this year be any different?" I heard my mom say to my father.

Cruz says that when Gramma dies he is going to live in her house. I like my room at home with the wood headboard, the bed that fits me and my stuffed German shepherd, and the closet that holds all of my clothes and most of my toys. I know Cruz needs a house more than me, but I love Gramma more.

Gramma roars into the living room, her eyes sort of shiny. "Stop picking my bones before I'm gone! I won't have it!" Her hands are on her hips.

Silence falls with the sunlight onto the entire room. "My son's married to *some* kind of addict," she says, her hands now moving in the air. "And my daughter to an illegal."

"Maaaa, he's from Puerto Rico," Mom hollers from the kitchen.

Gramma stops talking then, sits down in the armchair closest to me. She looks at Cruz, then stares right at me. And I stare back.

My lip trembles. "I am a U.S. citizen," I say. But she doesn't hear me.

"I bought them beds," Gramma says so softly her voice is getting shaky. "I bought them everything. I don't know where the stuff goes. What she's on . . ." Gramma babbles. Then she puts both hands on her knees and suddenly stands up. "They don't know how to live here," she says.

"But they *are* here," I say. "We're all here," I say.

And then Gramma's face goes out of focus as I look beyond her at the Christmas tree, in each of the little red and gold balls must be a tiny picture   of us surrounded by wrapping paper and ribbon, and the mess, like the only presents still unopened. Someone knocks on the front door.

With the back of her hand, Gramma wipes away a tear. "With this racket," Gramma says, "it's probably the cops."

We all turn to see who it will be.

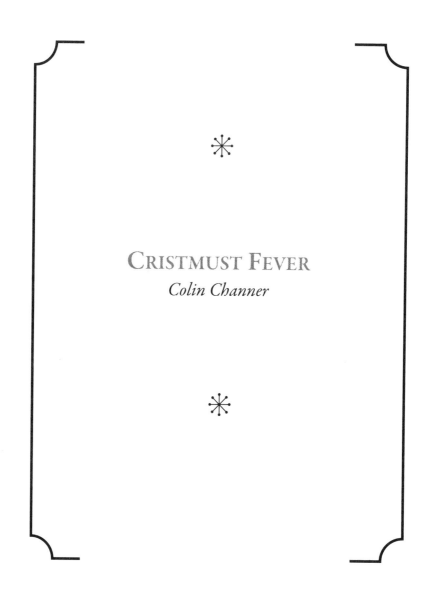

CRISTMUST FEVER
Colin Channer

t is not dark yet, but it will be soon, in the tent here it is hot, but it is hot everywhere, it is cooler outside but i no go go out, i am guarding

i am a girl and they have been saying for weeks that santa go be coming tonight for all girls who who don't know blood, if you refuse santa man them they go kill you, they say when the war is over santa will be something called president, from what i understand he is the one started the war what made all of us here refusees, they say his force is a stronger one than the evl or the ppm or the wsa, those force their bosses names are kernel kill them and major cat ass trophy,

here in the tent i feel alone although there is another somebody with me, the man i call my father, he thinks he cannot protect me from santa, santa is a bad man, his army is the boss one, his army they have all what they call mines, his army they have all the oil that pumps to make all the cars and trucks in the world stop or go, that is what people say,

there are people outside, not right outside, steps and steps away, there are a lot of them, i can see them through a tear in the tent, there are more of them than all the plaits in my hair added to the hair in the place where the woman blood go come from one day,

they are shooting rifles in the sky, they are singing too, the people them,

the people them are not really people, they are only boys, they are only boys who want to help santa fight, they want to help him because they go get more food if they do this, this is what i think, they no say that though, they say they go fight for santa for he is the bossest of boss,

santa go bring present is what they are singing, santa go give car to the father them who give him all the daughter them who no yet see blood, santa go

83

give ear to all of them who are singing who find girl who no see blood yet and take them from their father them,

i know all of those boys who are singing out there in the dust, the dust is red but it looks pink and gray because the full dark go come soon and time is getting short,

where they are singing is called the square, it is a new name, it is only a week old, shells bombed it and fifty tents they say were lost, i do not know exactly, i do not know how many, i do not know whose shells there were, if it was from kernel kill them or major cat ass trophy, all i know is that people were burned, some people just disappeared, some body them they tear up like our clothes,

i can smell their mouths from here, i can smell their armholes too, i can smell them over the smoke from the cooking wood, and the plastic bags of waste we throw outside,

i cannot smell them for true for they are maybe two hundred steps away, past many other tents but the smell of them it caked up in my head like something cooked too long in a forgotten pot,

these boys disgust me but i cannot take my eyes away from them, i am not a fool,

look at them there jumping in the graypinky dust, the rifles are taller than most of them, some of them are not even wearing pants, their front tails must be flopping up and down like fingers making threats,

my stomach twists inside me, but no water no come to my eye, even inside me there is drought,

cha!

look at them,

look at them,

they think they are big now but they are just boys, they did it to me two times so many of them and i have no baby to show, my hunger is still my own only, i no have to feed small mouth,

look at them,

me and them made by our mothers at the same time,

look at them,

they have guns but no power to bring life,

look at them,

the more i look at them the more i want to shout at them, i want to shout and say my belly no swell and it was so much of you who grab me that time when i was going for water, it was so much of you who push me in the dirty, it was so many of you hold me down, you wanted to be man, you wanted to swell belly, so all of you was saying, you go make me swell, you gambled among yourselves, betted who the child would favor, you lost, every single one of you, for my belly no swell, if fruit don't ripe it can't drop, you want to be man but you don't know seasons and times, what you go do when the war ends and you go have to keep wife, you no fit to farm,

cha!

the song they are singing i have heard something like that before from a doctor, not a swissland doctor, a doctor from cando,

you better watch out and you better not cry and somebody making a list of names,

i wish santa no go come, i hope these boys no go take me, there are forces all around the camp, they go kill me if i run, everyone here is afraid, no one go help me hide, i am a off hand, nobody thinks of me,

i wish the man i call my father go consider again what i put to him, this is my wish,

i wish more people could speak my language, i wish my language was one that could write and not just be said,

if my language could be write i would go write my story this evening and wish that when the swissland and cando people come back one of them would find my story on a paper or even scratch with a stick in the dirty and then rewrite what i wrote in their language,

this is my wish, someone to find what i say

i would not want it to be an african though, they only live in the refusee camp like me, the swissland and cando people take care of them, the swiss-land and cando people do the doctoring and bring the rice, africans suffer and kill,

but the cando and swissland people have been gone since late november, they don't want to fight santa and his people them, they say the boss of them says they must go away, this is what the swissland and cando people them say before they left me, the boss of them said and they have to do what he says,

one of them the one with the bent nose who gave me the doctoring after the boys said she was planned to visit her family in swissland for xmust, so she was not going because of santa, she was going for that,

i felt a different shame from the shame of the boys when she said xmust, i was thinking xmust was the same as cristmust, but she used to always say i was not only big in size for my age but also in the brain so i did not want to ask if they were the same and seem to be foolish,

cristmust i know is in the harm a tan time, when the dust comes and comes and does not stop, in the harm a tan time it is like the god of the ground lends dust to the god of the sky knowing he will be repaid with a profit, cristmust i think is close to ram down which is for horibs, for ram down horibs do not eat for many days then eat for all the days,

from the talking of the people from swissland and cando cristmust happens because a white man was killed,

the first time i heard this i was surprised, i used to think that white men did not die, only africans,

i see white people sick before, i see them hurt before, but i no see white people die, i know they must die, but i never see them do it, only black, not even the bombs kill them, before the bombs come the boss of them in swissland or cando tells them to leave,

i heard them say he wanted to die, the white man who was killed for cristmust to happen, but which man wants to die, all the men i see die were begging, if they were not begging it was because they were too weak to make a sound,

one time in this same camp here i went to look for firewood in one of the lonely parts, i had to go far far because there are many of us and we need to cook, half the day was gone and then i saw what was left behind of a man that died, what was left behind of him was dressed in ants and worms and after i walked past i heard a sound like when you are forced to blow air out of your mouth because no words are there to say what are you are sadding or paining about,

when i turned around a cloud of flies was rising from the black bones, the flesh between the bones was gummy,

that was the first time i saw a ghost and learned what they are made of, ghosts are made of flies, flies make a sound like the last wind that comes from a man's windpipe,

cha!

the light, i am being called,

i look behind me, i squeeze my eyes, the torch is bright bright, my mind fills in the shape of the man i call my father, he is on a piece on cloth on the floor, in the dirty, three steps from me, he is wearing a t-shirt like me, but his is own not long to his foots, it is long to his knee above,

his is white, mine is purple, or red

the man i call my father is like the tent, his skin is sagging, but unlike the tent he has fully collapsed, he is going to die, each sore is going to turn into a puff of flies, this man who took me long after the fever took my mother and father and all the brothers and sisters who came before me, there were fifteen of them,

they did not die here, they died after the war forced us to leave the city, that was four or five harm a tans ago, i was too young to remember, i was too young to understand,

we walked a long way, i remember this, it took us a long time, we walked until my teeth fell out and new teeth came back and many of my sisters got their blood,

when i came to the camp i came alone, there were many of us, more than a rich man's cattle but i was still alone, they put me with the other off hands,

the man i call my father is not even from my tribe, he took me after the boys had made their bet on me, i do not know why, he was the one who took me to the doctor from cando with the crooked nose, she was the one who used to give him the pills for the fever he said, now she is gone he is suffering again,

we used to sleep apart, but since i heard what santa is planning to do i lie with him at night, every night i say the same thing, i want him to save me from santa and the boys who help him, i tell him how and he tells me the same thing, he can not do it,

it is nearly dark now, more boys are there, more rifles are shooting more songs are singing, they are singing for santa, they are singing for girls without blood to surrender, they are singing that santa can see if you are sleeping, that he knows when you are awake,

santa is the bossest of boss, he knows everything for true, i believe this, the camp is full of spies,

eh eh!

the song has changed.

i take my eyes off the man i call my father and look through the rip in the tent again, the song is now a chant, the boys are chanting names, they are chanting names of girls, it is like they have the names written down but i know it is not so because they are boys, they must have told the names many times to each other, some of the names are pretty, some of them are strange, we are different tribes,

i wonder what girls of other tribes are thinking when they hear my name, when i hear it i go to the man i call my father, i do not walk, i go on my knees, i bend over him, i can make out that he is begging for water, i begin to answer him, he turns his face from me,

maybe when you are going to die you learn to see inside another person's head, it seems he knows what i go say,

they fraid for me now because the fever has come back to small him down to bone, they are afraid to touch me again because they think i live with him like wife, but their fear go only last for a time, already they forgot what tradition says will happen to people who do the kinds of things they did to me,

water begins to overflow my eyes now as i think of my fate, i wish i had paper and that my language could write, i want to write this down, i want to

write this down so a swissland or cando could find it and make it into words
that white people understand,

one time i heard a woman say when her baby when he cried for milk and
her breasts were small down like leaves i going go to the swissland man to
make him know no milk no there in breast for you for when white people
understand things they make good things happen,

i take the man i call my father into my arms and lean over him, i feel his
hair falling off onto my arms, it is scratchy on my wrist

cha!

i say this in my mind, it would hurt his feelings if i said it for true,

i once heard something about the white man they killed to make cristmust, they say he said that if you do something bad it is not bad forever, if
you talk about it in your mind and you feel bad about your bad thoughts and
you say that the thoughts were bad for true then it is as if you did not do a
bad thing at first,

i think this is what he said at least,

the man i call my father asks me for water again,

the water outside i tell him, you no hear the boy them outside, you no
hear them sing, you no hear them shoot, tonight santa go come to town, if i
go outside they go do again what they already do, i know them, i know them
good good, one of them use to learn with me at the priest man school,

my voice lowers itself with shame when i say this but i continue, i was the
one who learn him to count, i can count very well so i know how much of
them it was who tramped me in the dust,

my voice stays low but this there is a different feeling in my mind, i feel
like i am already talking to the white man they killed for cristmust in my
head,

i go bring water i say to the man i call my father, but i go do it only if he
make me lie underneath him like wife, i tell him i want wife from him, i tell
him i want wife from him outside in the dirty, i tell him i want wife from him
in front of those boys and their wicked eyes, i want public wife and if he no
give me i no go find him water for drink,

he say he no go do that,

i draw him closer to me like i go give him titty to drink then i take my other hand and fist him,

he gets it in the face, he makes no sound, his joints get tight then loose again, his skin is hot, his bones are tough,

every time he says no i fist him again, i am doing a bad thing, i know this, but i must do this bad thing to do myself some good, my fingers are wet, it is blood or pus, he has no spit,

you thirsty i ask him one time before the blow, he says yes, i am tired of him, i am tired of beating him for nothing, i am not wicked, i want him to do what i want

i let him go and swing one leg over him, i can feel his ribs between my legs, although he is on his back i feel the way i used to feel when i was little and they let me ride the goats,

he tries to move but i squeeze him with my knees

ahh,

this is what he says when the dripping begins, the hotness and the smell must tell him it is urine but he does not seem to care, it is wet and his throat is dry,

i let it fall on his neck, i reach down and wipe some on his chin, i touch a dry finger to his bottom lip to fool him, his lip feels like one of the bits you find on the ground after a man shaped a flute from a piece of wood,

he whispers to make him drink it, he so thirsty, i pass wind into his nose,

this time he cries,

cha!

no more time to waste with him, i feel around beside him, i find the torch, i go outside, my heart moved up to my head, this is how it feels, it is beating there beside my thoughts,

the noise is so much it feels like it is silent,

as i pass a lot of tents in the dark, they are all falling down, inside of them girls are crying, men are beating their wives, mothers are telling daughters there is no other way but to go, i can see the crowd of boys ahead of me as i am walking, no one is outside but me and them, i am for true an off hand, i am for true alone, i have no mother or father to prepare me for this,

when i get where the boys are i stand with one foot rubbing the other, it is better if they take me first, i don't want to hear what happens to the others, that would be worst,

but it is like am not there, i take off the t-shirt and throw it at them, it falls short, i know they can see me, i am not that far from them,

there are a hundred of them shooting and singing, their t-shirts are flapping like lips that have too much to say, i look at the sky, i see stars beyond the dust, i am remembering that cristmust and the white man they killed has something to do with a star,

the lights are beating like my heart, my eye keeps jumping as it tries to watch all of them, it is confusing, it is hard to look up at the stars and in front at the boys at the same time, but i am finding that i am less confused about the stars the more i look at them, i am thinking that some of them might arranged in patterns like tribes,

these boys in front of me are all of different tribes, if the world was upside down they would be a sky full of wickedness and hate shining for the spirits in the sky to see,

i feel a twist in my stomach, i am nothing, i shout, no one turns, i kneel, no one comes, i feel a new kind of shame, i have no word for it,

i run in the tent to find the man i call my father, i kick him in his side, i stomp on his chest, i stoop over him and empty my bowels in his face and hair, i drag him by the where the boys are in the square where fifty other tents used to be, i lie down there in the dust, naked in the dirty, i open my legs, he mans me, he does not want to be kicked and fisted again,

he is hot on me, and bony, this bloody man i call my father, inside though there is just a hint of him, it is not like it was with the boys,

i curse him, i scratch him, he begins to grow, the boys do not notice, they are shooting, they are jumping, they are singing, they are in a dance,

i close my eyes, i have the torch with me, i shine it at them, it is beginning to hurt, the thing i am doing, i am dry inside the way the man i call my father is dry in his mouth,

there is a change in the singing, the shooting stops, footsteps begin to shake the ground around me, there is right above my head,

the man i call my father starts to say bad things in my ear, he says it in a way that makes me think that when he says nice things to women he says it in the same way, he is grown halfway in me, i feel i am getting drier, i am lucky he is too weak to make me hurt much hotter,

i wonder if they know it is me, i shine the torch on my face, the heat of it is different from the heat of him, i push him off, i kick him with my heel, i sit up in the circle of the boys,

i open my eyes, they are dim with tears and dust and sweat, guns are looking down at me, i look up at the stars, the boys begin to talk, they are not talking to me, when i make to stand up a few that are close to me try to back away,

she have the fever for true oh, she have fever for true, this is what i think i hear their guns are still staring,

i might be saved tonight,

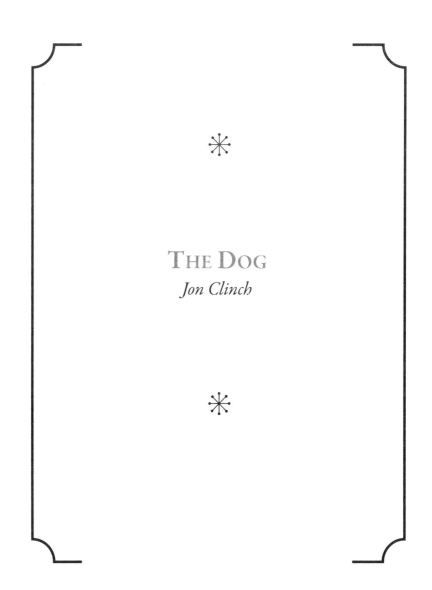

THE DOG
Jon Clinch

Into the riverman's life the dog enters like a thing freely given.

The man awakens in his frozen bed one morning and he stirs up the fire from weary embers and he steps out onto the porch all swept about with snow to assess the dawn, and from down along the riverside the thing barks up at him as if she has him treed. Such a howling he has not heard in the longest time. Joyous and intent all at once. As if all that remains to complete her nascent satisfaction is to see him shot.

He enters back into the house and makes his breakfast, and at his disappearance the dog leaves off. When he emerges later to run his lines she is gone and a fresh snowfall has obscured most of her tracks and to all appearances she has been taken up again into whatever heaven dropped her in the beginning. The water round about his skiff has thickened and taken on a greasy sheen in the dawn light, gone slow as churned butter with the beginnings of ice. The mooring lines droop hard as iron. He casts off and heads against the wind into the river, ice accumulating on his pole as he works it and the footing treacherous. He balances upon the slick planking and with the unbalanced pole and he would dream of summertime if he were to dream at all. Later as he kneels penitent to work the lines his knees go wet and his thin trousers stiffen and he takes comfort in the knowledge that at least his catch will keep.

He leaves off early and rather than sell what he has caught at some more profitable distance or risk the uphill walk to one of the hotel kitchens in the village he ties up at Dixon's. The tavern sits atop a high bank and the path to it has been carved from roots and raw earth by the tread of a thousand patrons come up this way. He knows it by habit and many a time has found it in the dark, so the ice and snow is little obstacle but still. He wraps the fish in a tarpaulin and brings them up darkly ashimmer like a sackful of green icicles. He hammers at the door until Dixon answers. To the rear of the tavern is the kitchen where Dixon's harridan wife fries catfish come noontime and beyond that the room where they sleep. She has forbidden her husband to have truck with one such as this but her usual sources are unlikely to appear today so Dixon purchases the little that he has brought up with her tolerance if not her blessing.

"Not fit for man nor beast," he says. Indicating the weather.

"I seen a dog out there," says the other.

"Ow."

He frowns and asks for a whiskey which Dixon offers up, handing the glass and the jug gently as a pair of matched gemstones and keeping himself between his visitor and the kitchen door that his wife might not see him encouraging this one whose unfortunate habits are so well and widely known.

The dog appears again in the morning, although where she may have weathered the night he cannot guess. He saves out some of his fatback for her and puts it on a tin plate and brings it out the back door and kneels with it in the dusting of snow. Whether the dog finds him or his bacon the more attractive or even differentiates between the two is unknowable but up the open stairs she comes. Her coat is dark and brindled and around her neck to his surprise is a collar, black as she is and hard worn. She eats as if she has only this day discovered meat. For a while he shivers on the elevated landing in her presence, warmed by it but only so much. She finishes the bacon and licks the tin plate clean and makes as if to nose the door, or else he just imagines it, but he thinks not for he has been around animals enough. And then in the absence of further invitation she goes.

Later he follows her track and finds her curled beneath the house in a low space where the snow eddies, her body black against the black woodpile. Ice in her claws and riming her brindled back. He calls her by her gender and she makes no particular response. Only when he reaches to touch her collar does she twist her neck and snap her jaws exactly once and offer up a growl that seems to come from her very lights and livers in defense of something that she once was but is no longer.

He has no use for a dog. If she is trained for squirrels he has no use for squirrels, and if she is trained for raccoons instead he cannot be expected to give over his nights to hunting raccoons for he has other habits already far more dear to his heart. Yet come the next morning he looks for her again and again he finds her alongside the woodpile and again he offers her a portion of his fatback, which she consumes like ambrosia. He waits until she is finished and touches her on the head and the neck and she permits him.

The next morning he removes her collar and by this unnaming he both frees her and claims her for his own. She will not enter into the house but he feeds her more frequently and she accepts it. The weather warms for a day or two and she vanishes with its improvement, and then it worsens all over again and she reappears and he wishes that she would come inside but she seems to possess other more solitary ideas. Her collar he keeps where he dropped it unclasped on the kitchen table. In the rising heat of the stove each morning it smells to him of dog and he does not mind in the least for it gives him a kind of company in the windbeaten riverside house.

One hardblowing dawn he feeds himself and the dog and before he knows it she has leapt into the skiff alongside him. For all his experience with hunting dogs he has never known a fishing dog and he tells her so with some begrudging amusement, but he is willing to give this new arrangement a try nonetheless. He finds the first of his lines and he runs it hunched over against the weather. One fish after another he throws onto the decking to spasm and freeze and endure as it either dies or merely grows deathly stiff at the chill wet proddings of the dog's black nose. He works his way upstream, the dog's enthusiasm driving him beyond his instinct. There is a short leftward bend to the north and he has let his lines upstream of it go untended during these difficult weeks, but bolstered by the dog's presence he vows that he will run them just this once. The wind blows fierce from the north bearing snow upon its back and he fights against it and against a current heavier than usual taking note of the added weight of the dog in the skiff but not minding.

Inches deep in a crusted shifting mass of icy fish they round the leftward bend and upon their turning the wind strikes them full from the side, blowing the skiff southward and heaving up a slow bulge of brown water to press against its shallow hull. The dog retreats to the left against the tilting weight of it and the man does likewise from instinct, treading upon the dog's frozen paw and drawing forth a howl that under other circumstances would be sufficient to break a person's heart. He curses the weather and the wind and the water and the craven yowling dog, and he jams his pole deep thinking to restore his balance for they are well to the left of the channel. Yet the pole finds no purchase and he nearly tips into the drink for he has miscalculated. The pole slips from his hand and vanishes briefly and bobs up to show itself downstream again coated with ice, and the man grasps the gunwale just in time to keep himself from pitching over. The brown wave passes beneath the boat and drawing near the snowy bank the man sees in time that it is not the bank he knows at all but a heaping up of ice, great sheets of it come from upstream and jammed against this turning in the river's course one after another. As if the very water itself has plotted against him in creating this obstacle and concealing the channel's true location both.

With the wave gone past, the dog reclaims the upstream side only to be surprised by another wave or perhaps a second instance of the same and she leans perilously out over the gunwale barking at the rising water in useless alarm, which causes the man to reach for her and lose his own balance in turn. With their weight thus shifted the wave builds against the skiff and takes it over, spilling the pair of them into water thick as buttermilk. Only the caught fish, safe in the bottom of the boat that has already gone spiraling back downstream, are immune to the predations of its icy and omnipresent teeth. The man for all his time on the river has never learned to swim and only by means of vigorous thrashing and initial proximity and a certain amount of luck does he reach the ice jam. The dog is more suited to this kind of adventure and her sharp claws carry her up onto its safer reaches first. She is there waiting for him and the sight of her gives him some measure of comfort.

She shakes off water in sheets and he wishes that he could do likewise and together they set out, the dog crusting over with ice and the man too. Up the jagged rise they scramble, falling back one step for every two. Blood drips from somewhere onto the ice in lacy red fannings-out and the man realizes that he has burst something in his nose or his forehead or above his hairline but he makes no effort to locate the source or to stopper it, for surely it will coagulate or freeze soon enough. When they reach the crest they discover that the downriver face of the ice jam is more steeply pitched than the front and mazed all over with the tangled limbs of a deadfall against which it took its root. The dog slips through handily and is on solid ground soon enough, but the man sees no obvious passage down. He places one boot-heel onto a jutting limb and follows after it with much of his weight but the limb snaps off at a hidden fault, almost but not quite letting him tumble to earth, which might have been a fate superior to being stranded up in the high open air with the wind howling and his clothes frozen hard to his pale and whitening skin.

The dog barks as if she has him treed and this brings a smile to his frozen lips in spite of his distress. Ice tugs at his beard. He reaches for another branch but his hands are frozen stiff and he can find no certain grip upon it, so he thrusts them to warm under his armpits and hunches forward and breathes for a moment or two but it does no good and only causes him to miss the departure of the dog. Disloyal cur. Given off with her barking and disappeared into the gale. After all he has done for her.

He studies the tangled branches and places a boot-heel in the crotch of two limbs and this one takes his weight. But the next step is not so easy and the limb he chooses for it proves in the end to be merely jammed into the ice and his weight breaks it free to leave him hanging. Crucified in that mazing of branches and ice, with one boot-heel jammed and one leg swinging free and his bare hands helpless athwart ice-crusted branches. Thus he stays for an eternity.

Until the dog returns, accompanied by two men bundled up like bankers costumed for a polar expedition. "My God!" says one of them or the other, either to his companion or to the dog or to the brittle air itself which coalesces around his words and makes them briefly visible before snatching them away for good. Warm and well fed the two of them scramble with surprising power up through the tortuous maze of branches and ice to the suspended man's side. Working together like a pair of comfortable old conspirators they pry him loose of the place where his boot-heel is jammed and free his frozen hands from the ice cementing them to the unfeeling treelimbs. Then they haul his vanquished figure down.

"Obliged," says the riverman.

"Not yet you aren't," says one of his rescuers, the heavier-set of the two. Hoisting him limp onto his shoulder and setting out for the village.

The other bends and claps the dog upon her rib cage, shaking loose a shower of icicles. "Good girl," he says. "Good girl, Queen."

Even in the snowlit day the cottage is all aglow. Candles sparkle in every window and pine boughs festoon the porch railings and the frozen man in his misery believes that he is about to be ushered into the banquet hall of some mythical king. Whether to eat or to be eaten he cannot guess. Nor does anything about the interior dissuade him. The place is redolent of allspice and cinnamon and apple pie and roast goose, the very air charged with song and laughter and the highspirited shrieking of children. In a place of honor stands an evergreen tree, much garlanded and set about with candles.

A woman stands rednosed and apronswaddled before the stove, a wooden spoon in her hand and a look of eager alarm upon her face. She is plainly relieved to see the two men safely returned, but just what ought to be done with the frozen man hung between them like wash is a mystery that her good Christian heart has not yet penetrated.

"Mother," says the heavy-set man, "fetch a blanket and some dry clothes before this individual succumbs." The two already dragging him to a chair by the hearth. With no ceremony on their part and no shame on his they strip off his frozen raiment which comes away in tatters. The children stand transfixed until the larger man shakes out a horseblanket in which to wrap the naked and white-rimed interloper and the smaller man shoos them back toward their games. To which they return only begrudgingly, for although Christmas comes but once a year, a sad shivering stranger agasp and agape has never previously groaned his life out before their hearthfire.

In time he warms and dresses himself beneath the blanket in clothing far too large but warmer than any he can remember owning. His flesh is mostly red but patched with white in places and even still he will survive all but scatheless. The heavy-set man brings him a dram of good whiskey which he sips like a gentleman for the warmth in it. The woman and another woman for all purposes identical to her feed him mutton stew and roasted potatoes and hot cornbread and baked beans and a warmed-over joint of venison for the goose is not yet done and his hunger will not wait. He licks his plate clean and combs out his moustache with his thawed fingers and licks down what he has collected there too and then holds out his greasy hand for the dog, which approaches without reservation and begins with her long tongue to finish such leavings as remain.

To anyone: "D'you say her name was."

"Queen."

"Yours, then."

"Five or six years now. She's practically a member of the family." As proud as if he has sired her himself.

"She ain't got no collar."

The heavy-set man bends to confirm its absence. "She used to." Pulling down the corners of his mouth. "I don't know what became of it."

"Good dog like that you best find her another'n."

"I will."

"I come upon the old one anywhere's I'll bring it."

"I'd be obliged."

The dog's tongue grows cold and desperate on his bare flesh and the river-man withdraws his hand beneath the blanket and the dog leaves off excluded. "I'm obliged for your kindness."

"You go on and keep the clothes if you like."

"You sure about that."

"It's no trouble. I insist. Go on."

"I will," says the riverman. Shaking himself free of the useless blanket and rising to go. "I'm obliged."

His has banked the fire in his own stove prior to leaving the riverside house and when he returns it has dwindled nearly unto death. He feeds it kindling and bends to blow upon it and he feeds it some more, standing there in his own cold house wearing another man's clothing altogether too large. When the flames begin to rise at last he adds a pair of split logs that send a shimmer of sparks up the chimney pipe and then he goes to fetch a glass of whiskey. This he carries to his chair by the stove and the dog collar he carries likewise from its place on the kitchen table, and the pair of them he addresses like sacraments, one into the flesh and the other into the fire.·

THE DOG

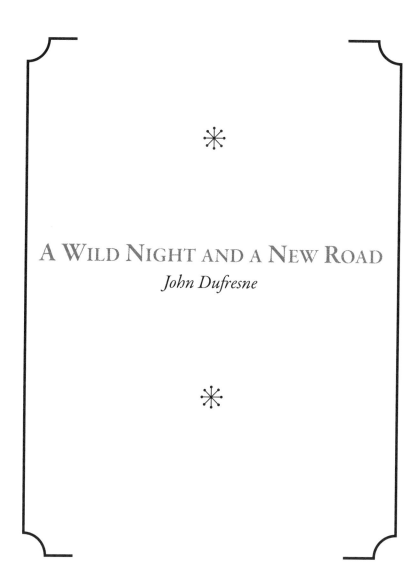

A WILD NIGHT AND A NEW ROAD
John Dufresne

S he drives home with her fake RayBans on and the radio blasting. Power
96! Amy Winehouse or someone like that. This is Saturday, Christmas
Eve, in South Florida, and, still, you could just die from the heat. At the
light on Federal by the high school, she changes the station to oldies. The
Stones' "Miss You." She cranks the volume up to twenty-nine. She sees a
woman outside the Dixiewood Motel, wearing snug red shorts, a Santa T-
shirt that says HO! HO! HO!, polyester antlers, and a Rudolph nose that
lights up whenever a car approaches. There's a toothless dude with an eye
patch sitting on a plastic milk crate in front of Room 4. He's feeding a red hibiscus flower to the absinthe-green iguana on his shoulder. A car pulls into
the lot. One of those cars that looks like a lunch box. Rudolph prances to the
car, sticks her head in the passenger-side window. Our driver hears the blast
of a horn. The light is green.

Her name's Roberta. Born Roberta Maybay. She was Bobbi as a child,
even Bobbie Jo for a time in preschool—her dad's idea. She tried Ro, then
Rob, then Bob. Bertie. Calls herself Robbie now. Robbie Bourassa. She's a
temp for Kelly Services. She spent the last week as a ticket agent for Air Tran
at the Fort Lauderdale Airport, checking photo IDs, issuing boarding passes,
wheeling old gentlemen through security and to the gate. You meet confident
people at airports. They have the poise of destination. Next week, who
knows, maybe back to Broward General recruiting blood donors over the
phone. About the boringest thing she can think of.

She swings by the Seminole Reservation, picks up three cartons of filter-
tip generics at Tribal Smokes. She writes "cereal" on her hand with her Air
Tran ballpoint. She stops at Publix for milk, bread, cereal, and beer. (White,
white, Jurassic Park Crunch, Lite.) She pulls into the driveway behind

Marty's pickup, puts the car in park, leaves it idling. She lights a cigarette, looks at her house, at the hard-water stain on the stucco wall, at the shabby pair of spiral Christmas trees by the walk and the cheerless icicle lights on the eaves, listens to Marvin Gaye. She puts her head back, shuts her eyes, and she's nineteen again, nineteen and blissfully high on Midori sours and wacky weed, and she's dancing like a dervish at that gay bar on Las Olas. She can't remember what it was called. It was called The Male Box.

Eventually she will have to go in and face it all. Face the two whiney kids, the Kool-Aid stain on the carpet, face Marty, lying on his bony ass with a can of beer in front of the TV, and the cat shit on the kitchen floor, and the dust everywhere, and the sorry mica furniture that looked so classy on the showroom floor, and the dishes from last night piled in the sink. Face the knowledge that it will always be like this. At least for as long as it counts. Robbie punches the cigarette into the ashtray. The three of them in the house. None of them waiting for her. And Marvin Gaye is dead.

"Marty the Bug Man." That's what it says on the side of his truck. "Good for What's Bugging You." Robbie married the exterminator twelve years ago. Her first marriage, his second. It will be her last. When she was dating Marty, Robbie would meet him on Fridays at Ocean's 11. Four-for-one Happy Hour. He'd complain about his wife, Jamie, the ER nurse. He'd nuzzle Robbie's neck, play her favorite songs on the jukebox. They'd dance, and later they'd wind up at her place, this place. She hears the dog barking out back like a lunatic. Probably hasn't been fed. The inflatable snowman is now a puddle of plastic on the brown lawn. Robbie wonders how her once favorite holiday could have become an annual disappointment.

Every day she suffers the family's exquisite indifference. Marty, a gristled lump of indolence, lost in his funhouse of electronic amusements, engages Robbie only when he's in need of sexual or culinary catering. And the kids simply refuse to clean up. Ever. No matter that she grounds them, slaps them, screams till she's blue in the face. The bugs will come, she tells them. Like they care. Some mothers get brainiacs, or their kids are good at one thing or another, or they're drop-dead gorgeous or vivacious, or they can charm the knickers off a nun or something. Anything. Robbie loves Tiffany and Nicole, of course, but she doesn't, she has to admit, admire them. Her bumper sticker might read My Dull and Sullen Child Is an Unremarkable Student at Mary Bethune Elementary. This thought makes Robbie laugh. She puts on her Christmas-mix CD and listens to Elvis having a blue, blue, blue, blue Christmas.

And then she recalls their first Christmas as a family. Nicole was just three months old and mostly oblivious, but so adorable in her *Dear Santa, I Can Explain* onesie. Marty spent the better part of the day parked on the Barcalounger, watching sports, and drinking his way through a six-pack of Christmas ale. And then it was time to visit the families, Robbie and Nicole off to see her mom, and Marty, if he stayed awake, off to his ex mother-in-law's to see his sons Kyle and Dale.

Mom's boyfriend, Ariel Kim, a secular Korean Jew who taught Russian and Chinese at FIU and who could not pronounce Robbie's name, did not observe the holiday. When Robbie smiled and called him a Scrooge, Dr. Kim said, "Cewebwate wife, not Cwismas, Woeberta!" And she held up Nicole and said, "That's what the baby's about, Ariel!" When she offered Nicole to Dr. Kim to hold, he folded his arms. When she gave her mother her Christmas present—a gold pendent with Nicole's opal birthstone, her mother thanked her with a kiss and set the unopened gift on the coffee table. "I'll open it later."

"You're not at all curious?"

"I know it'll be perfect."

The three of them played Dr. Kim's polyglot version of Scrabble while Robbie dandled the sleeping baby in her arms. Robbie couldn't stop staring at Nicole and could not believe how exhilarated she felt, how blessed. They had food delivered from Five Chinese Brothers: General Tso's chicken, Buddhist Delight, and Happy Family. Dr. Kim won the game when he turned the English word *flat* into the German word *flatterhaft* and earned a triple word score.

It's dark in the house. Robbie has to stand at the door and let her eyes adjust. All the verticals are closed. It's like a dungeon. Robbie opens the blinds in the living room. She plugs in the Christmas tree lights and the color wheel. In the kitchen she shoves the cat off the counter. The girls are in their room with the door shut and locked. Robbie knocks. "Are you girls doing your homework?"

"It's vacation," Tiffany yells.

Robbie tells her to do it anyway. She doesn't know why.

"Later!"

"Now!"

She checks messages on the answering machine. Her mother's bunion's inflamed. She needs a ride to Walgreens in the morning. She knows its Christmas, but Walgreens never closes, and anyway she needs to pick up a last-minute gift for Marty. "I was thinking maybe one of those Big Mouth Billy Bass, you know, the singing fish." The optometrist reminds Nicole of Monday's appointment. Mr. Jeffrey Knapp from AMEX would like Marty to give him a call at his earliest possible convenience. Robbie wonders how an empty life can seem so full. She tells herself to knock off the self-pity. Is her life really empty? Is it? Well, if empty means without content, then maybe yes. If it means idle, then no. Her life's not empty then.

Robbie figures she has time to bathe before they go out. She goes to the bedroom. Marty's on the bed in his underwear. He's watching TV, and he's pointing a handgun at Robbie. He says, "Bang!"

"You asshole!" she says.

"I can't hear you. You're dead."

"Marty, what have I told you about guns in the house?"

"It's a pistol, stupid."

"Get it out!"

"I need protection."

Robbie slams the bathroom door and looks at herself in the mirror. Do other people live like this? She opens the door, tells Marty, "You're picking up the sitter! It's *your* goddamn Christmas party!" She closes the door. Marty's work clothes are piled on the floor, smelling of cypermethrin. She checks the trouser pockets for cash, kicks the clothes to the corner.

In the bathtub she rests and looks ahead to tonight's party at Turbo Weedon's. Robbie and her girlfriends will sit around the living room, smoking doobies, talking about the movie stars they'd like to screw. And the husbands will sit on the deck and talk about the Dolphins or whoever the hell they are. The husbands are all mutilated in one way or another. They've all lost digits to meat cleavers, extruding machines, motorcycle spokes. And they all own dogs—pit bulls, Rottweilers, shepherds—and the dogs all have names like the husbands: Chipper, Duke, Buddy, Dave, Zonker, like that.

Finally, she's relaxing, for the first time in a week. She lets the hot water run slowly, falls into a fitful sleep, or something close to sleep. She's driving a Wonder Woman lunch box along an unfamiliar and uncrowded road. She doesn't know where the road leads; she's just driving toward the light. There's a sign ahead, but she can't read it, so she leans her head out the window. When her head hits the tile wall, she's back in the bathtub. She smiles. What was that all about? She hears the phone ring. Marty turns up the volume on the TV and ignores the call. She hears Barney Miller tell Fish to take Wojo and investigate a robbery in New Delhi is what it sounds like. Agnew's Deli, maybe? There was a time in her life when she had places to go. These days her life's confined to the house, the inconsequential jobs, the husband, the kids, the few friends, all nice enough, these friends, but tiring and complacent. Robbie feels like she's been driving in the breakdown lane.

There's a bright moment in the car on the way to the party. They're listening to Billy Joel on Classic Gold singing about how Catholic girls start much too late. Robbie, being a Catholic girl, says Billy's got it all wrong. She says to Marty, "Do you know the mating call of a Catholic girl?" He doesn't. She says, "I'm so drunk." Marty laughs. Robbie says, "What's the mating call of a not-so-beautiful Catholic girl?" Marty shrugs. "I *said,* 'I'm so drunk!'" Marty is tickled and touches her knee. He raises a lascivious eyebrow, and Robbie thinks maybe tonight he'll hold her. She tries to picture their embrace, but cannot. Sex with Marty has become infrequent, mechanical, coarse, and brief. It still feels good for the shuddering, but it doesn't carry her out of her world as it once did.

Turbo's wife Ronnie's wearing jingle-bell earrings and an elf's cap, and she tells everyone she told Santa she wants a tummy tuck for Christmas so she can feel craveable again. The Christmas tree is leaning six inches to the left, but no one mentions it. On the stereo, the Drifters are dreaming of a white Christmas. Annette Rafferty tells Robbie and the others that the Barnes & Noble on University has become like a singles bar. You browse a section, you send a message. If you're looking for a doctor, you might be over in Diet and Health. Looking for a mystic, New Age. Whatever you do, stay out of Addiction and Self-Help! Robbie says maybe they should start a book club. And they laugh. Justine Triplett says she'd like to take a stroll down the Bodybuilding aisle.

Robbie heads to the kitchen for another beer. Orlando Gonzalez is in there, leaning against the counter, sipping vodka right out of the bottle. He's wearing a sprig of mistletoe on his belt buckle. He tells her she's looking fine.

"Do you tell your wife that?"

"If I told her I thought you looked fine, she'd strangle me."

"You know what I mean, Lando."

He holds up the bottle. "High-test?"

"No thanks. Why aren't you out there with the boys?"

"You're more interesting, chica."

"That's not saying a whole lot, is it?" Robbie knows that the only time men take you seriously is when you're flirting with them. And she wonders if that's what she's doing. She takes the beer from the fridge, pops the top, smiles, and sips.

"You and me, Roberta, we should have lunch some afternoon."

"I don't think so."

"You don't know what you're missing."

"I don't need the calories."

"We could work them off."

She smiles. She wants conversation, not talk.

"Suit yourself." Orlando heads off to the deck. Robbie checks herself in the window's reflection. She's got her mother's upholstered hips. You have to be thin to wear anything worthwhile.

Later, after Robbie's driven the sitter home, after she's checked on the girls, kissed their foreheads, after she showers and puts on her nightgown, and after she's wrapped the gifts and set them under the tree, she makes herself a blue ruin—Sapphire and Schweppes—and curls up on the couch with the cat. She hears Marty come in from playing with the dog, and then she hears the drone of the television from the bedroom.

She remembers Christmases when the girls would set out cookies and milk for Santa, when they would swear they'd heard the reindeer clomping on the roof in the middle of the night. She remembers how easily they smiled when they were young, back before they'd taken to rolling their caustic eyes at everything she said. When she thinks about tomorrow, she feels a surfacing dread and the caution, which is its gift. This Christmas, she fears, will be much like the previous. The three of *them* will present her with another charmless and expedient gift, and she'll thank them for their thoughtfulness. Just what I wanted, she'll say, a FryDaddy. The girls will tear open their gifts, will not even bother to lift the clothes out of the boxes, and will mumble perfunctory thank-yous. Marty will say he likes the broken-in wallet he already has. You can exchange it, she'll tell him. He'll gush over the Ed Hardy T-shirt she and the girls bought him, but he'll stuff it in his drawer later and never wear it. And then the three of them will wander off to their caves and leave her to clean up the mess and to cook dinner. At Walgreens, she'll tell her mother she couldn't handle listening to an animatronic fish singing "Take Me to the River" every time you set off its motion sensor. She'll suggest buying Marty a razor and some aftershave.

Robbie sips her drink. Delish! She lights up a cigarette, strokes the purring cat, and remembers, as a child, getting all dressed up and going with her mom to Burdines to see Santa Claus and then sitting on his lap and reciting her wish list. When she was seven or eight, Santa brought her a pink and purple Princess Big Wheel, and her dad let her ride it around and around the dining room table. And every Christmas afternoon they'd drive to Aunt Missy's condo in Pompano for a turkey dinner. Aunt Missy who collected porcelain dolls and commemorative spoons and who always gave Robbie a chapter book for a present: *The Happy Hollisters*, *Those Miller Girls*, *Miss Pickerell and the Geiger Counter*.

These bittersweet memories, like industrious angels, work to revive Robbie's flagging spirits, and the blue ruin lifts the fog of trepidation. She can see now that the current domestic situation is unacceptable. If things don't change around here, she'll just explode. She will not tolerate this listless disdain in the house any longer, the incivility and spite, the disrespect and estrangement. This is no way to live. She'll sit them down, talk with them in the morning. She'll tell Marty it's time he started behaving like a loving husband and father, and if he can't do both, then maybe it's sayonara time. No, it's not a threat, Marty; it's a promise. But it will sound like a threat, won't it? So she'll need to phrase it more diplomatically. *Sayonara time*? Must be the gin talking.

This is what Robbie does whenever she decides, finally, to confront her troubles. She imagines the inevitable and obligatory scene of judicious confrontation and rehearses her lines over and over, revising them as she goes. And once she's started down this road, there's no turning back. She's so driven, she can't think of anything else, can't sleep for the anticipation. Maybe she'll tell him I want us to be what we used to be. I want the joy back in our lives. No, *joy* won't work. Marty thinks joy is for children and holy rollers. *Fun*! I want the fun back in our lives.

She'll tell the girls how much she loves them. She'll sit at the edge of Tiffany's bed, and she'll talk to them about their chores in a way that they'll understand. A family is a team, she'll say. We work together and we all win. And we need to start doing things with each other, going to the beach. Like that. Could you please put down the phone when I'm talking to you. Thank you. She'll hold their hands and ask them what she could do to make their lives more pleasant and meaningful.

So in order to get things off on the right foot in the morning, she'll cook them all a hearty breakfast. Before they open their gifts, before they revert to their desultory habits, they'll sit together, say a prayer of thanks, eat, and talk. If it goes right, if Marty praises his over-easy eggs, if the girls ask for seconds on the pancakes, then maybe the whole day will continue to be festive and cordial, and maybe that momentum will carry on into the next day, and so on, because the way we live our days is the way we live our lives. Isn't that right?

She carries her drink to the kitchen. She sets the table with the good dishes and the cloth napkins. She puts out the Mrs. Butterworth's and the Country Crock. She mixes up the frozen OJ and puts it in the fridge. She scoops the ground coffee into the filter basket and fills the reservoir with water. All she'll have to do in the morning is push a button. She knows she can pull off this Christmas miracle. What was born in Bethlehem was hope. She finishes the last of her drink, puts the glass in the sink. She scratches the cat on his silky head, cuts the kitchen light, and shuffles off to the bedroom.

Marty, who hasn't said a word since they left Turbo's, grabs her by the neck and shoves her against the wall, so hard the crucifix falls to the floor. She can't breathe. And he screams. "You wanted Lando's cock in your mouth, didn't you? You fucking whore!"

And then he pushes the gun into her face. "Here's Lando's cock. Why don't you suck on this?" He shoves the barrel into her mouth and cracks her tooth. She's bleeding, but she turns her head. "You like that Cuban cock, Robbie? What do you think, I'm fucking blind?"

"The neighbors, Marty. The windows are open. Jesus Christ, you'll wake the girls."

He puts the gun to her crotch. "I ought to pull this trigger."

Robbie weeps, chokes on her tears. He shoves her on the bed and says he'll give her something to cry about.

When it's over, Robbie lies with her back to Marty, who has his earphones on and is giggling at the TV. She wishes he would leave her. But who would have him? He's made himself so unappealing. And if it's always going to be like this, how will she ever survive? Well, she could stop noticing every little thing and get on with it. If you don't see the grime in the bathroom sink, don't see the busted futon in the den, don't consider the long, dull tomorrow, you can get by, and it won't even seem so bad. Just stop looking so closely, Robbie, she tells herself. Jesus, she thinks, it's not like you're a movie star or a rocket scientist or anything. Not like you're going to change the world. She worries the chipped tooth with her tongue. This will cost her a day's work and a month's wages to fix.

When she hears Marty snoring, she slips out of bed and sees Carson Sleeper next door, sitting at his kitchen window, twenty feet away, watching her. She turns off the lamp and vanishes from his sight. Carson doesn't know Robbie, Mrs. Bourassa, very well, but he does know that her disagreeable husband has abused her physically and emotionally over the years and seems to have done so again on this holiest of nights. When Carson got back from midnight Mass, he heard the husband's cursing and later heard the sobbing wife.

One night several months ago, Carson found Robbie crying on her front steps, and he went to her. The exterminator had locked her out of their house while he sat inside watching TV and drinking beer. Carson's knocking on the window and door was ignored. He took Robbie inside his house, lent her his terry cloth robe, brewed some coffee, fortified it with brandy, and set a box of tissues on the kitchen table. He offered to call the police. Robbie begged him not to. Ever. Never ever call the police. Promise.

Carson apologized for the day-old banana bread. It's all he had. She asked him about his limp. "Shrapnel," he said and waved a dismissive hand. No one really wants to hear your war stories.

Robbie looked around the kitchen. "So tidy," she said.

"It's just me and the fish," he said, "and they pick up after themselves."

She laughed. The aquarium sat on an iron stand beneath a framed print of Monet's field of poppies. "What kind of fish are they?"

"Flame angels."

"Gorgeous."

She spooned sugar into her coffee and admired Carson's flamingo salt and pepper shakers. She thanked him for his kindness.

He said, "Tell me it's none of my business if you want to, but why don't you leave your husband?"

She said she *was* leaving the SOB, she was always leaving, she just hadn't escaped yet. "There's a lot of gravity in that house."

He said, "It can't be easy leaving your life behind."

"I need somewhere to go. *Somewhere*, not just anywhere."

Carson hears the Bourassas' chained-up mongrel start barking. He shuts his window, draws the curtain, and goes back to his cognac and his book, B. H. Fairchild's *The Art of the Lathe*, a Christmas gift from his friend at work, Inez. He reads about "*the death of the heart . . . a kind of terrible beauty.*"

Next door, Robbie leans against her daughters' closed and locked bedroom door. She knocks with one knuckle. She doesn't want to wake them. She wants one of them to already be awake, to sense her mother's distress, and to rush to the door and rescue her. In the kitchen, she rinses her mouth with tepid water. She sits at the table and holds a can of frozen lemonade to her bruised and swollen lip. The place settings mock her vanity. This was all her fault, they say. She allowed herself to act like a child at Christmas, foolishly praying for a miracle. She cries, but the tears only anger her. Tomorrow she'll tell them all she's sick as a dog, and she'll stay in bed all day. She watches a leathery cockroach skitter across the table and climb the tub of margarine. The cockroach waves his long antennae like he's conducting a choir. If you have no place to go, you must be where you're supposed to be. Right? She'll be okay. She'll get through this. Not hope, but resilience is called for. She knows there's nothing so shabby you can't get used to it.

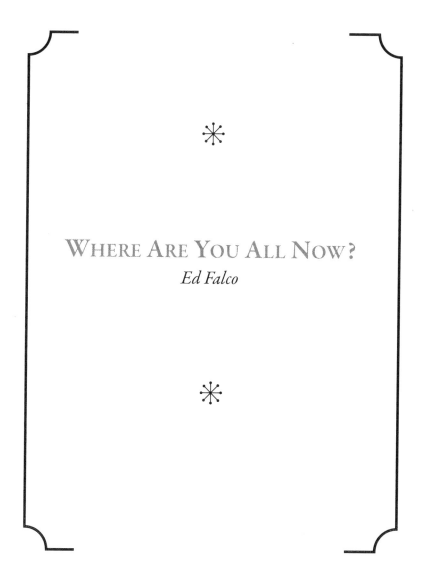

WHERE ARE YOU ALL NOW?
Ed Falco

T he house is still here, on Powers Street in Brooklyn, though now there are a pair of bicycles chained to the fence outside the basement apartment, where no doubt a couple of urban professionals live, or perhaps artists, the area is ripe with artists now. The building, a two-family dwelling with a concrete stoop that leads to the second-floor apartment, is worth around one point five million, a considerable sum more than the four thousand my grandmother sold it for fifty years ago, in 1961, when the neighborhood was mostly working-class Italians, and nearby McCarren Park was dangerous even to walk past at night. Brooklyn was different then, long before it got gentrified, when I was a ten-year-old altar boy, skinny and diffident, who walked along slate sidewalks with his eyes on the ground and his hands in his pockets.

I talked to God all the time back then. I was small and got picked on a lot. Now I'm an investment banker at Credit Suisse, and I've put on size and weight. Both my parents are long gone. My mother died and then my father died six months later. I don't talk to God so much anymore. I live alone. I'm sixty years old, three times divorced, the father of two grown children, both from my first marriage, the youngest already several years out of college, and, like his sister, on his own, independent, apparently having forgotten for the most part that he ever had a father—and here I am in Brooklyn again, back in my old neighborhood where I'm spending the night with my current girl-friend, a sculptor who lives nearby on Devoe Street, where my mother lived for the first twenty years of her life before she married my father and he moved her a few blocks over to the basement apartment in his mother's house. It's disorienting. Here I am, night falling, the houses all glittering with strings of multicolored lights, snow in the air—and a huge flat-screen television comes on in the basement apartment, the same apartment where I grew up. The set displays a fireplace with burning logs in a picture so bright it's almost three-dimensional, and when the volume comes on and the same round of ubiquitous Christmas songs starts up in surround sound, I finally move along, my hands in my pockets, my eyes on the ground.

Sinead is waiting for me, no doubt growing more sullen by the minute. We've just argued about the restaurant I chose for tonight's dinner, which I did, to her dismay, without asking her first. She's only a few years younger than me and she's far from her home and family in Dublin. She misses them, the whole rowdy, working-class clan, as she describes them—and that, in my view, is mostly the problem. She'd have loved to go back for the holidays, but she didn't want to go alone. She wanted me with her. I'm too busy for such a trip. There's too much work waiting. There's always too much work waiting. After weeks of cheerful hinting on the way to the holidays, when she realized it wasn't going to happen, I wasn't going to Ireland, her mood changed, devolving throughout Christmas week from quiet resignation to glum acceptance to this night's current sullenness and frustration verging on anger.

By the time I reach Leonard Street, it's snowing. The flakes are falling fat and white, drifting out of a rapidly darkening slate sky. On one corner, a statue of the Virgin Mary looks out from behind a glass-encased shrine, her arms open to the world. Except for the shrine, which is situated catty-corner behind a low stone wall, the house appears to be a private residence. When I stop to look more closely, I see my own reflection in the glass, and I'm surprised to find an adult looking back at me, a bald man in a black fedora and a London Fog overcoat with a white cashmere scarf wrapped around his neck and tucked into the black wool of his coat at the lapels. He's tall and stocky, a man with a weathered, craggy face that has about it a touch of something dumbstruck, perhaps in the eyes, which are dark and set back in the cave of the skull. I smile to try to change the impression, looking for a hint of the smooth-skinned boy I had half expected to see.

Already snow is sticking to the sidewalks, to the porches and stoops, as I move on from the Virgin. On Devoe a pair of boys charge down the center of the street pulling a long sled behind them, its metal runners scraping over rough pavement. They're shouting back and forth to each other in a language I don't recognize but guess is Polish. Nothing more than a dusting of snow has been predicted, but you'd never guess from their excitement and the size of the sled. They're bundled up in neon orange quilted jackets and bulky mittens and caps with furry ear muffs and straps that wrap around under their chins. They bang open a gate and bust through a garage door as it starts to snow harder, and I wonder if maybe I've missed a weather update and a blizzard is in the predictions. I stop and look at the sky, at a blur of white flakes speckled against a somber roof of clouds. I could be anywhere looking up at the sky. In the middle of the woods in Oregon. On a boat out at sea.

"Hey, Buddy," someone says, a guy, his voice husky but not unfriendly.

"Oh," I say, and laugh when I realize he's concerned about me. He's come out of his house in his shirt sleeves and he's hugging himself. He stands behind the gate. From inside the garage, the boys with the sled peek out at us. One of them is holding a miniature Christmas tree, a bright green pine with sparkling ornaments. In the few moments the man's been out of his house, his black hair has turned white on top with snow. He's young, in his early thirties. I ask, "Have I been standing here long?" I try to sound light-hearted.

"Awhile," he says. "You all right?"

"Yes, sure," I say. "I grew up in this neighborhood." He doesn't respond. He watches me. "When I was a kid," I go on, "my whole family, there were dozens of us, we all lived within blocks of each other, over on Powers."

"No kidding?" he says. He looks like a doctor observing a patient, trying to make a diagnosis. "Where are you all now?" he asks, and it takes me a moment to realize he's asking about my family.

"All over the map," I say, and I almost start to tell him the truth, that I haven't seen any of them since my father's funeral. Instead I open my hand in a friendly parting gesture.

I cross the street to Sinead's, where a plastic Christmas wreath blocks a line of small windows in the front door. When I knock, she doesn't answer. I knock again and the wreath falls to the ground. When I see that the guy and his kids across the street are still watching me, I lean over the railing to peek into the apartment through a pair of gauzy curtains. Sinead's coming out of the kitchen. She sees me in the window and takes a step back. She looks frightened. I'm a man in black coat covered in snow standing outside her door. I think at first she didn't recognize me—but then she does. She recognizes me, and she still hesitates. I can't read the look on her face. I call her name and it echoes up and down the street. I can't believe she's not coming to the door. I call her name again, and now it sounds like I'm begging for something. It sounds like I'm pleading. "Sinead," I say, thrown off balance by what's happening. "Sinead," I say. "Please.

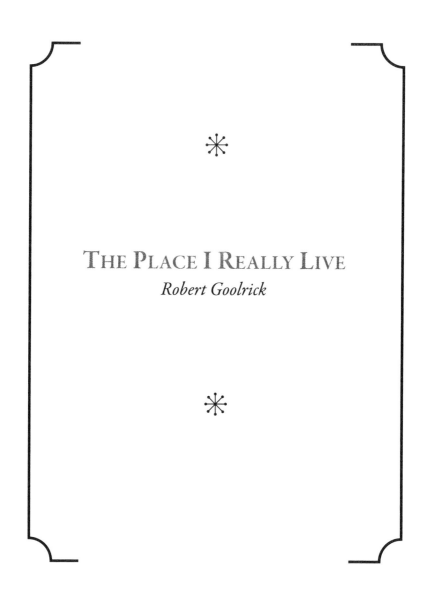

THE PLACE I REALLY LIVE
Robert Goolrick

I wake up in the dark. Au bout de la nuit. 4:06 on the LED. Take a leak. Cigarette. I know I shouldn't; I mean, in general, generally speaking, nobody should, not after everything we know, not after we've watched loved ones die, not to mention movie stars, but I do. I'm an addict. But I especially shouldn't smoke at 4:06 when I have a hope of getting back to sleep. It makes my heart race.

It makes the heavy covers feel like prison garb. It makes you feel like you live in a cheap bungalow in Los Angeles, California, in a noir decade.

If I did live in Los Angeles, I would never call it LA. But if I lived in Las Vegas, I would always call it Vegas. These are the games your mind plays when it's 4:07 and your heart is racing from the nicotine intake.

Sometimes, I turn on the radio and listen to alternative rock from the University of Pennsylvania for a while. My Morning Jacket. Placebo. Ray La Montaigne, the new wunderkind, who used to work in a shoe factory. Pink Martini, a twelve-member West Coast band that sold 650,000 copies of their self-made CD from their basement.

I keep the volume low, and I feel completely free of anxiety, even though my heart is racing and I'm excited about tomorrow.

Tomorrow, or today, actually, is the first Tuesday of December. On the first Tuesday of every month, I go look at apartments.

I work in a bookstore, one of those enormous chains, and I have Monday and Tuesday off, since I work on Saturdays, and I work the late shift on Sundays, after I go to church. I go to church every week, and put money in the plate, even though I have long ago lost my faith. I guess it's a kind of hope I feel, a hope that faith and a sense of the miraculousness of life will return to me. It hasn't, and the priests' voices drone on in that way that is supposed to be comforting but is actually kind of irritating, but I still go. Then I go to work, still in my suit.

I am the only clerk in the store who wears hard-soled shoes. Even though it makes my feet hurt, and even though nobody ever looks at my feet, I wear leather-soled shoes every day I work there. It makes me feel more like a member of the professional class, and less like somebody who just swipes your card. I'm very fastidious, and the kids in their Barnes & Noble T-shirts think it's weird, but I banter with them, banter is the word, and I know everything they know about alternative rock, and I'm good at helping them out with the inevitable glitches in their computer cash registers, and so we get along fine.

Let's not talk about what I do with my other days off, the other three weeks of the month. Let's not even get into that. I turn the phone off, for one thing, even though hardly anybody ever calls me, my sister from upstate once in a while, but let's not go into that.

I go to the grocery store and buy a whole week's worth of groceries, even though I mostly eat in the diner around the corner. I just like the way a full refrigerator looks, the endless possibilities. I pay for the groceries with my debit card. At the end of the week, I throw out stuff that's gone bad and go get other stuff.

But it's all just normal. You probably do the same things, on your day off. Take your shirts to the laundry. Run an errand. Take a nap. Work in your woodworking shop, whatever your hobby is.

My hobby is looking at apartments I will never move into.

On Monday, I go in and make the appointment. I always dress well, not too well, not a suit or anything, but a nice blazer and a pair of trousers with double pleats, fresh from the dry cleaners so the pleats are razor-sharp.

They make you fill out an application; how much you make, what you're looking for, how much you're willing to spend. I always lie.

I give them a fake name. Billy Champagne, a name I heard once in a locker room at a gym I used to belong to. This guy, Billy Champagne, was saying to a friend of his that the only reason he worked out so hard was he needed something to do with all his energy since he stopped drinking. He said that he used to drink a quart of Scotch every day before lunch, down there on Wall Street, and everybody, I swear everybody in the locker room said "Jesus" under his breath at the same time, with a kind of hushed awe. Billy Champagne was this guy's name, he was built like a linebacker, he had a beautiful, powerful body, and the irony of it never left me, so I use his name. I like the name. I'd gladly *be* Billy Champagne, drunk or sober.

I tell them I make $350,000 a year. I tell them I'm willing to spend $4500 a month on a one or two-bedroom apartment. I say this knowing they'll show me much more expensive apartments anyway. Or I say I'll also consider looking at lofts, live in a more open, abstract kind of way. I'd like to see as many apartments as possible on Tuesday, starting at ten a.m.

I don't go to the same realtor more than once every six months. Not that they care. Talk about hope. They live on hope. Hope and greed, those guys.

I lie awake in the dark for a long time. I smoke another Marlboro red. You should see me smoke a cigarette. I do it with a voluptuous finesse. Then I put it out in my mother's silver ashtray and turn off the radio right after the U of P goes off the air when The Blue Nile has finished their incredibly moving "Because Of Toledo." In the song, which pierces my heart every time, people talk about how lonely and misplaced they are. Like a girl, just a girl, that's all we know about her, in this diner, I guess, who's leaning on a jukebox in some old blue jeans she wears. Saying wherever it is she lives she doesn't really live anywhere.

I could weep for that girl, a fictional desolation living her one spark of life in a diner in a city I've never been to. Then I hear the line from Shakespeare: And girl I could sing / Would weeping do me good / And never borrow any tear from thee.

At five-thirty on the morning, the mind caroms around like a squash ball, hitting just above the line and then careening off in some totally unpredictable direction. You go from certain brilliance to absolute drudgery in a second. And, of course, it's Advent now, and after that comes Christmas, so there's that, too. I'd lean on that jukebox with that girl and tell her to cheer the hell up. She has no special claim to desolation, in my view.

I go back to sleep until seven-thirty. I've been awake for an hour and a half.

When I wake up, I'm groggy and I'm still tired, but I'm also excited, the way I always am. It's a new day. This is the day that the Lord hath made. Let us rejoice and be glad in it. I say that as I get into the shower.

I shave carefully. My hair looks brisk. I dress in clothes that are nice but not too nice, an investment banker or a lawyer on his day off, just a blazer and loafers, and then I have coffee. I make a whole pot, even though I just have a cup and a half. It just looks better. Cozier. Then I wash the cup and the pot and pretty much pace the apartment until ten o'clock. I like to be just a hair late.

The real estate office is a new one, very fancy. They have branches all over the city, but they've just opened a branch here because the neighborhood has gotten hot all over again. It's just gone wild, rents shooting through the roof.

When I fill out the application, I say that I'm a fashion retail executive. If they ask, I'll say I work at Saks. I put down that I make $375,000 a year. I put down an address where I do not live, and a phone number that is one digit off my real phone number. It's not like you have to show proof or anything. You could be anybody. Everybody does it, so you don't get the follow-up calls.

I wait, and then the shower comes out. That's what they call them, the people who show apartments. His name is Chris Mallone. He wears a nameplate on his shirt pocket. I almost slip, then tell him my name is Billy Champagne.

He's maybe twenty-nine, not good-looking, just a pasty-faced Irish boy, already going soft around the middle. It's sad, to see a person that age look so uncertain in his body. He looks like maybe he drinks too much on a regular basis. He looks like he maybe drank too much just the night before and stayed out too late, he was probably still out when I woke up to smoke, but he's all smiles, and he's got a good firm handshake, even if his palms are a little sweaty.

Six months from now, Chris Mallone won't be working here any more. He'll be selling sporting goods at Paragon. Six months after that, he'll be bartending in the East Village, selling double shots at happy hour. He'll move down the food chain so fast and so low he'll be sucking mud off the bottom of the river. And he'll stay there bottom feeding forever.

It's a shame. He should find his youth a pleasure. He should work out and see a dermatologist. He shouldn't drink so much. There's plenty of time for that later. And if he hates his job, and obviously he hates his job, who wouldn't, he should find something he likes better before the inevitable something worse finds him. It's not too late.

When I was his age, I had a job I loved. It made me feel rich and powerful and I dated girls who lived on the Upper East Side with roommates, and we did cocaine and drank Martinis and I bought my suits at Bergdorf's and Paul Stuart, suits I still wear because quality lasts, and we went out dancing at two o'clock in the morning.

I just got eaten alive. It was bad at the time, but it's not so bad now.

If you go swimming in a river, and you know there are piranhas in the river, and you get your leg chewed off or something, you can get mad, but you can't get mad at the piranhas. That's what they do.

So, it all changed. I work in a bookshop now. I wear a nameplate, like Chris Mallone. But I'm an American and I have health benefits and a 401K and every two years I save up money and go on a vacation to a country where I don't know anybody and don't speak the language. And I go first class. The best of everything, cocktails on the veranda at sunset, a view of the local monument. It reminds me of how it all used to be before it got all fucked up. Without the girls or the drugs or the phone calls.

The apartment I had then was beautiful. This wasn't so long ago, either. It had chic low furniture and the telephone rang all the time and friends dropped over to drink Heineken and leaf through copies of *Details* and *Wallpaper* and talk about whatever it was that was just about to catch the attention of everybody else. Girls with silken skin and sloe eyes spent the night there, and wore my shirts when they made espresso in the morning, in little cups they would bring to me where I lay naked in bed. I had the kind of body you see on the cover of *Men's Health*. My stomach was faceted. The girls, who all had great educations and foreign language skills and mostly trust funds, had the kind of bodies you see in *Vogue*.

Then the clock stopped ticking. The spring just wound down one day, and the getting stopped and the surprising and fascinating process of losing began. Not that I have nothing now. I do. I have a lot. You can learn to live with anything. You can do without so much. It's just irredeemably different and I go out looking for some vestige of my old life on the first Tuesday of every month, although I've learned to get along without it, like an amputee who is a marvel because he's adjusted so well.

As Chris goes through the various checkpoints on the form I fill out, I notice that the cuffs of my white shirt are unbuttoned. My mother once said you could always tell a crazy person because they didn't button their cuffs, but I disagree. I think it makes me look like a rock star from the sixties. Like David Bowie in the Thin White Duke days. I've seen pictures.

I think you can tell a crazy person because they always wear too many clothes in the summer and not enough clothes in the winter.

Chris looks eager to help, like he smells blood, although I'm betting he wishes he had a shot of vodka and an Altoids to get him through the next couple of hours.

I tell him exactly what I want. I want a pre-war building. I don't need a doorman. I need rooms with architectural details. I'd love a fireplace. I want to move because I've gotten bored with my apartment, it's too bland, although it's nice for what it is. Chris takes notes, then opens a book and begins to shuffle through the listings.

He says he's not sure I can get what I'm looking for at that price. I tell him I'm flexible, that the space is more important than the price, within reason. I'll go to 4500, if that's what it takes. I tell him I want a place where I can live for a long time.

The thing is, when I'm telling him all these lies, I don't feel fraudulent. I got over that a long time ago.

I feel an almost erotic thrill, deep in my body. I'm wearing hard-soled shoes and a Chesterfield coat with a green velvet collar from Turnbull and Asser that still looks almost as immaculate as it did the day I bought it, before the clock stopped. To Chris, there's no reason to believe I'm not all the things I say I am. This is America, and you can be whoever you want.

The streets are full, the Christmas tree people are already out, have been since Thanksgiving, but mostly they're just standing around in those gloves that don't have any fingers on them, drinking coffee and talking with the Korean flower people. Nobody in town is going to buy a tree the first week of December, but hope is just bleeding through everybody's pores, it would seem.

Chris has a fine mist of sweat at his hairline even though the day is brisk despite the bright white sunlight, and he talks on and on about the Knicks and about his girl friend and about how fast the neighborhood is changing. Meaning getting more expensive, filled with fathers in Barbour coats and horn-rimmed glasses leading their children around to private schools.

The sound of his voice is comforting, and I feel cheerful and ask all the right questions.

I take care to step lightly on the sidewalk. Another thing my mother used to teach us was that a light footfall was a sign of good breeding. I've learned it pretty well, pacing much of the time around my apartment, so the downstairs neighbors won't feel they're living in an Edgar Allen Poe story. "The Telltale Heart" or something. I expend a great deal of energy trying not to look or seem peculiar.

I've been to Puket, I want to tell sweating Chris, and China. I've been to Cuba. Stayed at La Nacional. I've had more money in my pocket than you have in your bank account most days.

His girlfriend works at the Chanel counter at Saks. She's a makeup artist. I tell him we've never met.

Chris keeps walking toward the first apartment. He's done this yesterday. He did it the day before. As far as Chris is concerned, he's been doing it forever.

We look at seven apartments, except that three are in the same building and two of those are identical, just on different floors. A long time ago, I went to a party in one of these apartments, or one in the same line, as they say.

There is something fatally wrong with every one of them. Well, naturally, there has to be. Like, for instance, one has this peculiar fifties miniature stove, so small you could barely fit a chicken into it. Chris asks me if I cook a lot. Oh yes, I say, I entertain pretty often.

The technique is to make some generally favorable remark when you first walk into at least some of the apartments, so that Chris doesn't get too discouraged. And, of course, with the first or second apartment, you have to say, Chris, this is exactly the apartment I don't want. Just so he knows.

Seeing apartments is essentially a sordid business. Looking at an apartment that the tenant hasn't moved out of yet makes me really squeamish.

One time, I looked at this nice apartment, pre-war, doorman, nice, and the tenant hadn't moved out and when I opened the bedroom closets there were all his clothes hanging there and I realized the tenant was a midget. Boy, that was weird, and I imagined myself living this kind of miniature life, never forgetting the deformed little suits, the tiny shoes, always feeling like Alice after she's gotten really big.

I couldn't get out of there fast enough, and it was rent stabilized and had a working fireplace.

You spend about ten minutes in each apartment, each redolent with lives lived totally unaware of your own, each filled with the promise of an imaginary life you might live there, where your clothes would go in the closets, where you would put the sofa and the television, and how loud it would be from the street.

I always imagine, right off, where I would put the Christmas tree. I know it's trivial; it's two weeks of the year and, besides, I haven't had a tree for years, not a full-sized one, just a little table-topper as tacky people say, but I don't know what else you call it when it sits on a table and isn't even a tree, really.

But I try to find a spot and picture a majestic eight-footer, covered with all the extravagant ornaments I've saved from my old life, the days when everything glittered too brightly.

Somewhere in these lonely rooms there is the ghost of the life I might have there, of the life I really live. Somewhere there is room for a wife and two or three children and a Sussex spaniel and Barbour jackets and travel tickets lying on the kitchen table.

I know that that's what I'm really looking for. I know it has nothing to do with the apartments themselves or sweaty Chris or my own disdain. It has to do with the natural maturation of the life I fucked up beyond recognition.

I see her. Her hair is colored once a month by the best colorist in the city, tawny blonde with highlights. She's a partner at Debevoise & Plimpton and she never cooks so we eat out all the time, or order in, and the three children are in private school, the youngest girl at Grace, the boy at Collegiate, the elder girl at Foxcroft where we let her go because of her equestrian passions, and, face it, she's not ever going to be a Rhodes scholar. Every morning I kiss them and go off to McCann Erickson where I am a global creative director, working on some of their biggest accounts. I am pivotal. I am rewarded beyond the common imagination.

I see her. She looks sort of like Barbra Streisand at the end of *The Way We Were* and she works as head of one of the departments at the library and I work at a small publishing house and we are very leftist and the children go to the Little Red Schoolhouse and then on to Horace Mann when they get older. We only have two children. Our hearts would hold a dozen, but that's all we could afford. We use our Metro Cards all the time, and we take a subscription in the Family Circle at the Met and the children will grow up to lead lives intense with intelligent ideas and passionate views and commitments.

Every apartment grows other rooms, grows organically into a place where a family lives for years and years.

The girls with the silken skin are happily gone and fondly remembered, along with the nights drinking hard liquor and doing lines off the bar at neon lounges. I do not miss these things. That was another time, like summer camp. Like a very long spring break in Jamaica. I am happy with what I have. Proud even.

And there is always a Christmas tree. It's all covered with beautiful ornaments, Bavarian glass, that we have collected over the years and put away with care and never broken any of, except that one time the tree fell over, all mixed in with funny kids' stuff and a tree topper made out of rhinestones and Popsicle sticks that Kate made when she was six and which now fills her with both uncertain pride and mortification every time we take it out and put it right at the very tippy-top.

In one life, the Plimpton McCann life, we give each other extravagant fur and remote controlled things and bijoux and bibelots, and we leave Christmas afternoon to go skiing in Europe for a week, because the airports are empty on Christmas Day.

In the Library life, we share mittens and scarves and *The Letters of Leonard Woolf* and baskets made in Third World countries and then we eat a big dinner in the middle of the afternoon and then we go for a walk in the snowy, almost deserted streets.

In one life, we are giddy but anxious. In the other, we are happy. Just a happy family.

I live with a woman. She is tall, taller than I am, with the long, lean body of a swimmer. She is ten years younger than I am, and she wears designer clothes and shoes that cost a month's salary for most people. She is a graphic designer and the apartment is a monument to good taste. We are wholly happy in ourselves, and we have no children. I am a writer. I write novels that make people feel better about themselves, and they sell quite well. You'd know me if you saw me, from the dust jackets.

We entertain a lot, actresses, publishers, people from the arts and we discuss Tristan Tzara and the Dadaists and Le Desert du Retz around coq au vin and Muscadet.

She once wrote to me from Paris, "You are to me as water to a man dying of thirst in the desert."

In any case, every case, we are a tribe, a law unto ourselves, filled with quirks that have come to seem perfectly natural to us. We have the pride of knowing that there is no other group of people in the world with our unique qualities of beauty and intelligence, or kindness or grace or strength. We are only wholly ourselves when we are together. Each completes a part of the whole.

The apartments I look at couldn't hold any of this. They could hold me, and I feel bereft each time a door closes behind us.

On West 12th Street, we meet another broker with her client at a double brownstone. The apartment is composed of the back half of the ground floor and the first floor, what used to be called the parlor floor.

The other client is English, in his early thirties, and we all go in together and look at this peculiar apartment. He is eating a green apple.

We go into the space, as city dwellers say these days, the space. The ground floor is peculiarly divided into two small rooms, one a kind of office, I guess, and the other the dining room, which looks out into a large, wintry garden filled with Italian terra cotta urns. Then there is a handsome galley kitchen with its own washer/dryer combination. The ceilings are low and the rooms are dark.

There is a treacherous cantilevered staircase jerry-rigged to get up to the second floor, which is perfectly wonderful.

There is a ballroom-sized sitting room with fourteen-foot ceilings. You could have a twelve-footer in here, easy. There is simple but elegant plaster molding. The windows look out onto the garden, and would be just at leaf level in the spring and summer.

Behind this there is a large bedroom, which is closed off from the living room by elegant sliding etched-glass doors, and an art deco bathroom with a real deep cast iron tub. It is all magnificent.

I am trembling with excitement. You can feel the weight of the lives lived in these rooms. It has an upstairs and a downstairs, like a real house. Once the whole brownstone was home to a single family, now it is carved up into separate spaces, disparate lives. You can almost hear the rustle of their skirts as the other agent slides the glass doors back and forth.

She turns to her young English client. "But where would you put the baby?" she asks, and he says exactly and they leave right away.

I want to stay there, listening to the sounds of my wife and children, watching the tree glisten in the early winter afternoon, but my ten minutes are almost up, and I don't want Chris to get overstimulated or he'll never leave me alone.

But I can see them. I can smell them. I can lie down in the bedroom and sink into the comfort of twenty years of marriage to a woman I love. I can see the posters of the rock stars and the sports heroes on the walls of my children's bedrooms.

I'm not a fantasist. I know the place where I really live. The one room is comfortable to me, and it isn't so bad. It is dark and it is small but it's also pretty much free from memory. There's a lot you can do with a one-room apartment if you use your imagination.

I know what I do and where I am in the world, which is pretty far down the *People* magazine Most Beautiful People ladder.

But I want things. I miss what I never had. I'm sorry I threw it all away. I feel terrible about fucking it all up, all the time. I want to tell Chris all this, I always do, but I don't say anything. I just take another tour through the rooms, remarking mostly on how they cut these brownstones up in such peculiar ways, and then we leave.

I look again at the twinkling tree, so brief, so fragile. I look through the tall windows into the garden where I might barbecue for friends on a summer night, white wine and chevre. Diana Krall. *The New York Review of Books*.

I kiss my wife goodbye. I kiss my loving children on their foreheads and we go back out into the fading sunlight. It's really cold now.

This apartment costs $5500 a month, more than three times what I'm paying now.

On the way back to the office, I tell Chris that his job must be very frustrating, showing all these apartments to people who are so hard to satisfy. He says that it's OK, he likes people. He says he has one client who's been looking for an apartment for five months. He says he just takes it one day at a time.

That's the way you ought to take it, pal, I think. One day at a time.

I shake his hand, promise I'll call him tomorrow. I walk home through the chill afternoon, passing the tree stand again. Maybe this year, I think. Maybe next week.

The windows we look through to glimpse the happiness of families.

All the rooms we might have lived in. All the lives we might have led.

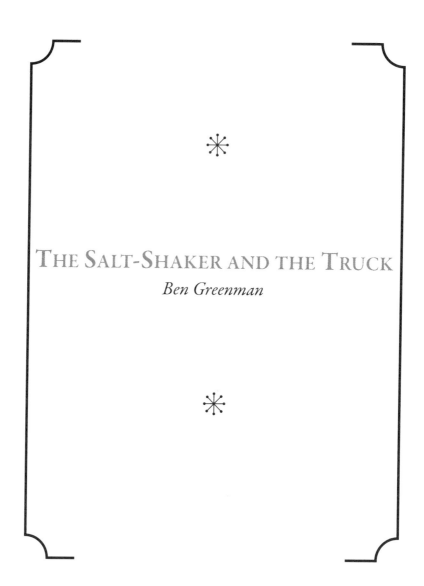

The Salt-Shaker and the Truck
Ben Greenman

The other day I was almost hit by a truck. But wait. I would rather tell you about the salt-shaker. That's a real story—it has characters and pathos and irony. Once I start I won't be able to stop, I don't think. Now it seems like a mistake to have brought up the truck at all.

It was two years ago, the day after Christmas, and I was nursing a hangover from a party I had attended at the home of a female friend. I had my eye on her, but she had her eye on someone else, so I drank too much, and eventually made a fool of myself, which didn't stop another woman—a tall elegant brunette in whom I had, somehow, no interest—from going with me into a back room and letting me take off her pants and taking off mine. It also didn't stop her from telling me, about ten minutes later, that she was pregnant. "So soon?" I said. She laughed and so I passed it off as a joke, but the fact was that I was just drunk and confused. My friend, the host of the party, scowled at me when I emerged from the back room with the brunette, both of us smelling like eggnog and sweat and poor judgment. "Here's my phone number," the brunette said as we walked out onto the street at the end of the party. "Okay," I said. "Thanks." Both words sounded stupid to me. I went home and slept the sleep of the unjust: shallow, fitful, perforated. The next morning my hangover clanged against the inside of my head. I boiled some water for tea, and steeped it until it was strong, but it was not enough. I needed coffee and eggs to beat my hangover, or at least battle it to a draw, and so I went to a restaurant down the street. The food wasn't any good, and the ambiance was bad, too, but it was where people in my neighborhood went for coffee. There were several regulars I recognized, and several strange faces, among them an old man with a comically long beard and a worn jacket. He pushed toast from one side of the plate to the other and was ignored, even by the waiters. "It's Santa," I said to myself under my breath. It was not. Another man, unbearded, younger, did the crossword puzzle with intimidating speed. A beautiful young woman ate pancakes by herself as music leaked out through her headphones.

They were solitaries, the old man, the young man, the beautiful young woman. I was one as well. Most of the people in the restaurant were there in groups, or at the very least, pairs. There were young couples feeling the swell of the holiday, older couples with children in tow, and quartets of middle-aged friends who recounted the week's events with high spirits.

I put away a few cups of coffee, and that's when I noticed the man sitting across the way from me, on the other side of a large empty table. His name was Maurice Breedlove, and he was something of a celebrity. He had become famous decades earlier as Sonny Breedlove, the child star of a television show called *In the Upper Room*, and after retiring from acting he began a second career as an entertainment manager, mostly for pop singers. He was more well known than several of the performers he represented, and affected an air of legitimacy as well: he owned and operated a theatre in the neighborhood, where he put on both classics and original work, some of which he wrote himself. Once I had noticed him, I became aware that others had, too; several other patrons buzzed his name and indicated him with their eyes, and he repaid their interest by appearing indifferent to it. The owner of the place, a tall, fat Greek whose mustache was dyed black, stationed himself near Breedlove's table, and he clasped his hands and bent forward with a helpless pleasure when the great man asked for more coffee or complimented the French toast or pontificated upon the decorations. He even sent his teenage son across the street to the bakery to get more of the seeded rolls that Breedlove had insincerely complimented. I was amused by Breedlove at first, but after a little while, his manner began to irritate me. I was relieved when a large group of teenage girls came into the restaurant and occupied the table between us.

The girls, six of them, took their seats in a precise arrangement: the lighter blondes on the left, the darker blondes in the middle, and the brunettes on the right. The three shorter girls sat with their backs toward me, and the three taller girls faced me. All six were bursting with energy. Maybe teenage girls in large groups always are. They had no fear of the other diners, and perhaps no awareness. They spoke loudly and quickly about the presents they had received, and their plans for New Year's Eve. A waiter came by with his pad, and he did his best to take their orders, though his best was not nearly good enough.

Most of the girls were pretty, but the tall brunette on the far right corner separated herself. Some women are so striking that when you look at them everything fails you: cleverness, descriptive power, context, everything but your awareness of their beauty, which hits you like a fist in the chest. She had a perfect mouth and everything else followed: eyes, hair, even body, which was not something that I felt comfortable noticing for too long. Not only was her appearance different, but her behavior distinguished her as well. The other girls fussed and chattered. The short blonde's sleeve was frayed, and she kept looking at it with hostility. The short brunette took the salt-shaker from the middle of the table and tried to balance it on its edge. The tall brunette held herself away from all of this, instead turning her chair just a few degrees away from the table and looking into middle distance. She had a necklace on, a cameo, which she fingered like it was new, and perhaps it was. There was a Christmas tree directly behind her, from my angle, and she was positioned just below a gold foil star, which served as a kind of lodestar. I stared at her, and she noticed me staring. It couldn't have been the first time that a man looked at her. But I felt ashamed. My coffee was on the table in front of me. It was cold, and even when it had been hot it had been terrible. I didn't want it. But I had to do something, so I drank it.

I was not the only one who had noticed the brunette. Her arrival buzzed behind me. "Her mother is Sylvia Merritt," I heard a woman tell her companion. "The Merritt Brothers heiress? This girl, whose name is Lucy, is in some television show about high school socialites." The tone tried for disparagement, but got caught up in awe.

Someone on Maurice Breedlove's side of the restaurant must have also recognized Lucy Merritt, for at that moment the sea of girls between us parted and I saw that he, too, was focused on her. There was appreciation in his eyes and something else, too, that I couldn't quite identify. Maybe he was aware that the energy in the room was suddenly flowing away from him. The owner had left Breedlove's table. He stopped two tables away to tease a regular about how he liked his omelets, stopped one table away to give two little boys lollipops, and then arrived at Lucy Merritt's table.

"Is everything to your liking, ladies?" he said.

The girls fell into a variety of behaviors. The shorter of the lighter blondes giggled. The taller of the darker blondes nodded. The shorter brunette, who was clearly the leader in some sense, answered for the group, in the affirmative. Lucy Merritt, whose answer was the only one that the owner had wanted—the only one whose answer anyone would want—stayed silent.

My meal arrived, and I ate it, letting the sound of the girls' conversation wash out against the broader noise of the restaurant. The eggs were overdone and too salty, just as I liked them, and the toast was sliced extra thick. My hangover began to recede. I thought about calling the woman from the Christmas party, not the one I had been with, but the hostess, the one I still wanted to try for. Maybe I would return the favor by inviting her to spend New Year's with me. Then, suddenly, I noticed Maurice Breedlove standing next to the girls' table, where the owner had been before. Lucy Merritt was too beautiful to notice him, I thought, and I was excited by the prospect of his comeuppance. I pressed my watch to my ear as if I was concentrating on it, so that I would not become part of the story. The tick of the second hand sounded like the tick of a pilot light, and then her smile went up like a blue flame, all at once. "I know you," she said to Breedlove.

"And I, you," he said. His voice went down in volume but up in everything else. "Or at least your work. I am pleased to meet you. What are you doing in my humble neighborhood?"

"I live just a few streets away," she said. "I'm here with my friends."

"These are your friends?" He frowned at the girls. He frowned, especially, at the salt-shaker. "Can I speak to you?"

"Of course." Her fingers were very long, and they unfolded and folded and came to settle on her lap.

"Years ago, I worked with your mother in a film."

"You know about my mother's movie?"

"Of course," he said. "I was a young actor there, fresh from television and trying to make my way onto the big screen. That movie, sadly, did not accomplish what I hoped it might. Have you seen it?"

"No, sir." Her politeness would have been easier to endure if it had been insincere.

"It is not a very good film, and I am partly at fault. Your mother bears none of the blame. She was exquisite."

"I have seen photographs from the set," she said.

"None of me, I hope," he said. "But I did not come over here to discuss my past. I'm more interested in your future. Have you ever thought of acting on the stage?"

"My mother is always telling me that I should," she said. "She says that my television work will be nothing without stage training."

"I must say that I agree," Breedlove said. "I don't know if you are aware that I own a theatre just a few avenues over. I would love for you to consent to appear in a play one of these seasons."

"Maybe," she said.

He raised a finger elegantly. "I could even write something for you," he said. "In fact, I have an idea I have been turning over in my head. It might be a play, or it might be a film. If inspiration hits me, I think I could be finished with it by Christmas of next year."

A teenage boy wandered over. It took me a minute to recognize him as the owner's son. He had the same features as his father, and large pale hands he had not yet grown into. He refilled the water glasses of some of the other girls and then tapped Lucy Merritt on the shoulder. "Lucy," he said.

This angered Breedlove. "Please," he said. "We are having an important discussion."

"Oh," the boy said. "I just need to ask one quick question."

Lucy Merritt turned toward the boy. "Hi, Sam," she said.

"Hi," he said. He revealed none of his excitement, revealing all of it. "Are you going to that party at the candy factory Saturday night?"

"I'm not sure."

"Oh," he said. "Okay. I was thinking of going with Lou and Greg and some other guys. It seems like it'll be fun." He filled the rest of the glasses and then headed back to the kitchen.

Breedlove had been bested, at least for a moment, and he chose that moment to take his leave from Lucy Merritt's side and follow the boy into the back of the restaurant. I decided to go, too. Breedlove and the boy were in the narrow hall by the restrooms, and Breedlove was lecturing. "You need to show more respect," he said. "We were doing business."

"I'm sorry," said the boy, without much surliness. He almost seemed to mean it.

"Sorry, sir, I think you mean," Breedlove said. "An apology is hardly the issue. You need to show respect, as I say."

Breedlove's tone had started off in sternness and hardened into something crueler, and the boy—for he was only a boy—was almost in tears now. Breedlove clenched his hand as if he was holding a handkerchief and backed off a few steps.

"Excuse me," I said. "I need to use the bathroom." To the boy I said, "Your dad's too angry. He's going to have a heart attack."

"That's not my father," he said.

"He's yelling at you like he is."

Maurice Breedlove turned toward me. The bottom half of his face was flushed dark.

I did not need to use the bathroom, but I stood inside there and let the water run for a minute or so. On the way back to my seat, I saw that Breedlove was talking to the owner, who was pointing toward the boy. "That's my son," the owner was saying. "He is a wonderful musician."

"There are no wonderful musicians any more," said Breedlove.

The owner laughed, as if at a joke. "If you know of anyone who could help him."

"There are always people. But I must say, your son was insolent to me." I was settling down at my table now, and Breedlove looked over to make sure that I was not going to interfere. "Nothing extreme," he told the owner. "But nothing that would make me want to help him."

The owner went off to speak to his son. His big hands hung at his sides, curling up angrily at the tips. The party of girls had broken up, and Lucy Merritt was standing out on the sidewalk. A big black car pulled up, and she leaned in the window. Maurice Breedlove hurried outside to renew his appeal. When Lucy Merritt's mother stepped out of the car, he introduced himself again and bowed. She crimsoned and covered her mouth with her hand.

I turned back to my meal and finished up my toast and eggs. When the owner's son came to clear my plate, he looked away as a form of acknowledgement. "I know you're not allowed to spit in food," I said, "but I think you can make an exception in his case."

The boy laughed.

We finished our breakfasts. The young man was still working on the crossword puzzle with the same alarming rapidity, though it seemed certain he would have finished already. The old man with the Santa beard had pushed his toast from side to side a number of times. The star atop the tree was still glinting in fake thin gold.

The other day, as I said, I was almost hit by a truck. I was on the way to visit my friend, the one who had hosted the party two years earlier, when I became distracted and stepped into the street against traffic. I heard the blare of a horn and hurried back onto the curb. My heart thumped in my chest.

I could not continue directly to my friend's apartment. I was too agitated and I needed to be calm to see her. It was a few days before Valentine's Day and I was bringing her a present that I wanted both to belong to the holiday and to exist apart from it. We had dated, off and on, for more than a year, never comfortably, sometimes for enough weeks in a row that it came to seem like an official arrangement. I had worked up the courage to ask her out more formally at the Christmas party that took place a year after the party where I had drunkenly moved into the back room with the pregnant brunette. That, in fact, had been the springboard: I had apologized for my malfeasance, laughed with embarrassment and pride both, and told her that I had always had the idea that the two of us would end up together. Over the course of the year, she and I had broken up repeatedly because she had told me that she could never be with me permanently, at least the way that I seemed to want. Then, at the Christmas party that took place two years after the party with the drunken brunette, I had proposed to her. We were at a party on a rooftop, and I was feeling, if not exactly romantic, primed for a revelation of that sort. I was stone cold sober and said so. She laughed gently and said that I had quite a talent for negotiating the ledge. I laughed just as gently because I did not know what she meant. She did not accept my proposition but she did not reject it either. When we were together in my bed I looked into her eyes and saw less fear than I had previously seen.

Almost hit by the truth, jumpy, flooded with relief, I calmed myself down by looking in the windows of the shops on the avenue. The first one was a gift store, and the windows were filled with gifts that made me anxious that the gift I was bringing her was inferior. The second one was a bakery, and I considered going in and adding a pastry to the present. The third one was an appliance store. There was a wide-screen television, and it was showing a replay of a recent awards ceremony. Actors, actresses, and singers glided across the red carpet. I could not hear the sound, but the reporter was excited. A starlet came up behind the reporter. She was in a sheer white dress that reached down only to the tops of her thighs. She looked unsteady on her feet and her eyes were tired.

The reporter shoved a microphone in her face. The starlet laughed, swayed, caught herself before she fell. She responded to the reporter's question with dead eyes. Suddenly, behind her, I saw Maurice Breedlove. He looked just as he had looked in the restaurant, years ago. I looked again at the starlet. It was Lucy Merritt, almost unrecognizable but for her perfect mouth.

She said something that confused the reporter, and then something that confused herself, and then she was gone down the carpet. Breedlove waited a few seconds and then followed, a look of concentration on his face.

GOOD FOREVER
James W. Hall

Bull Markham put up the Christmas tree every year on December first. Unpacking it from the long box that was stored in the attic. The center pole, the rotating stand that buzzed as it circled, one complete rotation every two minutes. Bull inserted the hundred and fifteen prongs with aluminum foil branches frilly with aluminum needles. He fit each branch into the holes drilled at the perfect angle to form the triangle of silver. Ten feet tall. Good forever. No need to buy a chopped down spruce every year, just so it could shed its needles on the terrazzo for a month.

Five years earlier he'd encountered the tree on the floor at Sears Roebuck. A salesman noticed him eyeing it and homed in.

"Never have to buy another tree," the salesman said. "This beauty will still be glittery and fresh when we're all in the grave."

"I'm old-fashioned," Bull said, trying to ease by the smiley guy.

"But you got a kid, right? You're a parent."

"So?"

"This is the future. This is where we're headed. Do right by your kid, mister. Step into tomorrow. Give her something she'll cherish forever. Every time she sees it, she'll think of her dear old dad."

When the tree was assembled, Bull set up the color wheel two feet away and plugged it in, switched on the revolving stand, and stood back to admire the green, red and blue colored light projected up through the shimmering tree. He felt warmth spread through his gut.

His wife came out from their bedroom, waving her fingernails dry, a cigarette in the corner of her mouth, wearing a slovenly orange bathrobe at seven o'clock at night. His fifteen-year-old Brenda sat on the couch smacking bubblegum while she paged through a movie star magazine, school books on the floor in a stack. Neither of them helped with Christmas. Neither gave a shit about decorations or the tree, or the Santa Claus and elves in the front yard. Every so often they glanced at Bull and were deadly silent. Both of them got the full benefit of his work, all that Christmas cheer filling the household, without ever twitching a goddamn finger to help.

Thirty days later, on December thirty-first Bull would dismantle the tree, put it back in the box, climb up the fold-down stairs into the attic and tuck it into the corner with the other decorations, alongside the plastic wreath, the jolly Santa and the six elves. There used to be seven but a kid down the street, a turdball friend of Brenda's, vandalized one, drawing a moustache on its face and poking a carrot through a knife hole in its crotch. An orange hard-on.

Bull dealt with the kid, and now the little shit took another route to school every day, didn't speak to Brenda anymore. Going three blocks out of his way to avoid Bull Markham's house.

The day after he gave the kid a solid swat to the rump, a police officer came to his front door. Bull showed the guy the desecrated elf and told the cop he wasn't interested in pressing charges against the little shit-eater because Bull was just brimming over with Christmas cheer.

"Are you admitting you struck Jimmy Flagstone? Your neighbor's kid?" The Miami cop was a foreigner of some kind. Didn't speak English right.

Bull didn't reply. And when the cop repeated the question, he didn't reply again. It made him angry, a cop who didn't speak good English. Enforcing the rules when he couldn't even pronounce them. Their native language disintegrating like the country's morals and respect for the past. Couldn't even spank a juvenile delinquent without a cop coming to your door.

The cop stayed on his front porch for ten minutes asking him over and over if he'd assaulted the boy, but Bull exercised his right to stay silent. That was three years back. The elves had been fine after that. Everything had been fine. Bull setting up the tree, taking it down, fitting the branches into their slots, taking them out four weeks later. Observing the holiday. Every night at dinner for the month of December drinking his homemade eggnog with two slugs of bourbon. Hanging stockings on the cork bulletin board in the living room, an electric candle in the front window, a wreath on the front door. The stockings staying empty all through the holidays. The candle burned all day and night.

"What's the point?" Brenda said, same as she did every December.

"Your father doesn't require a point," said Vanessa, the wife. "Your father is on a gerbil wheel."

"It's a tradition," Bull said. "Traditions are what keep the world running, they keep people stable and happy. Doing the same thing every year, it's how it is with church, the rituals and such. It's an observance."

"Gerbil wheel," Vanessa said.

Bull looked down at his TV dinner in the aluminum tray sitting on a China plate. Four sections in the tray, one with peaches, two chicken pieces in the main quadrant, mashed potatoes in another and then you had your mixed up peas, corn, and cooked carrots in the fourth. In a side dish Vanessa had thrown together iceberg lettuce with a clot of mayo. "We're Americans, descendents of the Pilgrims. We're keeping alive the rituals of our forefathers."

"Pilgrims didn't have aluminum trees," Brenda said.

"We've progressed," Bull said. "It's the modern era. The space age."

"Our own little Sputnik in the living room."

"Don't be smart."

"Don't be smart," Brenda said. "Don't be smart."

"Yes, dear," Vanessa said. "Be stupid like your father, the Pilgrim."

"Pick on me," Bull said. "Team up together and pick on me because I have a sense of history and the virtues of the past. I can take it. I'm tougher than the two of you. Bring in a gang of your friends and I'll take on all of you. Go ahead. Try it. Sneer all you want. But you got to keep one eye on the future and one eye on the past. Any other way, it won't work. Both eyes on the past, you can't move ahead. Always looking at the future, you stumble over what's right in front of you."

"One eye on the future, one on the past, that's cross-eyed," said Brenda

Brenda smiled at her mother, and Vanessa shook her head sadly at this blockhead she'd settled for.

Vanessa and Bull were in the eleventh grade when Bull fell in love, or lust, or whatever the hell it was. Back then Vanessa was a blonde. He fell in love, or whatever it was, with her hair. Long, silky, straight down her back, blonde. Folk-singer hair. All he could think about for months and months was how it would feel to run his fingers down the silky length of it.

Now her hair was short and curly and brown with frosted highlights. It looked like a discount wig. Things weren't going well between them anymore, not that they'd ever been super hot. More than two years since they'd screwed, and hadn't touched each other, not a kiss, not even an accidental brush of skin against skin since last November when that Catholic rich boy got elected President of the United States.

The last touch between them was a slap—her hand smacking his right cheek. Vanessa taking offense at Bull calling the president-elect a bead-rattling mackerel-snapping phony. She thought he was handsome and had magnetism, and thought the new president's wife was the most cultured and beautiful woman in the world. A fairy-tale president and his enchanted princess wife. Vanessa was working on getting her hair to look like Jackie's, and all her friends were doing the same.

Bull wore his black hair just exactly long enough to comb. For most of his life he'd had a GI flat top, bristles straight and even. Balance a wine glass on his hair, two or three wine glasses, full to the brim. Not a drop spills. But this longer hair, an inch, was his adjustment, a nod to current fashion. Willing to change, but only a fraction of an inch at a time.

Bull was a meter reader. Water meters.

A job that took him into the backyards and deep shrubbery of homes all over Miami. Ritzy, rundown, everything in between. Squatting behind hibiscus and ferns, flipping open the plate, wiping off the glass dial to read the numbers. In and out of yards in less than a minute, unless there was a bad dog. That's when he used the sharpened walking cane he wore like a sword in his belt. Jab them in the snout, get their attention, draw blood, even put an eye out if need be. Bad dogs and horny wives, that's all that slowed him down.

The wives appeared in the back windows, peeking through curtains or sometimes standing boldly in view. Dressed, or sometimes in just bras and panties, and four times in the last year there'd been those standing naked, showing everything the window allowed. Something was going wrong in America, causing the rise of slutty wives at windows. Fifteen years on the job, Bull started working for the county right out of Miami High, and it was only in the last year the women started showing themselves.

Bull believed it was linked to this new president about to take office. The handsome man was already sending hot-blooded signals to women across the land, making them lick their lips. Morals slipping. Putting housewives at their windows, presenting themselves to Bull Markham when all Bull wanted to do was write down their water use and get to the next house, the next house and the next one until he was done and could go home and watch his Christmas tree revolve and the colored wheel spin slow and Bull could sip his eggnog and feel the liquid warmth swell through him.

Bull was still making up for all the Christmases he'd missed. His drunk of a mother dumped little Bull with an elderly aunt, a shriveled-up woman who thought Christmas was a commercial abomination. Every holiday season her dark house stayed shadowy and airless while all around them, the neighbors were lit up with colored lights, fake snow and baby Jesus, all up and down the street, Jesus, Jesus, Jesus.

And it was just Bull's luck, here he was, a grown-up, trying to celebrate the holiday, inject some Christmas cheer and colorful radiance into his own home, and he ran smack into more bah-humbug women.

"We got to talk," Vanessa was saying as Bull watched the red tree turn to a green tree and then a blue tree, the tree rotating on its stand like a skater doing a slow twirl on the ice. Reminding him of the naked woman in the window of his last house of the day. Blonde, like Vanessa used to be, a real blonde. Showing him both halves of her blondness. Not smiling, not winking or primping or doing anything to lure him toward her as he stood up from behind the coco plum bushes. Just standing there with all her skin available in the late afternoon glow, not meeting his eyes but looking off toward the palm fronds, looking off like she was imagining some prince about to carry her off to a new land, a happy place, the kind of place she'd always deserved. And then she turned the same way the tree was turning, a slow circle, showing him her backside, the hair down her back, her narrow butt, and coming back around to face him again. Trying to entice him into her whirlpool of degeneracy.

"You listening to me, Bull?"

"You hadn't said anything yet."

"Now don't explode."

Bull set down his eggnog.

"It's about Brenda."

"What'd she do now?"

Vanessa tapped the ash from her cigarette into the palm of her hand then snapped the black dust toward the silvery spinning tree.

"She's sixteen. By her age I'd already been dating for two years." Vanessa took a drag on the cigarette, her eyes softening as if revisiting one of those early dreamboats before Bull charged into her world and hauled her off to this cramped two-bedroom house.

"A boy asked her to a pool party."

Bull watched the tree turn and turn.

"Don't even say it. You think she's got to have a chaperone till she's twenty-one and all that Puritanical bullshit, but the parents throwing the party, they're church people, Baptist, and they'll be there, so even by your caveman standards it should be okay. I said she could go."

"I don't have a say," Bull said.

"She's old enough to go out with a boy."

"A man in his own house without a say in his daughter's future."

"If it was up to you, you'd keep her ten years old forever."

"I didn't go out on a date till I was a senior in high school."

"Yeah, and look how good you turned out. Man of the world."

Vanessa smoked her cigarette down to the filter then walked the smoking butt over to an ashtray on top of the TV.

"The boy she's going with, his name is Jamal."

Bull picked up the eggnog and swallowed the last half of it.

"What is that, Cuban?"

"Not Cuban."

He set his eggnog glass on the table and drew a breath.

"Tell me he's not a Negro."

"He's a nice boy," Vanessa said. "And Brenda is a modern, open-minded girl."

"My daughter isn't going out with a colored boy. That isn't going to happen in the Markham family. Whites with whites, darks with darks, it's the natural way."

"I knew you'd come out with some dim-witted shit like that," Vanessa said. "I knew it, I knew it, I knew it."

Something happened in her eyes like the shutter on a camera lens snapping closed. No more light coming in, her brown eyes dead and sightless.

"Look, I'm not a bigot or whatever you want to call it. I got no problem with civil rights, but damn it, I got a few rights myself. My daughter isn't going to be a guinea pig in some big social experiment run by President Pretty Face. It isn't going to happen inside these walls. Let Pretty Face marry his cute little daughter off to a Negro, we can all sit around and watch on TV to see how that works out. But it isn't happening in the Markham household and that's final."

But it wasn't final. Vanessa drove Brenda to the pool party so she could swim half-naked with Jamal, the Negro. From that day forward Vanessa ignored him, Brenda ignored him, passing him by without a hello or good-bye.

Three months later in early April she was still dating the kid, coming in after ten o'clock on school nights, lolling around till midnight talking to him on the phone. Bull had lost total authority inside his home. Now Vanessa and Brenda were always confiding, whispering to each other on the phone when Brenda was off somewhere at night and needed girl advice.

Here it was, early April and the Christmas tree was still revolving. Don't ask him why, but at the end of December Bull couldn't bring himself to take down the aluminum tree and return it to the attic. It gave him solace, watching it turn, watching it go red and green and blue.

He knew it must be linked to Jamal. Some kind of protest, Bull's own stubborn stand against the revolution occurring in his household. Back in January he'd started to disassemble it, pulling out some of the silver flocked branches, then he stopped himself.

The tree was pissing off Brenda and Vanessa. Making them give Bull funny looks. Which was enough reason right there to keep the thing up. Plus he'd seen neighbors passing by on the sidewalk staring at the picture window, curtains open, tree lit up and revolving, and the looks on their faces made Bull proud. By god, he was experimenting too. Trying out a new approach to the yuletide season. Stretching it out, making it last into the uncertain future. Santa and the elves still frolicked on the lawn, their faces chubby and flushed.

Over the last three months he'd had to replace the bulb in the colored light wheel but otherwise the mechanisms were humming along fine. He sat in his chair each evening with two fingers of bourbon and a single ice cube and he watched the tree rotate and the two females moved around him as if he no longer existed. After all the fights and the yelling and the door slamming, it was peaceful again.

Tonight Jamal was coming over to meet Bull for the first time. Vanessa had decided it was time, announced it to him at breakfast and walked out of the room before he could reply. When he got home from work, Bull parked in the driveway and snuck the sharpened cane from his truck, his pit-bull sticker, and walked into the house with it hidden behind his leg. He lay it on the terrazzo beside his chair.

Now as he waited for Jamal, he felt the fiddle string in his chest tighten like it did when he entered some stranger's backyard and heard the hedges rattle and a badass critter came charging. Times like that, things turned simple and clear. He had to hurt the dog, maybe even kill the bastard, or else lose his own arm or worse. That's how he felt, that tight, that ready, that simple.

Bull had the TV on, watching the news people talk about the Bay of Pigs disaster. Some Miami Cuban idiots trying to invade, and the worthless pretty boy president being handsome and worthless.

Bull felt his chair rumble, the terrazzo vibrating beneath his shoes. Out the front window a car rolled to a stop. A Chevy, the chrome stripped off the sleek candy apple paint job, the car's body lowered on the frame to within an inch of the pavement. A chromed air scoop for a turbo charger jutting up through the hood. A goddamn drag racing hot rod.

Vanessa had come out of the back bedroom, and stood beside Bull's chair, looking out the window with him.

"How's a high school kid afford a car like that?"

"He's not in high school."

"They throw him out?"

"He graduated."

"And what's he do for money?"

"All these months, those are the first questions you've asked about Jamal."

"What's he do?"

"You're so curious, ask him. Face to face, find out who he is."

"I don't care who he is. It isn't right. White and black together. It isn't done."

"Oh, yes, it is too done," Vanessa said. "Things aren't like when you and me were kids. It's a new world dawning."

"It isn't going to dawn in this household."

Bull looked out at the car, still rumbling. Sally Harkness, the widow lady across the street was out in her front lawn watering her flowers. She was staring at the car, the hose spraying back onto her front porch.

The kid hadn't appeared from the car. It just sat next to the sidewalk. Motor running, the engine gunning every few seconds.

Vanessa moved around the chair and spotted the sharpened cane. She made an angry, startled sound in her throat, then a growl.

"You son of a bitch! What the hell do you think you're doing, Bull Markham?"

Bull was silent, staring past the revolving tree out at the hot rod.

"Are you crazy, Bull? You're planning to attack Jamal? Is that what you have in mind? Stick him through the heart because he's a black man."

Brenda walked into the living room wearing a tight blue sweater showing the shape of her new breasts. Blue jeans just as snug displaying her butt and her hips. All her private parts displayed like the women at their back windows.

"Goddamn it, Bull."

"What's going on?"

"Your father's a bastard," Vanessa said. "He was going to stab Jamal. Try to drive him away."

Vanessa kicked the dog-sticker across the terrazzo floor.

"Things aren't right," Bull said. "Little things, big things. It's there on the television every night, and I see it every day at work, nothing's reliable or trustworthy. It's falling apart, everything. The way people are, their values, it's slipping away."

"Out in the world? What're you talking about? You squat down in somebody's backyard checking their meter. That's where you see these big things falling apart?"

"I won't let it happen."

"You can't stop it from happening, you crazy son of a bitch."

Bull stood up and made a move toward the dog-spear.

"No, you don't."

Brenda punched him in the arm. Bull stopped and looked at her, his daughter in her tight clothes, showing her shape, her body so young and perfect.

Vanessa walked over to the tree and tugged loose a silver branch and walked back to Bull. Out the window, Bull saw the boy was still inside the car. Widow Harkness was spraying water on her cement front porch, glaring at the hot rod.

"You were going to attack the boy. Admit it, Bull."

"If need be," he said.

Vanessa drew back the silver branch and jabbed its base into Bull's chest. The prong penetrated his white T-shirt and lodged in his ribcage. Felt like a hornet sting. Took his breath away.

"I won't have it," Bull said.

Vanessa went back to the tree and plucked three more branches loose and walked back to Bull. Brenda darted to the tree and got a couple of silver branches of her own.

"Sit down in your chair, Bull. Sit down, you're hurt and bleeding. Don't make me hurt you worse."

But Bull took a step toward the front door and Vanessa thrust another branch into Bull's shoulder. Brenda stepped in close and jabbed a branch into his upper arm. He kept moving toward the front door. By the time he made it outside, he had seven branches sprouting from his body.

The pain jumbled together with the general turmoil inside his head. Bull walked down his sidewalk toward the car and a breeze ruffled the aluminum tassels on his branches. He was glittery and felt strangely strong and fresh.

He stepped off the end of the curb and stood in the street in front of the rumbling hot rod. He looked back at the house and saw Vanessa at the living room window watching her crazy husband who'd stepped off the gerbil wheel, stepped off it for good. Brenda wasn't beside her. Brenda, Bull knew, had retreated to her bedroom to sob.

The big engine switched off.

Bull felt the blood gluing his cotton T-shirt to his skin. The pain was a dark glow in his chest. Another breeze stirred his glittery branches, branches that would be good forever. Indestructible, non-perishable. No need to toss that tree out every year and go buy another. This was a tree for a lifetime.

The boy opened his door and got out.

He was wearing a uniform. A black tunic, white belt with a brass buckle, red piping on the edges, six gold buttons down the front, white dress hat with a glossy black bill. He had medals, three of them, on his chest. Bull didn't know what they were for. But the boy had been good. He'd shot straight or he'd got injured or he'd performed admirably under great stress and enemy fire.

"Are you okay, sir? You're injured and bleeding."

He had a strong handsome face, stood very straight, his chin pulled in. Bull thought the young man might be about to salute, so he raised his own right hand to his forehead and waited until Jamal returned the salute.

"I should call an ambulance, sir."

"Wounded in action," Bull said. "Defending a lost cause."

"You want me to pull those things out for you, sir?"

Bull looked down at the seven aluminum branches.

"No, leave them. I'll be fine."

"Pardon me, sir, but you look bad."

"It's a war we're in," Bull said. "We've got to be strong. We've got to be disciplined and brave. You believe that, don't you, son?"

"Absolutely, sir."

"We all have to be resolute, stay the course, stand firm for our beliefs in the face of overwhelming odds, the endless assaults by those who would over-throw all that is good about our nation."

"Were you in the service, sir?"

"I read water meters."

Jamal nodded.

"It's like sneaking behind enemy lines," Bull said. "I see things no one else sees. I see things that worry me."

Jamal was silent.

"This is a war with many fronts, son."

"Yes, sir."

"You're a Negro."

"Yes, I am, sir."

"And I'm a father of a white girl."

"You are, sir. A very nice young lady."

"Is that the way it's going? Is that where we're headed? Mingling the races."

"I'd like to think it is, sir."

"You and me, can we be on the same side of something like that? Some-thing so unnatural."

"I believe we can be on the same side, sir. I strongly believe that."

"But you agree it's unnatural, the races mingling."

"It feels very natural to me, sir."

"Does it?"

"Very natural, sir. I care about your daughter's welfare, whether she's white or black, that makes no difference to me."

"It doesn't bother you, being part of someone's big social experiment?"

"I've been smack in the middle of that all my life, sir. One way or another. I'm used to it."

"Do you and my daughter talk about any of this?"

"Any of what, sir?"

"You being a Negro, her being white."

"No, sir. I can't say it's ever come up."

Sally Harkness, the neighbor, had dragged her hose out into the middle of the street and was watering the asphalt nearby.

"You need assistance, Bull Markham?"

"No, ma'am. We're doing just fine here."

"That boy's not bothering you in any way? I could call for help."

"No, Sally. He seems to be a decent young man. Defending our country on many fronts."

Another flood of wind rushed down the street, a warm June breeze, and all the threads of tinsel on Bull's branches stirred and twirled and shimmered.

Bull Markham felt himself turning a slow rotation in the street. On his way around he saw other neighbors on alert in their yards, saw his elves and Santa looking on from his own grassy lawn, and for a half a moment Bull saw a long distance down his street into the fog of the indefinite future. A slow spin, coming back to Jamal in his full dress uniform. A young Marine.

"You okay, Mr. Markham? You're looking very pale."

"Never better," Bull said.

"I think I should call for a medic or an ambulance."

"Come on inside, son."

"If that's what you want, sir."

"I make a mean eggnog. You like eggnog, don't you?"

"Never tried it, sir. Heard it's good, but never had occasion to try it."

"Well, then, it's about damn time you expanded your horizons. Don't you think?"

"I'd like to give it a try. Yes, sir. I've always heard it's good."

Trailing blood, Bull Markham led the young marine down his sidewalk past Santa and his elves, the silver branches sprouting from his body like wings that him lifted off the earth, his feet brushing lightly across the concrete, Bull felt weightless, like Sputnik circling and circling in the empty heights of space, flying in endless orbits, free of gravity, yet firmly held in place.

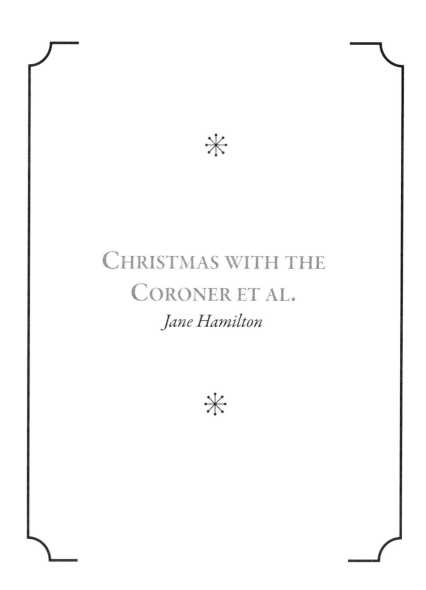

CHRISTMAS WITH THE CORONER ET AL.
Jane Hamilton

Wh_en I was twenty-two my father fell off a cliff. He was on a climbing trip at Devil's Lake, a Wisconsin state park, a place with fantastical, above ground geology. A billion years ago sand blew in and around the future town of Baraboo, and later heat and pressure did their parts to make quartzite rock cliffs from the sandstone, formations as if thoughtfully made for future climbers. A glacier came through for the finishing touches: why not a deep and sparkling lake right here? The park is considered by many to be the primo rock-climbing venue in the Midwest.

Recently, the subject of my father came up with an acquaintance. Tony said, "Is your father still living?"

"He died in 1980," I said.

"He must have been young."

It always sounds like a line, part of a standup routine: *He fell off a cliff.* I said, "The story is a little bit of a showstopper."

"Try me," my new friend said.

"He fell off a cliff!"

"Awful!" Tony paused respectfully. "I do hate to drop this, but I can one-up you." He went on to tell me that his twin brother died of an LSD overdose when they were fifteen."

"You win," I said.

I'm pretty sure it's accurate to say that, over thirty years later, I still think about my father every day. He was fifty-nine when he died, a real specimen, in stunningly good shape. After his most recent physical, his doctor had written, in a two-page letter, "The examination finds you to be in excellent health and no recommendations for changing anything are forthcoming. . . . Your habits are exemplary in every respect, particularly in the vigor with which you pursue the athletic life."

My father discovered rock climbing in his forties, and in suburban Chicago he ran most days, "working out," before it was called that, always in training for the next Mountaineering Club field trip. It didn't occur to him to buy running shoes and at the start of his enthusiasm he ran in hobnailed work boots. We joked about his mid-life distraction, no secretary on the sly for him, no red sports car, but instead a band of climbing brothers. He was an engineer, he loved Roman ruins, he read novels, he often went to the theater with my mother, the theater her brand of joy. My parents shared their interests and also set each other free into their obsessions. With the Mountaineering Club he went to Peru, to Ecuador, to Wyoming and Montana, and for local pleasures and challenges he and the gang often spent the weekends at Devil's Lake, a mere state away. At *Devil's*, as he called it, no one saw the fall that killed him.

It was the choicest of May days, the grass having turned green within a few hours, the Baltimore orioles suddenly back, the wild asparagus coming up, the violets unrestrained. I got the news, hung up the phone, and could do nothing but run. I ran out the door into the woods on our Wisconsin farm, and in all that running and tripping and running I heard a whippoorwill, something I've never heard at home before or since. I didn't take it as a sign, not being a sign-y sort of person, but it was a nice touch, a comfort, for a reason I can't even now explain. My mother, my siblings, the mountaineers who'd been with him—all of us walked around in a state of shock in those first days. For some of us, the zombie mode went on for months.

He'd gone up to set the ropes on a climb called Coatimundi, and he must have slipped. My doctor cousin insists he had a heart attack, as eventually happens to all the men in the Hamilton family, that autopsies are crude and do not always show a true picture. I think otherwise. His heart was perfect! The doctor who'd examined him in real life said so! The rock was slippery; he fell. Or, the rock wasn't slippery, and still he fell. My mother declined to drive the five hours to see him, to see the body. She'd been told that he was terribly beaten up, and she didn't think there was any reason for any of us to carry that final image around for the rest of our lives. One of the Mountaineering Club men brought her his wedding ring, his wallet, his shoes, his climbing gear, and later the crematorium in Sauk City sent her his ashes.

That summer she went to Europe, the time-honored grand tour for distraction. She wrote poems to him and about him. I had to finish up my Bachelor's Degree, had to take a geology class at the University of Wisconsin in Madison. On the bus trip to Devil's Lake for the field trip, I sat by myself wondering if I was going to feel anything. I didn't remember the name of the climb where the fall had taken place, and so all the bluffs circling the lake were the culprits. No one in the family had gone to the park since his death; no one had felt the need to make a trip up there into a pilgrimage.

During the field trip I examined the rock strata and tried to be as interested in water, and heat, and ice, and time passing as all those phenomena deserve. I kept waiting to be stricken with the enormity of The Place but I also didn't really want to be stricken on the geology outing. I didn't know my classmates, and certainly wasn't at the point where I could say to anyone, "My father? He fell off a cliff!"

I was taking the university class because at the small liberal arts college I'd graduated from the year before I hadn't actually received my diploma. At the ceremony, I'd been given a blank. I hadn't finished my distribution requirements because I hadn't been able to bear the thought of spending my father's hard-earned money at my expensive college on classes that held no fascination. Standing around looking at the features of geologic time at Devil's Lake, I was a failure on three counts: I was still not a college graduate; I didn't care about a subject my father would have loved; and, I didn't feel anything in a place that should have been wrenching.

A few years passed. Before my wedding my mother was helping me get dressed. We both understood we were thinking of my father, but we didn't say anything about him. I knew she wasn't thrilled about the marriage, and I knew also that although my husband and I had wanted to do all the preparations, she felt guilty about being excused from the typical mother-of-the-bride tasks. But what probably was most mournful about the whole enterprise for her was the fact that she couldn't discuss their youngest child's potential huge mistake with my father. She tied my sash; we didn't talk. She fiddled with the flowers in my hair; we didn't speak. The discipline of repression was required; all day we operated on Mute.

When I had my first child I had to have an emergency C-section. When I had my second, I was determined to experience natural childbirth. During the course of the labor I found the experience so appalling, so impossible that I appealed to my father. I don't believe in the supernatural, but I knew I wasn't having that baby without magic of some kind. And, if he didn't come through! He was absolutely with me, so loving and reassuring and visible—not exactly in the room, and not merely in my mind, but filling the space of my mind, which in the moment was the room. I was giving birth to a daughter, my father was visiting, *two, two, two mints in one*, as the old jingle goes.

My siblings and I had dreams about him, those dreams where the dead person is suddenly back, but there's always a rule: you can't touch him, he can't speak, he can only stay a few minutes, or he behaves in a peculiar way: he won't say why he left in such a hurry, won't explain anything. It was always so good to see him, the limitations notwithstanding.

Despite how much he was hovering in our psychic space, though, it became increasingly difficult to talk about him. It was as if, initially, in our shock, we were free to tell our stories because we were certain that the weird joke of his death would pass, and he'd return. As the years went on, the fact sunk in: he was dead.

We never talked about his experience of the fall, never conjectured together about what he might have thought about in those seconds—the brain in accident mode spinning out the moment to marvel at the fix you've gotten yourself into—but I'm sure we all wondered. Maybe for him, the fall took something like an eternity, a crazy song in his head looping over and over, or the whole good life whizzed by, or maybe a trivial horror flashed and flashed, an IRS form, a line not filled in. Anything, everything could have played in that stretch of five or so seconds.

My mother had comforted herself with the idea that the death was quick, but I privately guessed that for him it had to have felt slow. I hated to think that he could see the end point of the fall as it took place, and that in what time was left to him he felt terrible about the loss to my mother, and the loss to us—that he berated himself for making such a stupid misstep. A person who was as famously careful as he was, someone who observed the safety procedures to the letter was not someone who should have had such an accident. There was no way to know about those last minutes, I thought. No way, really, to even imagine them with any kind of specificity. Even years after, no one in my family, except for me on my geology field trip, had gone to Devil's Lake to think more about the step by step, You-Were-There account of that ever receding afternoon in May.

A few days before Christmas, ten years after his death, a large brown envelope arrived from my aunt, the sweet aunt, the addled aunt. "I've been cleaning," she wrote, "and I came upon some things of your father's." I put the goods away without looking at them, thinking to save the packet for a moment when I could enjoy the photographs, the letters—whatever it was that my Aunt had sent.

That was the Christmas my children were sick and we called off the relatives. They were three and five years old. On Christmas Eve, they both were feeling a little better but not so well that they wanted to fight. They were playing nicely in the living room, in front of the tree, the pale afternoon sun was shining in upon us, and I thought to open my aunt's envelope in that window of peace, to perhaps have a little Christmas moment with my father.

The coroner's report was the first in the whole sheaf of reports. *Things of my father's*. My uncle was a doctor and years before had probably requested to see the paperwork for his brother's death. My aunt had been cleaning. *I came upon some things of your father's*. The coroner's report was handwritten, factual, impersonal. "Subject had multiple contusions & abrasions over entire body. Laceration of chin—multiple injuries of head." My father, *the subject*. The coroner was doing his job, as he'd done many times before. Pronouns, unnecessary. He needed only to confirm that the death had occurred, and by accident. "No evidence of foul play.—Body donated to science." He later notes: "Late entry. Do [sic] to condition of body—rejected for research."

The first time, that Christmas Eve, when I read the reports I read them slowly. I wanted to remain in them, as awful as the scene was, as harrowing as the details were; this was the end of the line when it came to knowing my father. I'd read his journals, I'd reread the letters, I'd read his favorite books, I'd looked time and time again at the photographs. In this envelope were the last things that could be known.

The park ranger's report came next, an entirely different kind of reporting. He, too, had a form to fill out, but he's telling a story, no way around the story. He's telling it as responsibly, as thoroughly, as he can, based on the information he has personally gathered shortly after the accident.

"The victim was lying on his left side with blood and bubbles coming out of his mouth and nose. He was breathing a very shallow, rapid breath. The people on the scene advised me they were paramedics and wanted to know when the stretcher would be arriving. I told them that the stretcher was going to be coming up on the emergency road, on the top, near the walking path, and that I'd arrange for someone nearby to direct the officer with the stretcher to the scene." The ranger reports that after a stretcher arrived, somehow ahead of the ambulance crew, he asked the paramedics if they wanted to wait for the medical paraphernalia from the rescue vehicle. One of the paramedics said, "Time's wasting, we don't have much time to go, let's load him on the stretcher, there's no sense waiting for the other stuff that we need to be coming."

Needless to say in my quiet kitchen it was difficult to move past that small moment, that moment when time was wasting. There is still, in the story, a great deal of time to be spent, to be experienced, even when there is *not much time to go*. This is the point in the story to stop time—a feat made possible with each rereading. For a minute or two, you can hold the story still right there before you go on to the inevitable:

". . . About 4 PM Mr. S and Dr. C had examined him but nobody at that time made the determination as to whether he was dead or not. A short period thereafter (approx. 4:15) Dr. C stated that the subject had died."

How did time pass for my father? You can't be alive and out of the current of time, and yet in his condition I supposed that time might well have already ceased to exist.

"There was one other subject that was climbing with the victim which would be Scott Eckert," the ranger went on. "I tried talking with this subject earlier. He was so shook up, crying and hysterical, that he wouldn't give me his name or couldn't talk to me."

It's terrible work, being a ranger, I could see this, could see that our man was doing an admirable job, maybe even a heroic job. It was in the third or fourth reading, once I'd adjusted somewhat to the story itself, that the ranger's voice came through to me. It's his duty to tell the story, but he's in an unusual position: when he appears on the scene he's both in charge of the action, and he's recording it. He's both powerful and helpless. The pages read as if this might have been a first death for him, as well as a first big event in his tenure as ranger. That is to say, there is awe lurking in the account. The language is formal for the most part, but every now and then there's a poetic rhythm. He will not be rushed, he will leave nothing out, every detail a critical detail. You feel him saying earnestly, and humbly, *This is going to be the important document because it's my job to make it so, and because I was there.*

He finishes by saying, "Now after we'd gotten all the additional information and everything . . . I marked off the area on top where he did fall . . . I took a nylon strap and tied it around a tree and then carved into the tree as to the area in which he went down . . . I guess this about concludes my portion of it." (It's as if he doesn't quite want to leave it.) He adds, "It is now 5 pm. I was off duty at 4 pm." (He's putting in extra time!) "I might want to add also that there was rain earlier in the day . . . END."

Although the sheriff was not present for any of the aftermath, in his report there's a new piece of information:

"Dennis Bolt advised that Hamilton went up a climbing access route to the west of the area they were going to climb to set some anchors, and throw the ropes down. Bolt said once the rope came down it was approximately two or three minutes or at least a very short time passed before Bolt hollowered [sic] that something was coming down. Bolt then hollowered [sic] to two girls that were in the area that we have a fallen climber, and set the girls down the trail to get help."

Two girls, two new characters, two nameless girls who were *set down the trail*. What kind of fairy tale is this, I wondered, where girls suddenly appear in the narrative and are *set down the trail* to find help?

Dennis Bolt, the report said, "kept looking up for Hamilton, but finally looked and saw the blue jacket on the fallen climber, this was the first time he suspected it might be Hamilton that had fallen. Bolt said that he then went up, and saw the subject, and identified him as Hamilton, the fallen climber . . . Bolt said that Hamilton was a very safe climber and took no nonsense while he was climbing, and was very very careful."

In the section under random notations the sheriff writes:

"Hamilton was wearing shoes made specially for rock climbing. They look like high-top basketball shoes. The soles are made of black rubber. One witness was overheard to say these are the best shoes available on the market."

Is there anything more affecting than a dead person's shoes? Shoes always seem the most lonesome of personal affects, more than a hat or sweater or pants, I suppose because shoes were shaped by the very feet, and are not as easily given up to anyone else.

In the calm of that Christmas Eve I went on reading. Document number four was written by one of the paramedics. This account is the closest yet to the actual happening. After several false starts with his handwriting, several scratchings out on the form, he begins:

"I arrived at the scene about 5 min after we heard the man fall. When we arrived the man was lying unconscious. He was on his left side & his head was on a rock."

They *heard* the man fall? Was there a scream, a cry, or the sound of the landing? A thwump? Further, and most terrible, his head was on a rock? This is one of the saddest details, no pillow, that rock.

"Bill opened his mouth & the man was able to breathe, although with difficulty . . . His right pupil was dilated when I checked it upon my arrival and remained so until he was put onto the stretcher. The pupil did not appear to constrict when I raised his eyelid. It was approximately 4:10 when the stretcher arrived. By that time there were about 15 people present, and we transported the man to the car that was waiting at the top."

Fifteen people present! A swelling number, enough to count as a respectable audience. I didn't like to think about the pupil, how the dilation business must have meant the optic nerve was severed, or there was no brain activity, and yet, if there was no brain activity, perhaps he, the man, felt nothing.

There is another police officer's report, and another paramedic's account, and when I had finished the stack I began to read them again from the start. And when I'd again finished I read once more. What was moving, beyond, of course, the vivid details of the trauma to my father, was that so many people were holding the story, including, surely, the two girls who were *set down the trail*. Never to reappear. That a story is always first about the teller was plainly clear in these accounts, each report radiating the personality of the narrator. Were I to go to Devil's Lake again, I realized, the park would no longer be a generally mournful place, but would be peopled by all of those who carried the story. I would certainly, then, *feel* in a way I hadn't been able to during the geology field trip. That's what had been missing for years from the death: a party of narrators, the space of the story itself, a space wherein a person can, for a time, be.

I don't exactly feel connected to the sheriff, the ranger, the paramedics, and yet I've come to feel grateful to them, they who, in my mind's eye stand in a loving circle around my father. I don't know if it's strange, but, as much as I know the reports fairly well now, having read them many times, the fact is, I like to read them. I know that my heart will hurt when I'm living in the documents, and for a while after I'm done it will keep hurting, but I know, too, that the hurt is itself a deep and haunting pleasure.

And one last oddity. There is the messenger, my aunt, my aunt's thoughtful thoughtlessness in that brown envelope, the beauty of her craziness: *Here is the death of your father. Merry Christmas!*

LA VIGILIA

Ann Hood

Connie stands on the front steps of her childhood home, refusing to move forward. Her husband Vincent stands close behind her, breathing heavily in the cold air. He sounds like a dragon, or something about to explode. Like a geyser, Connie thinks. Like Old Faithful. Even thinking about Old Faithful fuels her anger. On the list of things she and Vincent were supposed to do but never have, visiting Old Faithful is number two, right after a honeymoon in Niagara Falls. Instead, they drove as far as Seekonk—only thirty minutes from the hall where her family still sat drinking wine and eating egg biscuits and *wandi*. Vincent stopped at the first motel he saw. So eager to take her virginity finally, he did not even wait for her to remove her pale green going-away suit and put on her champagne-colored negligee. Right then, she should have known. She should have picked up her American Tourister matching luggage and gone to Niagara Falls herself. Now, six years later, it was too late. Connie would never see Old Faithful. Or Niagara Falls. Or do any of the things on her ever-growing list of disappointments.

"I'm fucking freezing, Connie," Vincent says between snorts, which finally propels her forward.

"Davy," Connie says, nudging her five-year-old son, "ring the bell."

But Davy can't reach it. He stands on booted tiptoes, and reaches his mittened hand upward.

Connie sighs, worried that Davy will be a short man like his father, worried that this trip home for Christmas will be just one more misguided decision.

"Jesus," Vincent says and leans against Connie to ring the doorbell himself.

He doesn't move away from her when he is done. Instead, he presses against her back, making sure she feels that even in the below freezing temperature, even beneath his long wool coat and gray flannel trousers and white boxer shorts, he has a hard on. As if he has accomplished something special.

"Jesus," Connie says.

Davy turns his beautiful face up toward Connie and smiles his perfect baby teeth smile.

"Happy birthday, Jesus!" he says, and Connie's heart swells with love and pride. Davy is smart. He is beautiful. Despite being conceived on that very night in that terrible motel in Seekonk, Davy is the very thing Connie has always wanted for herself: Davy is special.

The door finally opens, and with it comes a strong smell of fish. Tonight, Christmas Eve, is the *festa dei sette pesci*, the Feast of the Seven Fishes, a reminder to Connie of everything she tried to flee when she married Vincent and moved to Connecticut six years ago. The *festa dei sette pesci* screams immigrant, *guinea*, *wop*. The smell of fish and the dread at this step backwards in her life make Connie's stomach do a little flip.

Her sister Gloria stands at the open door wearing a sweater that makes her breasts look as pointy as ice cream cones and a skirt that hugs her ass. Peeking out from behind that ass is Gloria's daughter Cammie, her hair in Shirley Temple ringlets and her dress a frilly white confection.

Cammie looks like she belongs on top of a cake, Connie thinks, even as she plasters a fake grin on her face and says, "Look at Cammie! So beautiful!" The girl, Connie decides, will have a hooknose like her father.

"Don't just stand there like guests," Gloria says, standing back to let them in.

Even then, as Davy goes inside, Vincent doesn't move right away. He has his hands on Connie's waist and he gives her the tiniest shove with his erection before releasing her. Like a teenager, he loves that thing. *I've got a chubby,* he whispers in her ear in bed at night. *A woody. A Johnson. Little Vinny,* he calls it. *Little V.*

Still grinning, Connie steps into the kitchen. The smells of fish and perfume and coffee percolating on the stove make her dizzy. All the faces looming toward her with their bright lipsticked lips flapping, their breath of cigarette smoke and anisette cookies, suffocate her.

The next thing Connie knows, she is going down hard onto the green and yellow linoleum squares, and someone—maybe her mother?—is shouting *She's fainting! Oh my God!* And then she is down, flat, her head throbbing and spinning at the same time, the sharp ammonia smell of smelling salts burning her nose.

She opens her eyes and tries to make sense of what she sees: Her sister Gloria with those ridiculous tits, frowning her skinny arched brows. Her sister Angie with what Connie hopes is a red wig and not her own hair, sprayed into a strange stiff flip, her eyes lined in heavy black liner and a fake black beauty mark beside her very red lips. Her sister Anna so pregnant she can hardly kneel without toppling over. Little Cammie, wide eyed, banana curls bobbing. Her own Davy, his face scrunched up the way he does when he tries not to cry. The smelling salts have been jammed up her nose by her mother, who is kneeling beside her looking pissed off, her faded flowered apron splattered with grease. On the other side, Vincent kneels beside her. Was he smiling? Was that asshole smiling?

Vincent looks up at everyone and announces, "I guess this confirms it. She's knocked up again."

Immediately, everyone's worry turns to squeals of happiness.

Connie watches their faces transform. Now they are smiling and their frowns are disappearing. Even her mother is smiling at her, stroking her cheek. Connie looks into her mother's face, the creases filled with some kind of heavy makeup that sits in the wrinkles like spackle and two round spots of liquid rouge on each cheek. She looks at Vincent, smug and proud, congratulating his chubby, his woody, Little V. And Davy, confused, trying to decide whether he should be happy or not.

"What's knocked up, Mama?" he says in a breathy voice. "You mean knocked down? Like, you got knocked down to the floor?"

Connie opens her mouth to answer him, but instead of words what comes out is a loud, painful cry that sounds like the cry their cocker spaniel, Ziti, made when he got hit by a car last fall. The cry seems to go on and on. Even after Connie is lifted to the green couch and covered in a hand crocheted afghan, even after Connie's mouth is long closed, she still hears that awful cry, echoing.

For the previous five Christmases, since Connie married Vincent Palazzo, she stayed home in their small white Cape in Middletown, Connecticut. She did not make seven fishes on Christmas Eve; she made a rib roast and roasted potatoes and string beans almondine. On Christmas morning she served Vincent and Davy french toast and maple bacon. Her family did not eat in the kitchen; they ate in the dining room on the china she bought piece by piece with S & H Green Stamps that she dutifully pasted into a book, filling one after another so that she could get the matching gravy boat and tea cups and salad plates, all creamy white with a border of off-white tiny raised flowers. All perfect.

When Connie first met Vincent, she believed he was a man who was going places. By that time, everyone considered Connie a spinster. Twenty-five, without even a prospect of a husband. Twenty-five and a virgin. The only men who asked her out were older, widows or bachelors with odd habits. There was the one who cried during dinner because he loved his dead wife so much. The one who had seven children to raise and needed a wife to do it. The one who could not leave his mother. The one who loved opera; who wore suspenders; who collected miniature porcelain animals; who raised standard poodles. The one who had been in prison. *Bad checks*, he'd explained with a shrug, as if that explained everything.

Then Vincent walked into the office where Connie worked in the secretarial pool with his case of Royal typewriters and Connie felt something she had never felt before. An almost unpleasant tug in her groin. It made her squirm in her seat. Vincent—dark olive skin and green eyes that bulged like a bullfrog's; stiff shoe-polish black hair that she would learn only after they were married was a toupee that sat on a mannequin head at night; short, just her height, and round like a barrel—Vincent sat across from her waiting to see the procurer of office supplies and Connie squirmed. She wished she'd curled her hair, freshened her lipstick, worn the sweater with the pearl buttons that looked so flattering.

He smiled at her, showing a row of white teeth as small as baby's teeth.

"How do you like that Remington?" he said, his voice smooth and silky, a voice you wanted to touch.

Connie cleared her throat. "My what?" she asked.

He pointed his chin in the direction of her typewriter. "The Remington," he said.

She realized her fingers, which had been busily typing when he appeared, had sunk into the keys like melted wax.

"It's a fine typewriter," she managed to say. Then she blurted, "I graduated from Katherine Gibbs, top in my class."

Vincent nodded approvingly. "Very impressive," he said. "Did you learn on a Remington?"

That tug in her groin. It was all she could focus on. An image of the rows of girls—*Katie Gibbs' girls*—in their business smart clothes, fingers sailing across the keys *the quick brown fox jumps over the lazy dog.*

"I'm a Royal man," Vincent said, leaning closer to her.

She caught a whiff of cologne, strong and spicy.

"Yes," Connie said, putting her hands in her lap as if that might subdue the tugging. She noticed his hat resting on one of his knees, black with a small red feather in the ribbon.

"Just got promoted to manager at the factory over in Connecticut," he said proudly.

His boasting, his confidence, only made the tug stronger. She found herself leaning toward him too.

He winked at her. "I'm on my way," he said, pointing his forefinger upward.

Every cell in her body was shouting, *Take me with you!* She wished he could read her mind.

The procurer came out of his office.

"Mr. Palazzo?" he said in his reedy voice. The procurer was allergic to nuts and wheat and shellfish. Connie knew this because she'd had three unfortunate dates with him, including the one spent in the Emergency Room of Kent County Hospital after eating a pupu platter at The Ming Garden. "*Nuts,*" he'd gasped, clutching his throat. His face had large purple welts on it and his lips swelled so much it looked like someone had shoved a baseball in his mouth by the time they'd reached the hospital.

Connie watched Vincent Palazzo walk away without looking back. She thought she might cry when the procurer closed his office door. Taking deep breaths, she went into the ladies' room, grateful to find it empty. Inside a stall, she leaned with her back against the door, wondering what would become of her. She imagined a life with her mother, the two of them crocheting at night, sipping an apricot brandy before bed. She imagined never feeling that tug again, that elusive something that her sister Angie seemed to feel all the time. Angie, who came home with smeared lipstick and a bruised mouth, smelling briny. Younger than Connie by seven years, she'd already broken off three engagements.

Connie knew she should wash her face, apply powder and lipstick, comb her hair. But instead, almost cautiously, she lifted her skirt and rubbed herself, lightly, over her girdle. That tugging, that yearning, would not go away. When she closed her eyes, the image of Vincent Palazzo filled her mind, and she could almost smell his cologne again. She rubbed a bit harder, surprised at the way her hips lifted toward her hand. Damn girdle, Connie thought, gripped unexpectedly by the desire to push her hand against her flesh. For an instant, she thought she had urinated on herself. She was wet, and breathing in short gasps.

Somehow she managed to squeeze one hand down her girdle, her fingers reaching, reaching, and then rubbing and rubbing, her eyes closed so that she could picture Vincent Palazzo, and then her breath quickening until something happened, something like falling off a rooftop. Something Connie had never felt before, or even considered feeling.

On wobbly legs she managed to get back to her desk.

Vincent Palazzo stood there, twirling his hat on one finger and whistling "Sentimental Journey."

"There you are!" he said. "I almost gave up hope."

Connie tried to smile. Could he tell what she had been doing by the way she looked? She would have to go to confession, right after work, she decided. Surely she had broken a commandment. But which one?

"You like Chinese?" he was saying.

She nodded.

"I like the chicken wings at The Ming Garden. And the chow mein. You like chow mein?"

Vincent Palazzo was asking her out, Connie realized. On a date.

She stood straighter. "Yes, Mr. Palazzo, I do like chow mein. And pork fried rice."

He grinned. "Good then. I'll see you Friday at six."

He walked off, whistling "Sentimental Journey" again.

I am going to marry that man, Connie thought as she watched his bowlegged strut. *I am going to marry that man and move to Connecticut and never ever come back here again.*

She smiled, sat at her desk, lifted her fingers above the typewriter keys, and typed.

"The baccala," Mama Jo says, "needs to be soaked three times." She holds up her thumb and the two fingers beside it. "For the Father, the Son, and the Holy Ghost."

Davy nods solemnly.

Even though one of the many changes Connie has made in her life includes not going to church, Davy holds a fascination for religion, and Jesus in particular. Vincent does the obligatory Catholic duties: Palm Sunday, Easter Mass, and—until this year—midnight mass on Christmas Eve. But enough of the kids at St. Alphonsus' kindergarten practice their faith that Davy has

ANN HOOD

gleaned some of the details.

"Is the Holy Spirit related to the Holy Ghost?" he asks Mama Jo as she begins to flour the smelts.

"They're all God," she answers.

Davy looks confused, but doesn't pursue it.

Connie, thick tongued and fuzzy headed, joins them at the table. Silently, she counts the fish spread out there in various stages of preparation. Baccala, smelts, snail salad, octopus, marinated eel, anchovies.

"Six," she says, after she's counted again. "There's only six."

"I've got shrimps in the icebox," her mother says primly.

Connie supposes that her mother will never forgive her for moving away and not coming home to visit. Until now. To Mama Jo, it is probably too late. But to Connie, she has come only out of desperation. There are so many things she wants to confess to her mother, so many questions she wants to ask her, but Mama Jo remains distant and cool. It's clear that she would not welcome any intimacy from Connie. The flush of joy over a new grandchild has already faded as Mama Jo remembers the disrespect Connie has shown her.

"Why do we need six fishes, Mama Jo?" Davy asks. He has put his hand over his nose and mouth to block out the strong fish smell.

Mama Jo shakes her head sadly. "This one, he knows nothing."

"We eat seven fishes on Christmas Eve," Connie explains. "One for . . ." She hesitates. "I almost said one for each apostle, but that's wrong."

For the first time since she's arrived, her mother looks right at Connie, her face so full of disappointment and disapproval that Connie has to catch her breath.

"So," her mother says evenly, "you follow a man to some fancy job and buy some fancy house and pretend you're American, and you actually turn into an American?"

"Ma, I am American," Connie says. She can feel Davy's eyes on her. "Italian-American," she adds.

Mama Jo takes hold of the rubbery white octopus and splays it on the table, slicing it with quick knife strokes.

178

The slap of the octopus against the enamel cuts through the silence.

"You know Vincent lost that job, Ma," Connie says quietly.

"Daddy is unemployed," Davy says with pride.

Mama Jo hesitates, the knife in mid-air.

"I thought he got a job with—"

"That didn't work out either," Connie says.

"And this is the time you decide to get pregnant?" Mama Jo says. "Is that what they taught you at that fancy secretarial school I paid for? I used to have to borrow from the other kids' lunch money for your bus fare to Providence."

"I didn't decide," Connie mumbles.

She wants to tell her mother that this is why she has not come home. Her own disappointment with her life is big enough for all of them. She wants to tell her how sometimes, when she watches Vincent feed his fat bullfrog face, she prays that he will choke. How when she finds him asleep on the sofa late in the afternoon, she watches to see if he is still breathing, and is always angry when his chest rises and falls in perfect rhythm.

"Mommy works for Doctor DiMarco," Davy says through his fingers.

Mama Jo's head snaps to attention.

"You work?"

"In the doctor's office," Connie says, trying to sound casual. "A few days a week while Davy's at school."

Her eyes meet her mother's.

"What?" Connie says.

"Vincent stays home, and *you* work?"

Connie's glance flits to Davy, and then back to her mother. But Mama Jo doesn't take the hint.

"What kind of wife . . . what kind of mother . . . works?" Mama Jo says.

"Dr. Marco looks like Montgomery Clift," Davy says.

Mama Jo frowns, but doesn't look away. Connie can feel her cheeks turn red.

"Connie," her mother says. Nothing more.

Connie picks up the bowl of smelts that still need to be fried and takes them over to the stove where a pot of hot oil waits. Through the window, she can see her husband drinking homemade wine with Angie's husband, Pat, and Gloria's husband, Rocky. The men have cigars clenched in their fingers and Vincent is holding court, talking and gesturing, happy to have an audience. She wonders what he is bragging about. His woody? Her pregnancy? The car they can't afford payments on?

She drops a handful of smelts into the bubbling oil. It splatters, burning her hands and arms.

"Montgomery Clift is a famous actor," Davy is saying. "Mommy's favorite actor, right, Mommy?"

The smelts sizzle. Connie fights back nausea as their acrid smell fills her nostrils.

Behind her, her mother slaps the octopus down hard once again, slicing it into small pieces.

"Mama Jo," Davy says, oblivious to the tension that fills the kitchen, "why are there seven fishes?"

"For the Holy Blessed Sacraments," Mama Jo tells him. "Your mother should remember that."

Three mornings a week, after Connie drops Davy off at kindergarten, she drives across town to Dr. DiMarco's office. He has given her what he calls *mother's hours*, working just while Davy is in school. She wears a white uniform that shows off her small waist, unbuttoned just enough so that if Dr. DiMarco wanted to, he could glimpse the white lace of her bra, the swell of her breasts. Connie hopes he is sneaking looks at them, at her. He is movie-star handsome, with thick dark hair and a high forehead, thick black eyebrows above piercing black eyes.

The diplomas that hang behind her in the office are from Williams College and Yale Medical School. Fancy schools. Connie imagines Williams College, which she knows absolutely nothing about, as a beautiful place with brick ivy-covered buildings and smart handsome men debating great ideas on brick-lined paths. She imagines pink dogwoods in bloom, and bright azalea bushes, and a clock tower that chimes on the hour. Davy will go there, Connie has decided. Davy will go to Williams College just like Dr. DiMarco.

Sometimes, Connie spends the ride from Davy's school to Dr. DiMarco's office, planning how she will seduce him. Maybe she will call him into one of the examining rooms on the pretense of something in a patient's file, and when he enters she will slowly unbutton the buttons on her uniform and take his hands and place them on her breasts. Or perhaps she should offer to cover for Bea who works on Tuesday nights when the office stays opened till eight. After all the patients were gone, Connie and Dr. DiMarco would be left alone in the office. It would be dark out, and just the two of them would be there with the hum of the fluorescent lights and the smell of ammonia and cough syrup.

So far, Connie has not executed any of her plans. Dr. DiMarco's wife Becky, Doris Day blonde and cute, calls several times a day just to say, *Love ya*. Every time Connie has to take one of Becky's calls, her chest fills with such jealousy that she can't breathe. How did Becky get so lucky? How did Becky get born into a family with a dentist father and a mother who bred golden retrievers? How did she get to go to Mt. Holyoke, an all girls college that is maybe even more beautiful than Williams? Connie hates Becky, hates her turned up nose and tanned cheeks and the tennis skirt she seems to have on every time she stops by the office.

One day Connie went so far as to call Dr. DiMarco into an examining room under false pretenses. She held a manila file in her hands. She unbuttoned her buttons one lower than usual.

Dr. DiMarco did not seem to notice the extra button.

Connie glanced down at the file to see whom it belonged to.

"The Pattersons," she said. "They're ninety days late with their bill."

He frowned. "Gee, that doesn't sound like Peggy, does it?"

Connie shook her head. Her throat had gone dry from being so close to Dr. DiMarco and she couldn't speak.

"Let me think. She brought Billy in for tonsillitis—"

"Whooping cough," Connie managed.

Dr. DiMarco nodded. "And Peggy had—"

"Gall stones. Or you thought she might have gallstones, but the X ray showed her gall bladder was clear," Connie said. She had so much to give him, so much information, so much of herself. Surely he must see that?

Dr. DiMarco smiled at her. "What would I do without you, Connie?" he said.

"Fall apart," she said, surprising herself with her boldness.

He laughed. "Probably," he said. "Just give Peggy a gentle reminder?"

"Peggy?" Connie said, confused.

Dr. DiMarco pointed a finger at her. "Aha!" he said. "What would you do without *me*?"

This was flirting, wasn't it? Connie thought. No one had ever really flirted with her before. But this must be it, the smiles, the joking, the double entendres.

"Fall apart," Connie said, shifting so that he could definitely see the white lace of her bra.

"I'm sure it was just an oversight," Dr. DiMarco said. "Thanks, Connie, for being so efficient."

Then he was gone. Just like that.

Connie felt her heart tumbling around beneath her ribs. She waited until she heard his deep voice greeting Pamela Sylvestri and her three kids, waited until she heard the door of that examining room close. Then she went and locked this door.

Alone in the room, with the colorful posters of the digestive system and respiratory system on the wall, Connie unbuttoned her uniform the rest of the way. She kicked off the white rubber-soled shoes and rolled down her girdle. Then she climbed up on the examining table, spread her legs, and closed her eyes, her own hands running up the warm length of her body, lightly pinching her nipples, imagining that it was Dr. DiMarco touching her, imagining him reaching his hands between her legs like she was doing to herself now, imagining he was whispering to her *What would I do without you, Connie?*

This was her shame. She was a sinner. Three days a week, in Dr. Di-Marco's office, she found herself doing this. In the bathroom. In an examining room. Once even in her car in the parking lot. Touching herself like this, so often, so desperately, was a sin. And wanting it to be Dr. DiMarco broke the tenth commandment: *Thou shalt not covet they neighbor's house, nor his wife, nor anything that is your neighbor's.* Worse, she would break the seventh commandment readily: *Thou shall not commit adultery.*

When she got home on the nights she worked, as she made pork chops with mashed potatoes and peas with pearl onions, and Davy practiced writing his letters, his careful A's over and over on the yellow papers with the wide blue dotted lines, and Vincent came up behind her whispering *Little V wants a date*, Connie thought about those stolen moments, that tug, that yearning that took over her body. She thought about Dr. DiMarco and how life with him would be, how different everything would be.

Dinner starts without Vincent. No one can find him.

"Really," Connie says, trying to hide her embarrassment, "let's eat. He'll catch up."

Her sister Anna, with her huge pregnant belly and her two-year-old son Nicky on her lap, heaps a pile of smelts onto her plate.

"Buon Appetito!" she says.

Nicky happily sucks on a smelt.

Mama Jo does not sit; she hovers. She frowns over each platter, sprinkling salt or squeezing lemon.

"Too rubbery," she announces over the octopus.

"Too much vinegar," she says over the eel.

Connie tries not to roll her eyes. This is her mother's way of getting compliments.

And everyone obliges her, saying at once, "No, it's perfect. All of it, perfect."

Everyone except Connie, who refuses to fall into the old habits. Bad enough she is here at this kitchen table, eating on these mismatched chipped plates instead of having slices of roast, medium rare, served on her creamy white china.

Vincent arrives just as Mama Jo starts to serve the spaghetti with anchovies. He sits down without apologizing and fills his plate high with smelts and eel and octopus and fried shrimp and baccala, then holds it aloft for Mama Jo to add the spaghetti with anchovies.

"Now I see how you keep your girlish figure," Pat says. His own belly is big enough to hang over his belt, and to quiver when he talks or takes a breath.

Vincent laughs and raises his jelly glass of wine. "Salute, my brother-in-law. To our girlish figures."

Mama Jo has left some spaghetti plain for the kids, but Cammie refuses it.

"I'll take it with the anchovies, Mama Jo," she says proudly.

Mama Jo beams, pinching the girl's cheeks. "Figlia mia," she says, and kisses the top of Cammie's ringleted head.

It seems they will never stop eating, Connie thinks, even though she touches almost nothing. The platters keep getting emptied and refilled. Vincent and Pat drink too much wine and grow sloppy and silly. The metallic taste of vomit fills Connie's mouth. When they get home, she will have Dr. DiMarco take a pregnancy test. No, she decides as quickly as she thinks this. She will go to Dr. Caprio. Somehow, the thought of Dr. DiMarco knowing she is pregnant embarrasses her.

Connie glances up at the clock.

"*Amahl and the Night Visitors*," she says, getting to her feet.

Standing so fast makes her dizzy and she clutches the edge of the table, the plastic her mother has placed over the polyester tablecloth decorated with fake looking poinsettias beneath it crinkling.

Angie stares into a small gold hand mirror, applying fresh dark magenta lipstick. "Amahl?" she repeats.

"The opera," Connie says. "It's going to be on television in a few minutes."

"Yeah," Pat says, "that's just what I want to do. Watch a friggin' opera."

"I've got your opera right here swinging," Rocky says.

Unexpectedly, tears fill Connie's eyes. She wants to go home. Now. Back to her small white Cape in Connecticut and her dreams of Dr. DiMarco falling in love with her. She wants to take Davy away from these people, who do not even seem to notice how special he is. But when she looks at her husband, it is clear he is too drunk to drive in the dark all the way to Connecticut. She is stuck.

Connie goes into the living room. Earlier that day, before she arrived, the family had put up a Christmas tree, its branches choking with cheap gold and red garland and too much tinsel. Her tree, standing perfectly centered in front of their picture window, has blue ornaments and blue lights that blink on and off, and a star on the top that changes colors, from white to yellow to green to blue to purple. Vincent hung blue lights in the hedges that border the house, and standing on the lawn, looking in, a person would think: *This is an orderly house. A beautiful, beautiful home.*

The opera is just beginning when Connie sits in her mother's worn easy chair, the powder blue upholstery fraying at the seams. She runs her hands over it, as if she can fix it.

Anna comes in too, but she is not interested in *Amahl and the Night Visitors.* She just needs to put her swollen feet up on the little footstool.

"He wants five kids," she says, almost boastful. "I am going to be pregnant for the next ten years."

But by this time, Connie is already too wrapped up in the story. The little boy, Amahl, is trying to convince his mother that there are three kings at their door. The mother keeps asking, *"What shall I do with this boy? What shall I do?"*

"Mother, Mother, Mother, come with me," the boy sings in the sweetest voice Connie has ever heard. *"I want to be sure you see what I see. …. . ."*

The boy's name is Chet Allen, and watching him Connie realizes that Davy could do this. Davy could be Amahl. He could be on television just like Chet Allen. She thinks of him in his kindergarten play back in October, how he came on stage in a floppy chef's hat and white apron, holding a tray of baked goods and singing *"Have you seen the muffin man?"* He had sung louder and more clearly than any of the other children. Why, no one could understand what Eleanor Patterson was singing. If she hadn't pointed up to a silver tin foil star, no one would have guessed she was croaking out "Twinkle, twinkle, little star."

Connie leans forward.

"*I was a shepherd,*" Amahl is singing, his voice pure and high, "*I had a warm goat who gave me warm sweet milk . . .*"

Others have come into the living room. The air is filling with the smells of perfume and cigars and sweat and wine. But Connie can only stare at Chet Allen.

"Cammie's going to do a little performance," Gloria says. "A little song and dance."

Davy climbs on Connie's lap and she holds him tight.

"See that boy on TV?" she whispers to Davy. "You can do that. You can be that boy."

Davy has his thumb in his mouth, sucking quietly. A habit she can't seem to break. Connie pushes the thumb from his mouth and holds it in her hand.

"Watch the boy," she says.

Vincent sits on the arm of the easy chair, holding a grease stained bag.

"For you," he says, offering it to Connie.

"What is it?"

He smiles crookedly and takes a white Chinese food container from the bag.

"Pork fried rice," he says. "From Ming Garden."

"But when—"

"I went and got it before dinner. I figured all that fried food might upset your stomach."

He is holding the container out to her, but Connie doesn't take it. On the television, Amahl's mother is agreeing to let him go with the three kings.

Mama Jo puts on the too-bright overhead light.

"Come on in, Cammie," she calls into the kitchen.

Cammie bursts in, dressed in a sea of sparkles. Her cheeks are rouged, her lashes thick with mascara, her lips reddened and shiny with lipstick. Even her tights sparkle as she tap dances to the center of the room. In her hands she holds a shiny red baton with white rubber tips. She holds it as if it weighs nothing at all, throwing it in the air easily and catching it without even looking.

"On the good ship Lollipop," Cammie sings in a squeaky loud voice, "it's a sweet trip to the candy shop . . ."

Her feet tap across the floor, the baton flies into the air, and is caught again and again.

Cammie points the baton right at Davy. ". . . and there you are, happy landings on a chocolate bar."

Davy is trying to pry his thumb from Connie's grip, but she holds on tight.

Chet Allen is singing. He is with the kings. He is following that star.

"Look," Connie whispers to her son. "Watch that boy."

Around her, her family is applauding. They are on their feet, surrounding Cammie, clapping and clapping until Connie thinks she cannot take it, not one more minute of it.

"Watch him, Davy," she says, her voice cracking as she presses her beautiful son close to her, holding on to him as tightly as she can. "Watch him."

ANYWHERE, PLEASE
Lee Martin

T he woman's in our backseat before I can say shoo. A skinny thing with too much eye makeup and a high forehead that shines in the glow from our Buick's dome light.

I've come around the front of the car and found the Mister talking to her, not flustered a bit. An old newspaper reporter, he's concentrating on getting the facts.

"Sweetbelle," he says when I touch him on the arm. He uses the pet name he's always had for me. "This young lady wants us to give her a ride." He says this in that calm, measured voice of his like this sort of thing happens every day—a strange woman in front of the Magic Wok on Christmas Eve, begging for our help. He's always been a gentleman, a soft-spoken man all his life, particularly now that he's become more feeble. He leans on his walking stick, the handle a carved head of a lion, its jaws open in a roar. The Mister is looking sporty in his charcoal corduroy trousers—an early Christmas gift from me— his chambray shirt with his monogram on the pocket, and his black baseball cap with the yellow letters that say, *Don't Tell Me What Kind of Day to Have.* He pokes his walking stick into the back seat and taps the woman on her bare knee. Her black skirt's too short, at least by my standards, and she doesn't have on any hose, so I can see the spider veins on her calves. She's not a young woman—I'd guess she's left fifty in the rearview—and it irks me that she's sitting in our car like she's entitled. "I told her we were just about to get a bite to eat," the Mister says.

The woman has her arms crossed over her stomach, and she's rocking back and forth. "The police are after me." She has a high, thin voice that makes her seem younger than she is. "I need to get out of here," she says, and I think,

Honey, why in the world would you tell us that?

It's Christmas Eve, and the Magic Wok is the only joint open tonight in this itty-bitty college town where the Mister and I have lived all the long time of our life together. Fifty-one years and counting, though lately we've had more than our fair share of mishaps and close calls, each of us at one time or another on the doorstep of the sweet hereafter. The Mister has a bum ticker on top of his other ailments. I'm diabetic, and back in the summer my blood sugar got too low in the middle of the night and next thing I knew I woke up in the hospital, the Mister sitting by my bed, waiting. "Glad to have you back," he said. "Didn't know I was gone," I told him.

I'm not crying over any of this. No need to call the wah-bulance. Just stating the fact. We're too damn old, the Mister and I. Time is short, and I won't squander another speck of it in the company of knuckleheads and ne'er-do-wells like this woman who's been so forward as to plant her bony behind on our backseat, tell us she's on the run from the law, and expect us to give her a lift.

"Where is it you need to go?" I ask her.

"I'll go wherever you want to take me."

"Why are the police after you?" It's the question someone has to ask, and I'm the gal to ask it.

She turns her narrow face to look me straight in the eye. All that makeup to try to give her plain face some pizzazz, to draw attention away from that high forehead. Maybe she should try bangs instead, but, of course, that's not my call to make. "Anywhere," she says. "Please?"

That's when I recognize her. "Lucy?" I say. "Lucy Keen?"

She ducks her head, gets all interested in her feet. She's not sure whether to own up to who she is, and for an instant I'm not sure whether to trust my eyes and my memory.

Then I hear the siren, and the woman swivels her head around to look out the back glass. Here we are at dusk. Out along Lincoln Street, exhaust rolls out of tailpipes. All down the length of the street, the traffic lights go from green to yellow to red. The air has that cold, wet feel that comes just before a snow, and outside the Magic Wok, I can smell the pleasures waiting inside, chief among them the lobster lo mein, and the snow crab, and, my favorite, the roast pork mei fun.

But here's this woman and the siren, and she lies down on the backseat, draws her knees up, and asks me to close the door.

"Please, Mrs. Schramm," she says, and I think, *Lucy Keen, lord-a-mercy, and on Christmas Eve.*

That's when the Mister says to me, "Why don't you go on in and eat, Sweetbelle?" He uses the tip of his walking stick to nudge the door closed. Not that it latches, but still it's enough to keep Lucy hidden. The dome light, on its time-delay, is now dark. To see her lying on the seat, you'd have to peer in through the car window. "You go on and enjoy yourself," the Mister says, "and I'll drive this young lady somewhere she'll feel safe."

Damn fool. He has these times when he just can't get the facts straight. He had to give up his driver's license a year ago. Macular degeneration. It's come to the point where I have to decipher the restaurant checks, count out money for him, read the newspaper to him, tell him the score from a football game on TV. Sometimes we go out driving in the country just before dusk, and I tell him what I see—a covey of quail lifting up from the corn stubble, a doe and a fawn coming out of the woods, a raft of geese overhead, dark against the sky as night begins to settle over Central Illinois. Sometimes he snaps at me. *I can see that,* he'll say. *I'm not all the way blind.* Even a soft-spoken man can turn surly once his health deserts him and he's no longer the man he always thought he was. Easy to lose his temper then. Easy to hold my feet to the fire. I'm not complaining, mind you. Would I want to be anywhere else? Well . . . I'm just saying sometimes it's hard.

Now he seems to have forgotten that he couldn't drive our Buick out of this lot without clipping another car, running over a curb, or—God forbid—smashing through the plate glass window of the Magic Wok where a string of paper lanterns—red and blue and yellow and orange and pink and green—make me feel like there's no place I'd rather be on Christmas Eve than there.

"You can't drive," I tell him.

He scrunches up his wrinkled brow, puzzled. "I can't?"

"Honey Bunny." Now I use the pet name I've always had for him. I touch him on his arm, and then I realize I've started out in a way that's too conde- scending, too full of pity. I let my voice go flat, kick it up a few notches to make sure he'll hear me. "Mister, you can't see to drive."

"Well, hell," he says, and there we are.

I can see the red lights of the police car coming out Lincoln past Old Main at the University, the original building on campus where, when the Mister and I were students, we all gathered each morning for assembly. A cas- tle with towers and battlements and turrets. White lights outline the top of the central tower, the one you can see from miles away as you come into town. They'll put Christmas lights on anything these days, even a building as historic and as stately as this. I wouldn't call myself a Scrooge—not exactly— but I swear if I ever see inflatable lawn ornaments around Old Main at Christmas time, I'm buying a pellet gun and getting to work.

Lucy sits up and opens the car door. "Please, Mrs. Schramm," she says again.

I say, "The police are coming all right. What's the story?"

The cold is creeping into my aching knees, and I'm tired of standing out here when there's a warm place to go and food to eat.

"It's my mother," Lucy says. "She called the cops."

"Your mother?" I can't keep the surprise and the disgust out of my voice. "Lord-a-mercy, I didn't know she was still alive."

Hetty Keen. A woman I don't care to ever see again.

"Lucy, what did you do to make your mother call the police?"

"Nothing, Mrs. Schramm. You've got to help me."

The police car is just about to turn into the lot. I can't say what compels me. Is it a basketful of sorry for this plain woman and her high forehead, this woman I knew when she was a girl? Or is it my desire to finally have my re- venge on her mother? To be honest, I'm stumped. I'm not sure exactly what it is—probably a little bit of all the above—that makes me overlook the fact that the police are coming for Lucy. I only know what I'm about to do, and it seems good and right like a choice already made. Nothing I can do to stop myself.

"Come on." I hook Lucy by the arm and tug. She comes out of the Buick, eyes wide with surprise. "Step, smart," I tell her, which was what I always told my fifth-graders when I was still teaching. "If you fail to plan, you plan to fail."

"Where we going?" the Mister asks.

"Going to eat," I say. "Going to have our Christmas Eve dinner."

The lights are dim inside the Magic Wok, and we take a booth in the back near the kitchen. Lucy slides in next to the wall, and I squeeze in beside her. The Mister sits across from us, tapping at the placemat and the chopsticks and the water glass with his trembling fingers. He's taken off his cap and laid it beside him on the bench seat, hooked his walking stick on the table's edge. He bows his bald head—only a few strands of hair laced across the top of it—and keeps touching first the placemat, then the chopsticks, then the water glass, always in that order, over and over, acquainting himself with things he can't fully see, making sure he knows what's what.

I don't know why I've chosen to plop down here beside Lucy. Maybe I'm afraid she'll take a notion to bolt, and I'm not ready for that to happen. Not by a long shot. She's not getting past a stocky gal like me, no matter that I may be on my last legs. I've got something to ponder, and I want her close by while I do it. I want to look at her face and remember when she was a girl and how her mother changed my life for the worse. I don't care if it happens to be Christmas Eve. Just another date on the calendar, if you ask me.

"Honey Bunny," I say to the Mister, "do you remember Hetty Keen?"

He moves a chopstick a smidge to the left until its point taps up against its mate. "Hetty," he says. "No, I can't say I recall that name."

I slip my arms from the sleeves of my parka and leave it around my shoulders. I tell the Mister to take off his Levi jacket. I start to tell Lucy to take off her coat, too, to get comfy because we're going to be a while. We're going to eat and eat, and maybe we'll end up saying the things that need to be said. Then I notice that Lucy isn't wearing a coat, a fact that somehow didn't register with me when we were outside, and I was surprised first by the fact that a woman was in our backseat and then with the knowledge of who that woman was.

"Had to leave in a hurry," Lucy says, taking note I suppose of the way I'm studying her. "No time to grab a coat. Had to skedaddle."

Now there's a word I like—skedaddle—and hearing Lucy say it makes me feel kindly toward her. Then the old story from the past comes hot behind my eyeballs, and I say, "Hetty Keen. Lucy, I'm not sure your mother ever liked me much."

"Why, Mrs. Schramm. Whatever makes you think that?"

She's genuinely puzzled, and it comes to me that the thing I've carried all these years—the moment I've done my best to give the heave-ho—has barely stirred the air around her, hasn't mattered a speck, and maybe it's the same with her mother. Maybe Hetty doesn't even recall the reason I have for wishing her ill.

"Just a feeling I've always had," I say, and then the police car drives past, its lights swirling and tossing a nice tint of red onto the Magic Wok's plate glass window. "How'd you get here?" I ask Lucy.

She slumps down on the bench seat until her high forehead is just above the tabletop. "Told you," she says. "I skedaddled."

It was another Christmas, thirty-two years ago, this time I've never been able to fully forget. The Mister and I lived on Seventh Street then, right across from Old Main, in a two-story clapboard house with a wraparound porch and gingerbread trim. He was City Editor at the *Times Courier*, and I taught at the Lincoln Land Elementary School. To make a dollar go further, we rented out rooms to students at the University. One of our borders was Hetty Keen.

We had a little girl of our own, Pattianne. A blond-haired girl with green eyes and a sweet smile. A miracle child who came to us after we'd given up hope of ever being a mommy and a daddy. She was our one and only, and we thought the sun rose and set on her. Now she lives away from us with a man we've never met. Lives in Washington state, about as far away from us as she can be. Lives in a yurt, for Pete's sake. I didn't even know what that was. Had to get on the computer and look it up. She'll call tomorrow, just like she does every Christmas. She'll be all bubbly—all *Merry Christmas, Mother!*—but it won't mean anything to me. I'll know she's just putting on. The last time I saw her was ten years ago just before she divorced her husband, a kind man who grew orchids, and left for Washington to be with the new man in her life, Burt—Burt, who lives in a yurt. "You won't always have me," I screamed at her during our last row over what in god's name possessed her to leave the life she had with her husband and set out for the Pacific Northwest. "This is my life," she screamed back. "You've never understood that, Mother. You've always wanted me to live yours. Well, now I'm making my own." Like that, we got shed of each other, and though we've had time now to return to a certain measure of civility, what we mainly do is ignore the fact that we're barely mother and daughter and haven't been for years.

Now here's Lucy Keen, come into my life again to call back the one moment I'd change if I could, the day—I'm firmly convinced of this—when everything started to go wrong between Pattianne and me.

"Lucy and Hetty boarded with us," I tell the Mister. "On Seventh Street. Remember?"

"We had a house on Seventh Street," he says.

"Yes, we did." I want to go on. I want to tell him everything I remember. The college kids walking past, book bags slung over their shoulders. Pattianne and Lucy in the porch swing, leafing through *Tiger Beat* magazines and squabbling over who was cuter, Scott Baio or Shaun Cassidy. The Mister coming home from the paper and standing in the foyer, arms open wide, saying, "Where's my girl? Where's my Patty Cake girl?" He refused to acknowledge that she wasn't a little girl anymore, was thirteen in fact. Like me, I'm sure he remembered the sweet smell of her after her bath when she was younger and came to kiss us each good night. The first sound of her feet on the stairs each morning. All this and more. Everything about being a family. "We were happy in that house," I say to the Mister. "At least for a while."

Hetty Keen didn't have a husband. He was a soldier who died in Vietnam. She came to the University to get a degree in journalism, so naturally she and the Mister hit it off right away. They had common ground. Some Friday evenings, when he had to cover more than one high school basketball game, he'd send her to a gym—maybe in Mattoon, Arcola, Neoga—and ask her to keep a scorebook and some notes and then bring it all back to him so he could write the report. I'd go to another gym and do the same thing. Sometimes I took the girls with me, and sometimes Hetty took them with her. They drank Cokes and ate popcorn and watched the cheerleaders, dreaming about the day, fast coming, when they'd be in high school. Not fast enough to suit them, though. Like all girls that age, they had no patience with time and little tolerance for grownups. Still, around the dining room table at the end of those Friday nights, they'd have hot chocolate and cookies and gab with Hetty and me while the Mister brought out his portable Smith-Corona and typed up his stories about those basketball games. Just like that we formed a little family in that house on Seventh Street.

One night, when Hetty and I were clearing off the table, carrying the hot chocolate mugs and the saucers speckled with cookie crumbs into the kitchen, I turned back from the sink and noticed her lingering in the archway that led to the dining room, just standing there, watching the Mister as he reached for one of the non-filter Camels he smoked in those days. His shirt collar was open, the knot of his skinny black tie was loose, and the curl of his brown hair tumbled onto his forehead in a way that made him look dashing and, yes, maybe even a little dangerous. He reached for that Camel, shaking it up from the pack with that bounce he always gave it with the flick of his wrist, intending to catch the cigarette with his lips. It was a little trick he had, one he surely learned when he took up smoking in WWII, a little flair that I'm sure served him well at the newspaper office when the boys were being boys.

On this night, though, he botched it. The cigarette came out of the pack with too much force and flew up above his head. He tilted his head back to catch that Camel, and that's when I noticed that Hetty was tilting her head back, too, that her lips were parted. I even saw her lift up on her toes. She was wearing a denim skirt and her calf muscles tightened.

Then the Camel came twirling down, and the Mister caught it in his lips. Hetty got down off her tiptoes, and I heard her sigh. She turned, then, and saw me watching her. She glanced down at her hands, still holding a stack of saucers, and I knew that she harbored something in her heart for the Mister, something I could have been jealous of if I'd taken the notion. After all, she was a pretty woman, more than a few years younger than the Mister and me, a tiny little thing with dainty features and skin that nary a wrinkle had touched. She had this long, brown hair that she parted in the middle and let hang over her shoulders and a perfume she wore that smelled musky. Once, I saw the Mister picking up a winter scarf she'd left draped over the sofa arm. He brought it up close to his face, just for an instant, just long enough to tell me that he was smelling that perfume, that he was more than a little enchanted with Miss Hetty Keen.

I've had years and years to think on what the story was between the two of them, and for the most part I've convinced myself it was nothing more than a little crush that never got out of hand. Still, truth be told, I have this nagging doubt, one I do my best to put away from me.

It was the Christmas season on that night I'm recalling. Soon the University would let out for its holiday break. I had a tree up in the living room decorated with the snowflakes I tatted from lace, the glass ornaments that had belonged to my mother, the tinsel, and the lights. The Mister had strung lights around our porch, and I liked to watch the college kids coming past and stopping a bit to take it all in, thinking, I'm sure, about how soon they'd be going to their homes where their families were waiting. I liked being able to give them that good homesick feeling, that longing for the company of the people who loved them best. There was a time, you see, when I adored Christmas, loved everything about it.

So when I saw the way Hetty looked at my Mister, I made a choice to just let it go. I said to her, "Hetty, you don't have to do that." I was talking about the saucers in her hands. "I can take care of cleaning up."

"I want to," she said, and still she couldn't look at me. "I want to help."

The Mister was lighting his Camel, no thought in his head, I'm sure, of what had just gone on.

We went to bed that night, and I lay awake a long time, thinking about how flimsy our hold was on everything that we thought we owned. The Mister slept beside me. That was so long ago, but it seems like only yesterday. I didn't know anything about the days ahead, though I convinced myself I did. Didn't know that eventually the Mister would have bypass surgery, start to lose his eyesight, and then his memory. Didn't know I'd slip into that diabetic coma that summer night and nearly die. Didn't know Pattianne would marry two different men, never give me a grandchild, move so far away I barely felt I could find her. Sure as heck didn't know that Lucy Keen would come back into our lives—Lucy and Hetty. Here we are—the Mister and I—almost at the end of things, and now I have to go back and live it all again. The Mister, though, is blessed. He can't recall it, can barely conjure up that house on Seventh Street and what happened in it the morning after I saw Hetty looking at him that way. It was such a small thing—what I still have in me to tell—but in the end, it was everything.

"Do you remember?" I say to Lucy, but just then the door to the Magic Wok opens, and a police officer steps inside.

We're the only ones in the joint except for the owners, Mr. and Mrs. Moy, who are sitting at a table in the corner, snapping green beans. The beans are spread out on a newspaper on the table, along with two blue bowls, and Mrs. Moy has a bunch of beans on her lap in the pouch of her white apron. She's a round-faced woman who wears rectangular glasses. The glasses have red frames—*red*, for mercy sakes—nothing I'd ever have the nerve to try. Mr. Moy is slightly built with stooped shoulders and scraggly gray chin whiskers. He has a paper hat on his head, the kind soda jerks used to wear, and someone has pinned a spring of mistletoe to the peak. The Moys have been talking quietly in Chinese while they wait for us to place our order. No buffet tonight. "Not enough customers," Mrs. Moy explained when we came in. "Just menu. You order menu."

Now the Moys lift their faces to see who's come in the door, and the dim lights in the dining room make Mrs. Moy's glasses glisten. The little silver ribbon tied to the mistletoe on Mr. Moy's hat sparkles.

"You want eat?" Mrs. Moy is on her feet, unfurling her apron so the green beans she's been holding fall into the bunch on the table. She waves her hand at the police officer, beckoning him toward her. "Sit, sit," she says. "You eat."

I can feel Lucy's arm trembling against mine.

The police officer is bareheaded, a tall man on the young side. Even from where we're sitting, I can smell the cold air that he brings into the restaurant. His blue jacket has a black fur collar. He has a neatly trimmed moustache the same color. He strokes it with his fingers and explains to Mrs. Moy that he's not there as a customer.

"I'm on duty," he says. "I'm looking for someone."

Like I've said, the lighting in the Magic Wok is what I guess you'd call "subdued," and we're so far away from the front door, sitting in a high-backed booth mind you, for an instant I convince myself that the officer won't spot us.

Then Lucy says in a whisper. "Oh, please. Please. Oh, please. Oh, please."

I don't quite know what to feel at that moment. Part of me hears her fear and trembles with her, and I remember the way I thought I might come apart that night all those years ago when I caught Hetty making goo-goo eyes at the Mister. Another part of me travels back to what happened that next morning when what I felt had nothing to do with mercy at all.

I slept in that morning, and by the time I came downstairs, Hetty had made pancakes for the girls. They were sitting at the dining room table, the girls beside each other on one side and Hetty across from them, smoking a cigarette. The Mister's Smith-Corona was at the head of the table where he'd left it the night before. He'd gotten up early and gone downtown to the newspaper office.

The girls were singing along with a record that was playing on the hi-fi in the living room. They'd turned the volume up so they could hear it where they sat, and it was that noise, actually, that had jolted me from sleep and brought me down the stairway where I stood in my robe and slippers, my hand resting on the newel post, taking in the sight of the girls at the table with Hetty and the Mister still staking his claim at the head with that Smith-Corona, and for just an instant my breath caught as I recalled the way Hetty watched him the night before, and I felt like I was looking at how their life together might have been. He would have been singing along with that song, too, because he was like that, easygoing and indulgent with Pattianne. I was the strict one, the parent who always told her no, told her to conduct herself like a young lady, to refrain from vulgar behavior, to remember that I expected from her the same sort of sterling comportment I demanded of my pupils. "Ugly is as ugly does," I always said. Ever since Hetty and Lucy moved in and the girls became best friends, Pattianne had taken to rolling her eyes at me and saying, "Oh, Mother."

The song on the hi-fi was "Ring My Bell," a record that Pattianne had been begging for me to get her for Christmas. I told her I would most certainly do no such thing because that song wasn't proper for a girl her age. When the woman singing it invited her man to ring her bell, I think it was pretty clear what she was really talking about, and that was the sort of junk I didn't want my thirteen-year-old daughter to have in her head.

Now, clearly, Hetty had bought it for Lucy, and there was Pattianne singing at the top of her lungs, pretending that her fork was a microphone, and Hetty was laughing, and it would have all been just fine on a Saturday morning close to Christmas when the sun was shining on the snow outside if not for the fact that I was still smarting from the night before.

I told myself to just let it go. Then Hetty took a last drag on her cigarette and pressed the stub out in the crystal ashtray the Mister had left on the table. I noticed then that Hetty wasn't smoking the long Virginia Slims she usually smoked. No, she'd smoked one of the Mister's Camels instead, and I was left to wonder how she'd gotten one from him before he left the house. Had he offered, or had she been bold and asked? Had he lit it for her from his silver Zippo? Had she leaned close to him, put her hand on his as she held the Camel to the flame? My mind ran wild in ways I didn't need it to, and I couldn't tolerate the sound of that stupid song any longer.

When I jerked the tone arm off the record, leaving a scratch in the vinyl, I'm sure, I barely knew I was in my own house. It was like I'd gone off somewhere I hadn't planned to be, but there it was, this place, and I didn't know how to get back to where I'd been just seconds before.

It can happen that fast, your life.

Pattianne screamed. "Mother," she said, embarrassed in front of Hetty and Lucy.

I turned to face them. I said, "Pattianne, you're not to listen to such trash. Haven't I told you?"

Snowmelt was dripping from the porch roof. I could hear it hitting the railing. The sun was coming through the big bow window in the living room, splintering through the Christmas tree and dappling the oak floor. I heard a girl's bright voice outside, one of the college girls walking past, talking with her friends—"Can you believe it? It's almost Christmas!"

Hetty and the girls sat at the table looking at me like I was a lunatic stranger who'd wandered into their home.

Pattianne bowed her head, but I could see that her lip was quivering the way it did just before she burst into tears. I should have said something to make things all right—should have made a joke, should have said I was sorry. Not a day goes by that I don't think about it, think how I was about to call my daughter by her name, make my voice go soft, tell her she should just forget her dizzy old mom who'd obviously gotten up on the wrong side of the bed.

But just then Hetty said, "Well, now really, Mabel." She'd never called me by my first name before and to hear it gave me a shock. "I hardly think it'll hurt her to listen to that song."

Pattianne lifted her face, and I saw that her lips were now pressed together and not quivering at all. She narrowed her eyes, and as much as I wanted to believe that she was squinting at me because of the sun, I knew that wasn't true. I knew she was looking at me with heat.

"My God, Mother," she said in a tone of voice she'd never used with me. "Honestly," she said, and I thought, *There she goes, years and years ahead of me.* All because of what started the night before and had nothing to do with her. Only now it did. Now it was about what I'd done with that record and what Hetty had said. "You heard Hetty," Pattianne said. "It won't hurt me."

Then she got up from the table and walked with slow, deliberate steps to the hi-fi, where she put the tone arm back on the record, nudged it over the scratch I'd left, until the house again was filled with that woman telling her man he could ring her bell.

Pattianne didn't even look at me. She went back to the table and she started singing. I can still hear her voice, a little throaty, a little angry, and then Lucy joined in, and Hetty gave me a smug look, and for the time being that was that.

But not really. After that, Pattianne was never mine again, and I'm convinced Hetty knew it. She and Lucy stayed through the holidays, and then just after New Year's they moved into an apartment downtown above the newspaper office. The Mister came come home from work sometimes and said he'd seen Hetty, and I told him to keep it to himself. I wasn't interested.

Just like that, we all made the turn toward the rest of our lives.

The police officer comes to our table. He's so close I can smell the polish on his shoes and the pine-scented aftershave he's wearing. He puts his hands on the table's edge and leans in toward us. The Mister's fingers make a little move toward the officer's as if he's cataloging that hand along with the placemat, the chopsticks, the water glass. Then the Mister stops. He puts his hands in his lap and hunches his shoulders forward like a boy at his desk, eager to behave.

"I'm looking for a woman," the officer says. He studies Lucy. "A woman about your age, ma'am."

My voice surprises me. "Are you looking for Lucy Keen?"

"Yes ma'am." The officer takes his hands from the table and stands up straight. He looks at me a good while. "How did you know that?"

"She was in our car out there not but a few minutes ago." I don't know why I'm protecting her. I'm not even sure why she's on the run. Surely, it's not just nothing like she told me. What if she killed her mother? What if it was as bad as that? "She wanted us to give her a ride," I tell the police officer. "When I said I couldn't do that, she skedaddled."

"Took off, did she?" the officer says.

I nod. "Yes, sir. Lickety-split."

He leans in even closer. The leather of his gun holster creaks. "She might be in trouble." He stares directly at Lucy, who now, like the Mister, is very interested in her placemat and chopsticks and water glass. "She *will* be in trouble if what her mama claims turns out to be true."

Maybe it's the old newshound that stirs inside the Mister. "What's she done?" he asks. "That girl. What's the report?"

"It's a sad story," the officer says. "Not something you'd want to hear on Christmas Eve. Not something you'd want to hear ever."

"Nothing new about sad stories," I say. "Read the paper. They're everywhere."

I guess my heart has gone hard. Everything about the way things turned out between Pattianne and me—all that distance between us—has closed me off to all manner of sad tales. They're nothing special. Dime a dozen. None more boo-hoo than the rest—except to the people living inside them.

"Wait until you hear this one," the officer says, and then he tells it.

Seems that Hetty's not long for this life. "Terminal," the officer says. "A cancer in her lung."

So her daughter—oh, Lucy, I know my heart should break for you—has been living with her, making sure she ate something, helping her with her "necessaries." That's the word the officer uses, and for the first time he looks away from us, embarrassed by this mention of all things private. Then he turns back and stares right at me, as if he wants my approval.

"It's not every daughter who'd do that much for her mama," he says.

I look him straight in the eye, don't give him a glimpse of how much it hurts me to know if and when that time comes for me, I won't expect to see Pattianne as much as darkening my door.

"What's that old saying?" I ask. "A daughter's a daughter all her life?"

The officer nods. "Yes, ma'am," he says, and then he goes on with his story. It's the pain pills, he says, the ones the doctor prescribed for Hetty. Turns out—or so Hetty claims—she isn't always getting them when she's supposed to. Has a suspicion that Lucy's been sneaking them off and selling them. Oxycodone. As much as fifteen dollars for a single pill. "Imagine if that's true." Now the officer stares at Lucy. "And her mama lying there hurting." He finishes his story. "Finally, she got hold of a telephone and called 911. That's when the daughter . . . what was it you said earlier, ma'am? . . . oh, yeah, that's when she skedaddled. "

"Now you're looking for her," says the Mister.

"I found her car just a block up Lincoln." The officer points toward the paper lanterns in the front window, out into the dark where I can see the taillights of cars heading into town. Folks going to Christmas Eve services at their churches or to relatives' homes to exchange gifts. Lord love them. I mean it. I don't bear them any grudge. "Busted fan belt," the officer says. "She took out on foot. Folks saw her come into the parking lot here. And now you tell me she took off. Usually folks don't run unless they've got something to hide."

It's so quiet inside the Magic Wok. The Moys have stopped talking so they can eavesdrop on our conversation.

I can tell the officer is suspicious of my story, and now that I've heard about Hetty's sickness and how Lucy may have been treating her—probably *has* been treating her; like the officer said, why else would Lucy be on the run?—I'm tempted to go back and change it. I guess it shouldn't matter what I've always thought of Hetty and what she said all those years ago about that record doing Pattianne no harm. Or how I was convinced that Hetty had eyes for the Mister. We're all old now. That's what I know for sure. We're too damned old and one by one we'll leave this world, and the children will stay behind—Pattianne and Lucy—to continue their own journey to the sweet by and by. Good luck to them. That's all I can say. Nothing I can do to help them, any more than they've helped me.

"I'm afraid I'm going to have to ask to see some identification," the officer says to Lucy.

She's sitting up straight now, a puzzled look on her face.

The Mister says, "Hetty Keen," as if suddenly he remembers everything.

Lucy says, "I've left my purse back at the house." She reaches over and puts her hand on mine. She squeezes with her fingers so hard it hurts. "Didn't I, Mom?"

That word comes near to breaking me.

"Ma'am, is this your daughter?" the officer asks me.

I can hear the quiet murmur of a radio somewhere in the kitchen, the faint sound of a Christmas carol. I strain to listen, imagining it's "Silent Night," but I'm not really sure. I know I'm in the Magic Wok, but really I'm not. I'm in that house on Seventh Street, a woman who loves her husband and daughter. A woman who loves her life. Then she jerks the tone arm off that record, and she wants to disappear into the silence that follows.

If Hetty hadn't said what she did, maybe the rest of my life would have been different. Maybe Pattianne and I would have been as close as close can be. Maybe I wouldn't be in the Magic Wok on Christmas Eve, overwhelmed by the feel of Lucy's hand on mine, about to say yes, yes she is. She's my girl.

And once it's said, the officer gives us all one more good, long look, trying to decide, I can tell, whether to buy what I'm selling. Then he takes a step back from the table.

"You folks have a good holiday," he says, and we wish him the same.

I know what I'm doing. Where will Lucy go now but where I'm about to send her? Where will she go but back to her mother, a woman in need and I with nothing to offer. Nothing I can manage anyway on this cold night before Christmas. No help at all.

Mrs. Moy comes to take our orders. "You ready?"

Lucy and the Mister don't say a word. I pick up my menu, my fingers trembling. So hungry now, so starved.

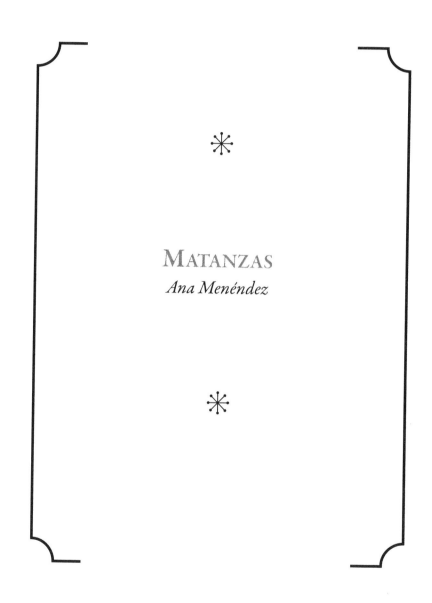

MATANZAS

Ana Menéndez

That year the men decided to get a live pig. It was our fifth year in Miami, our fourth Christmas Eve, and the year my brother turned thirteen, becoming a man.

The first Christmas-in-exile, we'd had chicken. The second, pork chops. It wasn't until the third year that the family had managed a whole pig. But it was a shared holiday with the Colón family, who had bought theirs already slaughtered. My father complained the whole time as the pig lay roasting in its hole in the ground. It wasn't a proper Christmas Eve without the slaughter. And he didn't come to this country to turn his back on the correct way of doing things. The following year, he promised, it would be a live pig and my brother would participate in its preparation.

We were sharing a rambling, charmingly crumbling house in Shenandoah with my mother's mother, her brother and his wife and three teenaged boys. I was the youngest, and the only girl, though my isolation never occurred to me until I was older. Back then, I still preferred the world of men.

It was a large house, which made us feel rich, even though ten people shared it. Best of all, for my father, it came with a backyard already overgrown with fruit trees: a lemon tree, a sour orange tree, two orange trees and a mango tree that began giving fruit our second summer. In a corner of the large yard, my mother kept a few chickens. Summer nights, with the windows open, the house filled with the smell of gently rotting fruit and chicken shit, and you could almost imagine we were back on the farm in Matanzas.

The men brought the pig home in a borrowed pickup truck three weeks before Christmas. I was upstairs, reading in my small room, the windows open to the season's first cold front. It had been a quiet afternoon. And then, a flurry of noise. The men were shouting, as usual. But the high-trilled scream, I later learned, came from the pig, who knew it was going to die.

Today, I buy my pork boneless. It comes already sliced and wrapped in plastic and its diminished state has nothing to do with the living animal, which I suppose is the point of all that elaborate packaging.

A live pig bristles with power and will. It is neither meek nor cuddly nor given to the performance of humiliating tricks. A pig does not seek to please, not with its looks, nor with its odor and certainly not with its personality, which falls far short of the ideal championed by the children's books.

The pig the men brought home did not ask to be loved and I complied. I didn't give it a name and I didn't give it food. My poor brother, ever the victim of my father's quest to make a man out of him, had to rise every morning at five to feed it acorns and corn mush and then go out again in the evening to slop in whatever leftovers we had from dinner.

I avoided the animal. If I caught a glimpse of it fattening in our back yard-backyard, it was inadvertent and I always quickly looked away. The pig didn't so much disgust me as scare me. But though I skirted it during the day, I could not help hearing it at night through the open windows. Can I call it a voice? Disembodied there in the dark, it seemed to speak to me alone, and I thought I recognized something in its discordant wailing. The lonely grunts of early evening always gave way, by dawn, to cries that vibrated with a memory of wilderness.

The morning of the twenty-third, the men rose early. I was not allowed to see the killing. My father ordered me to the kitchen, where the black beans hissed on the stove. I sat at the table, sulking, while the women gossiped. I hated their weakness. It was only many years later, after I had given birth to a girl of my own, that I understood that what I had mistaken for passivity was but a kind of indulgence, a concession to the vanity of men.

Blind to the slaughter that morning, I followed it with my ears. High strangled screams. Ancient cries that seemed to swell out of the ground. A desperate trampling, the low moans of elemental fear. Some time ago, when I told my father that I had heard the doomed pig cry out at the moment of his death, he laughed and said my imagination had served me well in my line of work. He has chosen to forget.

In the afternoon, the men filed back into the house. They had washed with the garden hose, but the smell of blood hung on them, persisted for days. My brother did not look me in the eye. The men were jovial and after their showers, they sat out on the porch to drink beer. But my brother stayed in his room, alone.

After dinner, the slaughtered pig, smelling of singed hair, was brought inside. This silent beast was not the same animal who that morning had bargained so viciously for its life. The men had conquered and subdued him—hollowed him out, scooped up heart and liver and entrails, exposing the giant cavity of his chest. They lay him, head intact, but body splayed open at the ribs, on the kitchen table. He glistened with marinade. The only reminder of what he used to be were his jelly-like eyes, open and unblinking beneath the ruined chest.

That night, everyone went to bed early. The following day was Christmas Eve and the roasting would start after breakfast. I lay in my room in the dark, unable to sleep. I had the windows open, though it had grown uncomfortably cold now. The night seemed strange, electric. And then I realized it was quiet. A dead quiet for the first time in weeks, the only sound that of distant crickets and the occasional rustle of a roosting hen. I had lain awake for an hour, listening to this new silence, when I heard the stairs below me creak. It took a few moments for my heart to calm. After I started breathing normally again, I got out of bed and went down. My brother stood at the threshold to the kitchen, looking in at the animal who lay still and cold in the quiet dark.

I stood behind him for a long while, thinking he hadn't heard me. But then, without turning around, my brother whispered my name. I came up next to him and we both stood looking into the kitchen, the great shadow on the table.

"Dare you to touch his eye," my brother said.

"No way."

"I'd do it," he said.

But my brother didn't move. Both of us just stood there, barefoot on the cold tile, shivering.

SHUT UP, HEART
Les Standiford

——*For Zander*

L et's say you're a writer. And that you have just finished a book about a couple whose son was kidnapped and murdered back in 1981. Your story is not so much about the couple, though, as it is about the cop who spent almost thirty years trying to prove who did it. Because he's the kind of detective who won't take "No" for an answer, this cop managed to accomplish what many other cops—the FBI and the Florida Department of Law Enforcement included—could not, and that's one of the main reasons you wanted to write the book, to show that there are people living outside the pages of novels for whom there is no such thing as "impossible."

When the police department and the state's attorney in whose jurisdiction the crime had been committed called a news conference to announce that the killer had finally been identified, it was well along into December. After the announcement had been made and the networks were packing their cameras, the detective's wife found herself walking alongside the couple on the way out of the building. "I hope you have a Merry Christmas," she found herself saying.

The woman who lost her son so many years before stopped, an odd look on her face. "Thank you," she said. She took her husband's arm. "This *will* be a Merry Christmas, the first one we've had in a long time."

This is a conversation that took place in 2008. And now it is more than a year later, Christmas Eve of 2009, to be exact, and the book is finished, and once again, everyone is hoping for the best.

If you are the writer in question, you are a big holiday person, maybe because you were born in the minutes leading up to Halloween and your mother always threw your party on that day, possibly to save on decorations, who can say? In any case, your enthusiasm for holidays did not stop there. Thanksgiving and Easter, Fourth of July, President's Day, St. Patrick's Day, Memorial Day, Veteran's Day, New Year's and Christmas. Especially Christmas. The world stopped, you ate different, sometimes you dressed strangely too.

The writer had a conversation with a Jewish guy about it once. He said, "If you like holidays, you should have been a Jew."

All this about holidays is, of course, subtext or backstory, or call it what you will. That is fine, because this is a story, and besides, one of the main characters is a writer, who has, the way it worked out, actually married a Jew. Hardly a week goes by that there is not something to celebrate.

But back to our Christmas Eve. The night that is the most hopeful of them all. Christmas itself might not be so wonderful, but the night before is all about possibility. No matter what the circumstances, on Christmas Eve you can always hope.

What the writer is hoping for on the Christmas Eve at hand is some good news about his own son, his youngest, eighteen, and away at college for his freshman year. Ordinarily—if there really is such a thing as ordinarily—his son would have been sitting around the table with the rest of the family, eating through the menu (always something new, always printed in fancy restaurant font and tied up like a scroll). But there has been something of a family blowup and the son has driven back to his apartment in the town in the northern part of the state where his college is located.

How forlorn is a college town in the middle of winter break? the writer thinks as he picks at his dinner. Though his son assured him in a phone call of a few days before that it wasn't so bad. Since most of the students had left the town, he'd landed a plum job delivering take-out orders for a popular restaurant, his son explained. He'd make plenty in tips.

Still, to the writer, it sounds like a lonely holiday season. But his son is a stubborn sort. What is to be done?

The call comes after the appetizers and the first round of drinks. The person on the other end of the line identifies herself as a police officer and asks if the writer knows where his son is. The writer is puzzled, but he says that he believes that his son is in the town where the call is coming from.

The officer explains that she is outside his son's apartment in that town and that his son's car is in its parking place but that no one is responding at the door. When the writer asks why the officer has gone to his son's apartment in the first place, she says that someone has called the department expressing concern that his son has not been answering phone calls.

This is the point at which it occurs to the writer: of them all, which is the perfect night for things to fly terribly off the rails?

The officer has promised to call again once the building manager can be located. Since this is a story, it is required that this person—who carries the only master key in his pocket—be sharing a Christmas Eve dinner with family in a place that is some distance away.

And it is also required that the officer does not call back. It is in fact an hour or more later, and only when the writer thinks to check the Caller I.D. left behind on his own phone and places the return call himself that everything is revealed.

Were the story more highly plotted, perhaps the police officer would have had her phone blocked to incoming calls, or she would have checked the number of the caller and simply chosen not to answer, thus heightening the tension. But she did pick up the call, and though she would not respond when the writer asked, "Are you in my son's apartment?" all was clear enough.

The officer told the writer that she could not answer his questions at that moment, but insisted that someone would call him back soon, and, as she spoke, the writer heard the droning of a television in the background, and the hubbub of several other voices not involved in television drama, and the writer knew.

Once a story begins, it rarely ever stops.

This being the type of story that it is, the writer next calls the detective with whom he has worked on the book that recounts the details of the long investigation. The writer knows that though the detective has retired, he keeps up his various connections and that if anyone can pry an answer from a police officer in a distant town, this detective can.

There is a long-standing set of television commercials featuring a mechanical rabbit beating a drum and powered by a set of batteries that simply will not die. If the story were of a different nature, the writer would liken the detective to that advertiser's dream.

It is late, but still short of midnight on Hopeful Eve when the car enters the drive of the writer's home, and though he is the first out the door, the rest of the family is there to see it too.

The writing of the book about the investigation has gone on for the better part of a year, and everyone knows the detective by now, and the familiar shape of his car, and the cadence of his unhurried stride. He is coming quietly up the driveway, his feet crackling on the gravel, and, following behind, there are two young officers from the suburb where the writer lives, their caps tucked under their arms.

"The news is not good," the detective begins, and in some ways, that is how the story ends.

Writing is nothing without its convergences, however. Before the book about the dedicated cop who gave a family some sense of justice, the writer had written one about the ultimate holiday itself, the true story of a down-trodden, dispirited Dickens, who gave it one last shot with what he called a "ghost story about Christmas." Christmas was a second-tier holiday at the time, and Dickens was on his way to joining the ranks of the has-beens himself. But the story struck a chord, as they say, and everything changed, for Dickens and his beloved holiday.

Planted in the mouth of one of Dickens's characters is a sentiment of the author's describing Christmas as "the only time . . . in the long calendar of the year, when men and women seem by one consent to open their shut-up hearts freely."

But it is a dangerous business, opening a shut-up heart.

Some significant time following the detective's visit, the writer was able to revisit the book they had worked on together. Fearful that he might have taken the smallest thing for granted in the record of a family's loss, the writer pored over each scene, striking out this ill-conceived phrase, crossing out that.

Towards the end of the account the writer re-read the scene containing the chance exchange between a detective's wife and the mother of a murdered boy. *"It* will *be a Merry Christmas,"* the mother had said.

The writer worried that it seemed improbable, no matter how true. How do you manage to open a shut-up heart, after all those years of suffering? But still, that is what she said. That is exactly what she said.

CONTRIBUTORS' NOTES

DIANA ABU-JABER's newest novel is *Birds Of Paradise*. Her novel, *Origin*, was named one of the best books of the year by the *LA Times* and the *Washington Post*. Her novel, *Crescent*, won the PEN Award for Literary fiction. Her first novel, *Arabian Jazz*, won the Oregon Book award. *The Language of Baklava*, her memoir, won the Northwest Booksellers' Award. She teaches at Portland State University and divides her time between Portland and Miami.

PRESTON ALLEN is a recipient of a Florida Individual Artist Fellowship and a winner of the Sonja H. Stone Prize in Fiction for his story collection *Churchboys and Other Sinners*. His work has been anthologized in *Las Vegas Noir*, *Miami Noir*, *Brown Sugar*, and many literary journals, including the *Seattle Review*, *Crab Orchard Review*, *Gulf Stream*, and *Black Renaissance Noire*. His novels *All or Nothing* and *Jesus Boy* received rave reviews in the *New York Times*; *O, the Oprah Magazine*; *Kirkus*; *Library Journal*; *Feminist Review*; and *Florida Book Review*.

STEVE ALMOND is the author the story collections *My Life in Heavy Metal*, *The Evil B.B. Chow*, and *God Bless America*, the novel *Which Brings Me to You* (with Julianna Baggott); and the non-fiction books *Candyfreak*, *(Not That You Asked)*, and *Rock and Roll Will Save Your Life*.

LYNNE BARRETT's third collection of short stories, *Magpies*, is just out from Carnegie Mellon University Press. Her work has appeared in *Delta Blues*, *A Dixie Christmas*, *Miami Noir*, *One Year to a Writing Life*, *Ellery Queen's Mystery Magazine*, *Night Train*, *The Southern Women's Review*, and many other anthologies and journals. She co-edited *Birth: A Literary Companion* and *The James M. Cain Cookbook*. She lives in Miami and edits *The Florida Book Review*.

TRICIA BAUER's new book, *Father Flashes*, won Fiction Collective 2's Catherine Doctorow Prize for Innovative Fiction and was published in 2011 by the University of Alabama Press. Tricia has published four other books of literary fiction. She works in educational publishing in Manhattan and lives in Connecticut with her family.

COLIN CHANNER is a fiction writer, occasional essayist and failed reggae musician. Although he's taken one fiction writing class in his life, he's taught lots of them at pretty good places, including Wellesley College, where he was the 2008-2011 Susan and Donald Newhouse Professor in Creative Writing. He was born in Jamaica, which is obvious once you speak to him. He's lived in America for most of this life.

Author of the novels *Finn* and *Kings of the Earth*, JON CLINCH has been an English teacher, a metalworker, a folksinger, an illustrator, a typeface designer, a housepainter, a copywriter, and an advertising executive. He and his wife live in the Green Mountains of Vermont.

JOHN DUFRESNE is the author of four novels, most recently *Requiem, Mass.,* two collections of stories, and two books on writing fiction. He teaches at Florida International University and lives in Dania Beach, Florida.

ED FALCO's latest novel is *The Family Corleone*, developed from pages extracted from screenplays by Mario Puzo for *The Godfather III* and *IV* (unproduced), due out in June 2012. His previous books include the novels *Saint John of the Five Boroughs* and *Wolf Point* and the short story collections *Acid* and *Sabbath Night in the Church of the Piranha: New and Selected Stories.* In 2008 he was awarded a fellowship in fiction from The National Endowment for the Arts and the Robert Penn Warren Prize in Poetry from *The Southern Review.* He lives in Blacksburg, Virginia, where directs the MFA Program in Creative Writing at Virginia Tech.

ROBERT GOOLRICK is the author of the critically acclaimed memoir, *The End of the World As We Know It.* His first novel, *A Reliable Wife*, was a

#1 New York Times bestseller, and winner of both the NAIBA and Book of the Month Club First Fiction Award. He lives in White Stone, Virginia.

BEN GREENMAN is an editor at the *New Yorker* and the author of several acclaimed books of fiction, including *Superbad, Please Step Back*, and *What He's Poised To Do*. His most recent book is *Celebrity Chekhov*. He lives in Brooklyn.

The taciturn JAMES W. HALL is the author of seventeen novels, the most recent of which is *Dead Last*.

JANE HAMILTON lives, works, and writes in an orchard farmhouse in Wisconsin. Her short stories have appeared in *Harper's* magazine. Her first novel, *The Book of Ruth*, won the PEN/Ernest Hemingway Foundation Award for best first novel and was a selection of the Oprah Book Club. Her second novel, *A Map of the World*, was an international bestseller.

ANN HOOD is the author of nine novels, most recently the bestsellers *The Red Thread* and *The Knitting Circle*, which is soon to be an HBO movie; a collection of short stories, *An Ornithologist's Guide to Life*; and a memoir, *Comfort: a Journey Through Grief*, which was a *New York Times* Editor's Choice and named one of the top ten non-fiction books of 2008 by *Entertainment Weekly*.

LEE MARTIN is the author of four novels, including his most recent, *Break the Skin*, and the Pulitzer Prize finalist, *The Bright Forever*. His stories and essays have appeared in *Harper's, Ms., The Georgia Review, Creative Nonfiction, The Southern Review, The Kenyon Review, Prairie Schooner, Glimmer Train*, and elsewhere. He teaches in the MFA in Creative Writing Program at The Ohio State University.

ANA MENÉNDEZ was born in Los Angeles, the daughter of Cuban exiles. She is the author of four books, including, *Adios, Happy Homeland!*, which was published in August 2011. She lives in Miami and The Netherlands, where she is a lecturer at Maastricht University.

LES STANDIFORD is the director of the Creative Writing Program at Florida International University and is the author of fifteen books and novels, including *Bringing Adam Home*. His son Alexander—vibrant spirit, gifted athlete—died in 2009 at age eighteen.